Oh Great, Now I Can See Dead People

Sam's back and now
she can see dead people

Oh Great, Now I Can See Dead People

Sam's back and now
she can see dead people

Deborah Durbin

Winchester, UK
Washington, USA

First published by Soul Rocks Books, 2013
Soul Rocks Books is an imprint of John Hunt Publishing Ltd., Laurel House, Station Approach,
Alresford, Hants, SO24 9JH, UK
office1@jhpbooks.net
www.johnhuntpublishing.com
www.soulrocks-books.com

For distributor details and how to order please visit the 'Ordering' section on our website.

Text copyright: Deborah Durbin 2012

ISBN: 978 1 78099 979 1

A CIP catalogue record for this book is available from the British Library.

Design: Stuart Davies

Printed in the USA by Edwards Brothers Malloy

We operate a distinctive and ethical publishing philosophy in all
areas of our business, from our global network of authors to
production and worldwide distribution.

OH GREAT, NOW I CAN SEE DEAD PEOPLE

Deborah Durbin is a British journalist and author.
Oh Great, Now I Can See Dead People is her second novel.

Visit Deborah's website at
www.deborahdurbin.com

Acknowledgements

Throughout the writing of this book, I've discovered that writing a sequel is a lot harder than I thought it would be, so I would like to thank my three beautiful daughters, Becky, Georgia and Holly, for their inspiring ideas when I've hit a brick wall and for their patience when I've said I'll be just five more minutes, which invariably turns into an hour! To my wonderful husband, Rich, who constantly reminds me that I'm the world's best procrastinator and tells me to just get on with it. To my friend and fellow author Caroll Arnall for all her support and encouragement. To my lovely, amazing proofreader, Judith White, who can be found at http://www.sfep.org.uk/directory/ordinary/entry547.html

And of course to my mum and dad, who helped make me the person I am today.

This book is dedicated to my best friend, Annie – a wonderful lady who makes me laugh on a regular basis.

CHAPTER ONE

Capricorn: There will be testing times ahead and you will need the patience of a saint to see you through them.

Hum... yer think?

You would have thought by now that I would have got used to being a messenger for dead people and would have been forewarned in some way by someone up there, or at least been given some sort of a sign, that it would not actually be a good idea to move back in with my mother while we waited for contracts to be exchanged on our new house, wouldn't you?

In fact, you could be forgiven for thinking that someone up there would say something along the lines of, 'Hang on a cotton-picking minute, Samantha. Do you really think it's a good idea to move back in with your mother, having lived independently for the past five years, even if it is just for a few weeks?'

But no. After all the messages I have passed on over the past year – some rather reluctantly, I hasten to add – not one person has advised me that, sure as eggs are omelettes, I would be locking myself in the downstairs bathroom, with my fingers in my ears, in a bid to escape my mother.

That's the problem with spur-of-the-moment decisions. They never, ever, work out how they're supposed to. I naively thought that seeing as my husband to be, Jack, is spending the next God knows how long in London rehearsing with his band for the Vibe Awards, and Valerie, my landlady, has decided to sell her house, the ideal solution to solving my accommodation crisis would be to move back in with my mum. It's just until our solicitor confirms that I can have the keys to our lovely little cottage in a tiny village on the outskirts of Bath, but it is already driving me bonkers.

The reality of it is that our solicitor is from the school of Make-Em-Wait, and is in no particular hurry to sign contracts with the vendor, preferring instead to send me letters at £30 a shot. Which is why I am currently playing hide and seek in the bathroom in a bid to escape my mum and the twenty-plus back copies of *Bride* that seem to be permanently stashed under her arm.

My mum, however, is a dab hand at hide and seek – having played numerous games of it when we were children – and has already found me. It only took her fifteen seconds this time.

'Sammy love? Are you in there? What are you doing in there?'

What does she think I'm doing in here? Standing on the loo with my fingers in my ears, trying to avoid her for five minutes?

'Nothing. Just coming!' I yell as I step down from the toilet seat with its fluffy pink cover and flush the loo so that she thinks I've been doing what you're meant to do in the bathroom.

'There you are. Now listen, I borrowed these from Marjorie. You remember Marjorie from the WI. Her son Jonathon got married last summer. You remember Jonathon, her son? Nice boy. Went into medicine ...' my mum begins. 'I had high hopes for you and Jonathon at one time. He's a doctor now, you know. At St Luke's,' my mum continues. 'Anyway, Jonathon married that Indian girl ... now what was her name? Fauna? Florence? Oh, that's it, I remember now, Fleur. Anyway, Marjorie, who is very good at organising events – she arranged the flowers for Mr Samson's funeral; they were beautiful. She got the display just right. She's nothing if not a perfectionist. Now, where was I? Oh yes, Marjorie said that because Fleur wasn't accustomed to our culture and way of doing things, she would be happy to arrange the wedding and she spent months collecting magazines and working out place settings. Not that the girl was grateful, mind you. She told Jonathon that she wanted a quiet wedding in a registry office, of all places. I think, between you and me, she was you-know-what and wanted a quick wedding. Marjorie had even gone to the trouble of booking Thorpe Manor ...'

Now can you understand why I locked myself in the

bathroom?

'... but no, they wanted to do it their way and ended up getting married at Bristol registry office...' my mum continues, pulling a face full of disdain. I don't like to point out that Fleur was in fact born in Hampstead and is as British as British can be, or that Jonathon-the-doctor-at-St-Luke's probably didn't want his interfering busybody of a mother taking over their special day for them.

'Well, they might just have wanted to organise it themselves.' I venture – take the hint mother!

'What, and have everyone dressed head to foot in saris? Really, Sammy,' my mum laughs.

'So, are they still together?'

'Who?'

'Jonathon and Fleur.'

'Oh, yes, but Marjorie refused to go to the wedding. She was ever so upset. It broke her heart,' my mum muses. Now I feel guilty.

Personally though I can understand why Jonathon Harris and his bride to be decided to do their own thing. Ever since Jack proposed to me in Australia, my mum has officially gone into Mother-of-the-Bride overdrive and spends every waking hour filling in an 'ideas book' with information for *our* wedding.

And it's not as though I can escape from it either. Since having to vacate my flat, Missy, my wonderfully loyal cat, and I have been knee-deep in copies of *Your Wedding*, *Hello* and *OK*. Everywhere I look in the house there is a magazine devoted to blushing brides, who grin from ear to ear at me from the glossy pages.

I say Missy, my wonderfully loyal cat. In truth Missy couldn't give a rat's arse about the wedding. In fact, I don't think Missy has even noticed that my mum has turned into a woman obsessed by celebrity weddings given that Missy is herself madly in love with a tomcat called Spencer. Spencer doesn't have his own home and lives the simple life between various houses – it's all very *Lady and the Tramp*.

No sooner had Missy unpacked her belongings – cat bed and toy mouse – than Spencer was scratching at the back door asking if Missy wanted to come out and play. Being a bit of a snob, Missy decided that Hell would freeze over before she went out with some common old alley cat, but when Spencer returned a second time with a dead mouse and dropped it on the patio for her she had a change of heart. I've told her to play hard to get, but will she listen? Will she heck. Always a pushover for the corpse of a mouse is Missy.

And now there is no stopping them. Missy only returns home for her tin of Sheba, which she duly shares with the new love of her life. She is far too preoccupied doing whatever it is that cats do for fun to notice that my mum is quickly taking over my life!

'I still don't know why you don't agree to Larry's suggestion of selling your wedding to *Hello*,' my mum mutters as she flicks through back issues of the glossy celebrity magazine. You're a celebrity now, Sammy. You're the psychic to the stars! You should make the most of it while it lasts.'

'I do not want the whole world at my wedding, thank you, Mum. It's my big day and I certainly don't want press photographers there. You know how I feel about them and Larry's only suggesting it because he's my agent and will get a nice commission out of it,' I add, recalling the fight I had last year to prove myself and clear my name, thanks to my best friend Amy selling a pack of lies about me to the tabloids.

'Yes, but that's all over now. You proved that you're an authentic psychic and people believe you now. You've even got celebrity clients, Sammy. They will want to come to your wedding, surely?'

'And look at how much stress I had to go through to clear my name, Mum. No. I do not want a celebrity wedding. I don't want any celebrities there, so don't even think about it,' I warn. 'Now,

I've got to go to work. If the solicitor phones, tell him I don't want any more letters telling me what he's already told me in the last one; I want to know when I can collect the keys to the cottage and make a start on getting it ready for when Jack comes home. If Jack phones, tell him to call my mobile. I need to sort out who we are inviting from his side of the family – not that there are going to be many from his side – and if Larry does call, *do not* tell him that I am interested in my wedding being featured in any magazine, celebrity or otherwise. Mum?'

My mum nods in agreement, but rather like a sullen teenager who has been told that she can't have an extension on her curfew.

'Mum?'

'Yes, yes, OK, but I still don't see why you are so opposed to the idea. I just … I just want you to have the best day of your life. Just like your dad and I did,' she adds quietly.

'I know you do, Mum, and I will, which is why I don't want the world and his wife seeing my big day. Now, if you really want to help me, you can ring round the local florists and get some prices on winter flowers. Oh, and I don't want a unicorn either,' I say with a smile. I know she is only trying to help and wants my Christmas wedding to Jack to be the best it can possibly be. After all, she only has one daughter and it's an exciting time for her, but sometimes she can get a little carried away with it all. I mean, where on earth does she think she's going to get a unicorn, for that matter?

'Oh, and don't forget to phone your publisher back. You've got another book to get on with,' I remind her, just in case she has got so carried away with wedding malarkey that she has forgotten that she and her new beau Colin are now under contract with their publisher to write a new book before the year is out about the importance of organic vegetables.

'Oh, yes, I almost forgot about that!' she laughs. 'Oh, I didn't tell you, did I? You know Colin's cousin, Clive?'

'The one who stalked me. Hum, how could I forget?'

My mother is referring to her new partner's cousin Clive-the-weirdo, who I tried to treat for his phobia of vegetables last year in my previous career as a psychologist. Clive took an unhealthy interest in me and yes, for a while I had my very own stalker.

'He's dead,' my mum says matter-of-factly.

'Dead?'

'Yup, as a dodo. Now what colours do you want in your flowers again?'

'Hang on. When did this happen?'

'A few weeks ago. Apparently he was in the supermarket and one of the veg racks came loose from its fitting. Fell straight on him, according to Colin; killed him outright.'

'Oh my goodness!'

Talk about ironic. See, Clive always said vegetables were dangerous.

'Why didn't you tell me about this?' I ask my mother.

'Well, let's be honest, Sammy love, he wasn't your favourite person, was he?'

'Well no, but I wouldn't have wished any harm on him. Did you go to the funeral?'

'No. Colin did. Said it was a quiet affair; family only.'

How strange.

'So, flowers? What colours?' my mum asks.

'Oh, um, whatever you think best, Mum.'

Oh, I do wish Jack was here to help me.

CHAPTER TWO

Despite it being the end of September and the weather forecasters constantly telling us to get our winter woollies out because a brisk Siberian wind is on its way, it is absolutely stifling in the Town FM radio studio today. I find Annette sitting at her desk, in a pair of shorts and a t-shirt, with her feet submerged in a bucket of ice, which is rapidly melting between her red-polished toes.

'Oh, Sam, I'm having another one of my hot moments,' Annette sighs, as she lazily flicks a few switches so that the listeners can hear yet another Town FM jingle.

Since I was reluctantly thrown into the spotlight as a radio psychic, the producers at Town FM have received so many requests for readings that they asked if I would be prepared to do the show three times a week. Considering that my wonderful DJ friend Annette was the only one in the media industry who was prepared to stand up for me when the rest of the world did their very best to try and ruin me by claiming that I was a con artist, I felt that it was only fair to give Annette and the team first refusal on my employment. And it suits me just fine. I no longer have to travel up and down the motorway to work for the BBC, and what with launching the Psychic Café Academy with Miracle, my friend and previous boss, and book and magazine deals coming in all the time, it means that I can work as and when I want, within reason.

I have also discovered that I now have a spirit guide called Andrea, or Ange as she likes to be called. I always thought that spirit guides were meant to be wise old sages, or at the very least a Native American Indian called something interesting like Hopping Moonlight, but apparently not always, and certainly not in the case of my own spirit guide. Ange is a young and vibrant Essex girl, who died while out on a night on the town.

Someone put a kerb in the road when she wasn't looking and she went flying over it in her platform shoes.

'One minute I was having the time of me life, the next I was up ere!' she said the first time she came and introduced herself to me. *'I have to say I was well pissed off about it. I'd just met this gorgeous guy and got his number and everything. He was well fit, Sam. I thought, I'm well in 'ere! The next thing I know I'm in bloody heaven! Oh, I'm your official guide by the way – not a girl guide – a spirit guide. I could have been a girl guide if I wanted, mind you ...'*

Having reluctantly learned to live with hearing voices inside my head, I figured another one wouldn't make too much of a difference. Ange, however, is a rather high-maintenance spirit and can be somewhat time-consuming. She pops up at the most inappropriate times and comes into my head for a chat about things such as why she thinks I should buy a pink feather boa or why it would be a good idea to have my wedding dress made out of cake. Another example is when I'm in a meeting and she starts singing 'agadoo-do-doo' to me, or worse, when Jack and I have been in bed together and she decides to tell me all about her past lovers!

Ange is also a fashionista and likes nothing better than to chat about who's wearing what. She insists I get a copy of *Heat* magazine every week without fail, just so she can keep up with what's in and what's out, who's dating who and what her idol Cheryl Cole is up to. Ange's fashion sense leaves a lot to be desired though, as I discovered when she informed me of what she was wearing on that fateful night – a denim miniskirt, which was originally a pair of jeans; a white halter-neck top (without a bra, of course); a pair of pink bunny ears; and her all-time favourite shoes – a pair of clear plastic platforms that came accessorised with real goldfish swimming around inside the wedges!

'Poor Boris and Doris,' Ange said solemnly, *'poor buggers died too. No sooner had I hit that stupid kerb than my left shoe flew off into the road and got mushed by a passing bus! Boris was killed instantly.*

And then when they finally retrieved what was left of my other shoe and buried me, the silly sods forgot that Doris was still in the other shoe!'

Oh cripes!

Unfortunately Miracle still hasn't told me how I make the voices go away, so for most of my day it's much like sitting on a train listening to hundreds of people on their mobile phones and hearing all their conversations at once.

I fan Annette down with the pages of my *Heat* magazine – quite appropriate really, considering it is about ninety degrees in here at the moment.

'And how's my favourite DJ then?' I ask, as I plonk myself down next to her, kick off my fluorescent pink flip-flops and plunge my own dainty toes into her bucket of nicely chilled water.

'Oh, you know – hot!' Annette says as she lets the faint breeze from my magazine waft over her face. 'You know, I don't know what we women did to deserve this. I mean, not only do we have to put up with bloody periods for God knows how many years but we also have to go through excruciating pain to have bloody babies who turn out to be bloody ungrateful and useless bloody teenagers, and then some smart-arse decides it would be a terribly good idea to give us the bloody menopause!'

'Not a good week then?'

'Not a good week,' Annette confirms. 'Anyway, how's yours been so far?' she says as she signals to Liam the sound tech to switch the jingle off and play the introduction to my *Sixth Sense* programme.

'Almost as good as yours by the sound of it,' I sigh. 'My mother is driving me bonkers with wedding plans; the solicitor is driving me bonkers by refusing to do anything to close the deal on the house; clients are driving me bonkers because they all think I have the meaning to life, or, at the very least, the winning numbers for the lottery and I'm keeping them to myself;

and Jack is nowhere in sight!'

'But you're not going through the change,' Annette says. 'Is Jack getting on alright in London?'

'She ain't going through the change either. She's preggers,' Ange informs me.

Oh crikey! I hate it when this happens and I am still not used to it. And there's Annette thinking that she is menopausal!

'Sam?' Annette shakes me from my thoughts.

'Sorry?'

'Jack. How's he getting on in London?'

I've learned now not to question the information I'm given, but I have no idea how I go about telling Annette that her hot flushes are not a sign that she is going through the change, despite being in her early forties and with two teenage sons. I don't even know if I'm supposed to say anything or not. I decide not is the best option right now. Instead I say,

'Oh, Jack, yes, he loves it! It's a dream come true for him, rehearsing for the Vibe Awards with some of the world's best musicians.'

'Well, he's a talented young man and I am so pleased that the two of you are getting married. You're made for each other.'

I feel a warm glow wash over me. Annette's right, Jack and I are made for each other and the sooner I can get the keys to our lovely cottage, the sooner I can make it our first real home together. Okay, I know we did share his flat for a while, but that was only because I was in hiding from the paparazzi, so that doesn't really count. Plus, at the time we were just good friends. Now it all seems so much more real. The mere fact that we have enough money to buy our own property is enough to make me want to burst with excitement and I can't wait!

'Oh well,' Annette says, as she slowly pulls her feet out of the bowl of water and dries them on a paper towel on the floor. I quickly scan her stomach to see if there are any visible signs of pregnancy – there aren't. 'I guess we'd better get on with the show.' She pops her headphones on, signals to Liam and flicks the 'On Air' switch.

'Right, folks, that was 'Bump in the Night' by Allstars and as our regular listeners will know that can mean only one thing - we have the lovely Mystic Crystal in the studio today and she's here to answer all your calls, so get phoning in,' Annette says as she winks at me. I put my own headphones on and wait for Liam's signal of a thumb up to signal that there's a caller on the line.

Ever since my attempt at dating the gorgeous sound tech and then realising that he wasn't The One, I'm happy to say that Liam and I have remained very good friends. Ironically, Liam is now going out with Jack's ex, Jasmine, you know, the skinny one with the big nose that resembles Concorde, and it is now Liam who has to bear the brunt of taking her to see arty noir French films.

'And first on the line we have Petra. Petra, have you got a question for Crystal?' Annette asks into her mic.

'Um ... yes ... please,' the caller mutters quietly.

'How can I help you, Petra?' All of a sudden my eyes mist over. I blink a couple of times in a bid to make them water. I must have some dust in them or something.

'Um ...I wondered if you could tell me if my mum is OK.'

As I look up at the smoked glass screen in front of me that separates Annette and me from the sound studio, the mist in my eyes starts to clear, but instead of seeing Liam and Jeff, the newsreader, on the other side of the screen I see a strange hazy image. It's not my reflection and it's not Annette's. I hear a voice inside my head.

'Tell her I'm just fine and I'm sorry that she had to see me like she did,' an elderly woman's voice says. *'I didn't want to go in there. I had a bad feeling about that place. I knew that I would never leave there. Can you please tell her that I know it wasn't her fault, but it wasn't what they led her to believe either.'*

I relay the strange message and hear the caller gasp.

'Does this mean anything to you, Petra?' Annette asks,

looking at me with concern.

'It was my brother's fault, not mine. He wanted our mum to go into a home and I was too preoccupied with work to give it much thought. He suggested it and I just agreed,' Petra says quietly. 'She was only seventy and full of life before my brother put her in that horrible place. The last time I saw her, she looked as though she had aged by twenty years.'

'What do you think your mum means by it wasn't what they led you to believe?' Annette asks.

'I don't know,' Petra says. 'The last thing I heard was that she had died peacefully in her sleep.'

'I didn't, you know. That's not the truth. It was a cover-up. Tell Petra to demand an inquest,' the woman's voice urges me. She seems very agitated.

'Petra, can you do something for me?' I venture. 'Can you find out if you can get an independent inquiry into your mum's death?'

'Why? Do you think something happened there?' Petra asks nervously.

'I ... I don't know what to think at the moment, but your mum is telling me that something has been covered up about her passing.'

Annette looks at me as if I may have just opened up a huge can of worms, but I can't let this drop. Something happened to this lady and I have a feeling that it's been covered up and someone is not telling the whole truth here.

'OK, I will do that,' Petra says.

I look in front of me and where I should be seeing my own reflection in the smoked glass screen I see the image of a pretty, grey-haired woman smiling back at me. I gasp and put my hand to my mouth.

'Are you OK?' Annette mouths to me.

'Um ... yes ... yes, fine. Right, who do we have next on the line?' I ask, as I look at the glass screen again, only to see my own reflection looking back at me. Oh, heck. Was that Petra's mum I just saw? Until now I have only been able to hear dead people in my head and, as strange as it might seem, over time I've actually got used to that.

Oh, crikey! I can't say I'm a hundred per cent confident or happy at having psychic abilities, but I've learned to live with them, and it's not only become my job, it's now my life, but I'm not altogether sure that I want to be able to *see* dead people. Miracle did say that the more I learn to trust myself, the more I will be able to pick up. I make a mental note to phone her later and tell her what I've seen.

Annette looks concerned for a moment and then flicks a switch up to signal that the caller on line two is on air and ready to speak.

'And caller number two, what can Mystic Crystal do for you?' she asks.

'Yeah, er, hi. Yeah, I'd like to know how Mystic Crystal does it so convincingly,' a young man says through the speakers of the radio. Oh, great, another sceptic to add to the list.

'I mean, she's very convincing and everything, but we all know it's a load of bollocks. I just wondered how she does it so well,' the male caller continues. 'Take that woman just now. You're not telling me that she's for real. That magician, what's his name? Darren something or other. He said psychics are a load of crap. I don't blame you, mind you; if I could carry it off I'd be earning a fortune convincing people that there is life after you're six feet under.'

'*Oh boy, is he gonna get a shock when he goes!*' An Irish woman's harsh voice comes into my head. '*Silly sod, where does he think we go? Frigging idiot!*' she continues. '*Mind you, I thought I'd be going straight to Hell, me!*' she cackles.

Who are you? I mentally ask.

'*Oh, sorry pet, I'm his Aunt Marion. Tell him you've got me here; that'll scare the pants off the little bugger!*' Aunt Marion cackles again.

'...and that's another thing, how come, if they're really up there, how come they can't give her something useful like the lottery numbers for Saturday night?' the caller demands to know.

'Tell the idiot that he will still be an idiot, no matter how much money he's got in the bank!' Marion laughs.

'Can I just stop you there a moment, love?' Annette says. 'Crystal, would you like to enlighten the gentleman, or shall we just cut him off now?'

'No, that's fine. Everyone is entitled to their own opinion on the subject. And I don't feel that I have to justify myself to anyone. However, there would be no point in giving this caller Saturday night's winning lottery numbers as he will always be an idiot, regardless of how much money he has.'

'Eh?' the caller responds, and Annette looks at me as if I might just have overstepped the mark, again.

'His Aunt Marion has just told me to tell him that.' I smile smugly and poke my tongue out at the microphone in front of me.

'No way!' the caller says.

'Way,' I reply.

'Nah, nah, you don't even know me Auntie Marion.'

'Maybe I don't,' I shrug, 'but she's here with us now.'

'She can't be. She's dead. Yeah, see, you didn't expect that, did you?'

Boy, and to think there are people like this out there on the streets!

'Err, yes, and this is a psychic show,' Annette says, pulling a face at her microphone. Liam and Jeff are wetting themselves laughing in the booth in front of us.

'Yeah, well, if she's that dead then ask her to give me the lottery numbers.'

'I do apologise, pet. He's a right ignoramus is our Damien. Tell him he'll see the winning lottery numbers if he looks properly for them. I

ain't going to do all the work for him, you know. He's a lazy sod that one, but he's so bloody thick, you can't help but feel sorry for the silly bugger and give him a bit of a helping hand. He can't even hold down a job for five minutes. I don't know what my sister Janet makes of him. The runt of the family I used to call him. Bloody hopeless, he is,' Marion cackles again.

I pass on the message with a chuckle to myself.

'What's she mean by that then?' Damien asks. Has it not sunk in yet that I have been speaking to his dead aunt, therefore proving that there is life after you're six feet under? Obviously not. I despair of people sometimes, I really do!

CHAPTER THREE

Having spent three hours in the radio station talking to people both very much dead and very much alive – and believe me, it's the living ones who are the ones to worry about - I decide to call in to see Valerie, my ex-landlady. Despite her insistence that I call her by her Christian name, it still feels wrong somehow and I have to stop myself from calling her Ms Morris all the time.

Valerie decided to sell her lovely Victorian house to a young couple who have convinced themselves that they can become property developers after seeing a property development programme kidding everyone how easy it is. I blame Sarah Beeny myself.

Valerie has now moved into Sunny Valley Retirement Homes, a block of posh retirement apartments for people who wish to live out their autumnal years in luxury.

And luxurious it is! Just to gain access to the building you have to get past Donald, the official security guard assigned to the complex. Despite being on first name terms with me, Donald still insists that my identity is checked at the gate every time I visit Valerie. First this elderly gentleman, dressed in a smart uniform of burgundy and gold that would not be out of place at The Hilton, looks me up and down and nods, and then he says, 'Who are you wishing to visit, Miss Ball?' followed by 'Have you got any ID on you?'

I thought he was joking at first. I mean, Valerie is the only person I have any intention of visiting and the only person I *do* visit, so I'm hardly going to say, Oh, hang on, I wish to visit the funny old man who collects butterflies in apartment seven instead today, please, Donald. And considering he knows me by name and knows all about me, it's highly unlikely that I am an impostor impersonating me, now is it?

'Afternoon, Donald,' I say as I hand over my driving licence to him. I've given up trying to explain that this regular identity checking to ensure I am not a terrorist is really not necessary.

'Good afternoon, Samantha, and who would you like to see today?' Donald asks.

'Oh, now let me think … Um … I would like to visit Valerie Morris, please.'

'Very well. Yes, you're clear to go,' Donald says, as though he works for the SAS. Having scrutinised my driving licence again he presses a button to allow the large, reinforced gates to the complex to open.

'Well, I suppose it is his job. I mean, if he lets people in without checking them properly, his job could be on the line,' Valerie replies to my current moan about security conscious Donald.

'I suppose. Anyway, how are you doing? Settling in OK?'

'Oh yes. I love it here … well, apart from her next door. As mad as a hatter she is,' Valerie says as she pours us both a cup of tea from a china teapot. 'You know she was up until four this morning playing that bloody jazz music. I told her, I said, I know a young man who plays in a band, he'll show you music. I've got a good mind to ask Jack and the band to come and rehearse in my apartment.'

'You'll have a job. He's currently in London rehearsing for the Vibe Awards,' I say glumly as we listen to the tones of Ella Fitzgerald and Louis Armstrong thumping through the walls.

'Ah, are you missing him, love?'

'Yes, I am. A lot. I'm trying to hold things together and get things sorted for the wedding and chase up the solicitor, but this is proving harder than I thought.'

'Can't your mum help?'

'Oh, don't mention my mum helping! She's gone into overdrive ever since I told her we were getting married. She is driving me to distraction!'

'Well, that's what mothers do, dear,' Valerie chuckles. 'I would be just the same if my son decided to get married. It's a mum thing.'

'I guess so. It's just I want everything sorted out for when Jack gets back and it's not going as I had planned it. The cottage is taking ages to sort out – have I shown you the photos?'

'Yes, you have, Sam. Now, listen to me. Take a deep breath and relax. You'll do yourself no good tying yourself up in knots about it all, you know.'

'I know. You're right. Deep breath,' I say, inhaling deeply while trying to forget about all the things on my to-do list that are not getting to-done.

'Have you thought of who will give you away?' Valerie ventures.

Valerie is far from my initial perception of a bitter battleaxe of a landlady. She's actually a very sweet and wise lady who has had quite a hard life, and venture she might. I mean, it's not every day a girl gets married, is it? And the one person who is meant to give me away is no longer here to do so. Every time I think about the fact that my dad won't be able to give me away at my wedding, tears fill my eyes.

'I don't know yet.'

And I don't. I mean, I like Colin, my mum's 'friend', as she likes to call him, and there's always the option of one of my brothers, Matt or Paul – although Paul is bound to forget to turn up, knowing that there was something he had to do but couldn't quite remember what it was. Whilst Matt's three years younger than me and it just doesn't seem right for a twenty-four-year-old to give someone away at a wedding, does it? I just wish my dad was here. He would have everything sorted out by now. He would already have his father-of-the-bride speech organised. He would have booked the cars and made sure everyone who was meant to be on the guest list was on the guest list. My dad would have had everything sorted – if he'd been here.

Valerie pats me on the arm.

'It'll all be just fine,' she smiles.

'Right,' I say, quickly changing the subject. I don't want Valerie to see me cry *again*! 'I must go and see Miracle before I head home.' I place my cup in the sparkling stainless steel sink. 'Oh, by the way, Frank's just told me, he suggests you turn the electricity supply off to number five.' I chuckle.

'Well, you can tell my dead husband that he was the one who always did the electrics, so he can bloody well do it,' Valerie laughs.

You may think this is a rather peculiar conversation to be having, but ever since Valerie's late husband, Frank first contacted me, I find that most days I have a message to pass on to her from him. I still don't know quite how this happens, but it does. I've given up questioning why this has happened to me.

Suddenly the jazz harmony that had been acting as our background music comes to an abrupt halt.

'See, he was listening to you!' I say with a smile.

As I leave Valerie's new home and wave to Donald, my mobile rings. It's Jack.

'Hey baby! How's it all going?'

'Not too bad. Still no news from the solicitor, but I did have a good show at the station today.' I am so pleased to hear from Jack. 'How are rehearsals going?'

'Good. We've got all the tracks sorted, but Dillon keeps insisting that we're not going to have enough time to do the full version of 'Holiday'. I keep telling him it's going to be fine, but he won't have it.' 'Holiday' was the song that Jack wrote when we were in Australia.

'Well, Dillon is a natural born worrier. Tell him Mystic Crystal says it will all be OK. Trust me, I'm a psychic!'

'And a sexy one at that!'

'You're not so bad yourself,' I laugh. 'Come home soon, Jack. I really miss you.'

'I will and I miss you too. Loves ya.'

'Loves me too, darling.'

See, that's all it takes to put a spring back in my step. As I drive to the Psychic Café Academy I feel as though I'm back on cloud nine.

'Someone looks very pleased with herself,' Miracle says as I sashay my way into the office of the Academy as if I'm auditioning for *Strictly Come Dancing*, with a big smile on my face.

'That's because I am!'

'You just heard from Jack.' Miracle says.

'Ooh, you're good. You should be a psychic.'

'Very funny. Now, before you head off there are cheques to sign and we're going to have to put on a new course. We've had so many people apply for the Beginners' Psychic Experience that we have too many for the one course.'

It was Miracle's idea to set up a psychic academy in Bath, when she saw how confused and frightened I felt when I first discovered that I had this unusual ability to talk to dead peeps.

It's alright for Miracle - she was born into a bohemian family who positively encouraged her from a young age to talk to the deceased. Unlike me, Miracle wasn't brought up in a culture where voices in your head meant that you were a sandwich short of a picnic. Miracle's own mother, Destiny, was a fortune teller for a travelling circus, and she encouraged Miracle to develop her 'gift' from an early age. I think, between you and me, Miracle just assumed that everybody could speak to dead people and was somewhat surprised that this isn't the case.

The Psychic Café Academy is situated in a huge Georgian building in the centre of Bath. It cost us a fortune, but as Miracle's new hubby, Max, is an estate agent, we managed to knock the price down by a few thousand pounds on the grounds that the old building was riddled with woodworm. And so the Psychic Café Academy was born and is going from strength to strength. My job is to help people new to psychic experiences accept that they are hearing dead people and are not actually going mad, although I have my suspicions that a few of our delegates are in fact the latter and just want somewhere to hang out. Like Alistair Thomas: a young man in his twenties who claims that Elvis Presley possesses him. He periodically bursts into song during our meditation time and keeps adding "Uh-huh" to the end of every sentence and announcing "Elvis has left the building" whenever he goes to visit the bathroom.

'So when is Jack going to come home?'

'Still don't know. The concert isn't for another five weeks, but their manager wants them to lay some new tracks for the new album because they've got the best music producers over from Holland, or something like that.'

'Well, it's no good you sulking, young lady. Get on with chasing up that solicitor and before you know it, you'll be up to your eyes in paint and wallpaper and have that house of yours looking perfect for when he comes home – and hopefully have all the wedding sorted out by then!'

'Yes boss. Right, must get back to Missy and my mother,' I say, as I quickly sign the cheque book and hand it back to Miracle.

As I pull into the drive at my mum's house, I see a familiar figure walking quickly down the street, avoiding my gaze.

'Clive?' I call out as the figure turns the corner.

The figure disappears.

'Did anyone call while I was out?' I ask my mum as I plonk myself down in the chair.

'Well, our publisher called to say that she wants to change the title of the book – again. I don't know what Colin is going to make of all this, I really don't? Then I had *My Garden* magazine call to say they want to run a feature about growing miniature vegetables on your windowsill. Oh, and then Marjorie called about us doing a tombola for the autumn fete. She's not sure whether we should have bottles of wine on there …'

'I meant, did anyone call for me, Mum?'

'Oh yes, Mr Jarvis called to say that you can pick up the keys to the cottage tomorrow. Larry called to ask if you would be interested in talking to *Hello* about letting them cover the reception. Oh, and the florist in town said that red and cream are very popular for a Christmas wedding. I always thought it was unlucky to have red flowers at a wedding, or is that ivy?' My mum reels off the list in front of her.

'What? I can pick up the keys for the house?'

'Yes dear,' my mum says, nonplussed by the fuss I'm making, and continues reeling off her list to me.

'Fantastic! And no, I do not want to sell my wedding reception to *Hello*,' I add as an afterthought.

'So, I said that would be fine by you,' my mum says as my mind starts wandering as to whether I should paint the bedroom in magnolia or lilac. Despite my intentions to marry the love of my life, I actually have no idea which colour he would prefer. Is that wrong? Mental note: call and ask Jack what's his view on interior design. 'Hum? Yes, whenever,' I mutter, looking out of the window to see if Missy has decided to come home for her tea or whether she is going to stay out all night again with her new chap.

'Oh, that's wonderful. Marjorie will be pleased! I thought the 31st would be the ideal time.'

'Yes, fine.'

What my mother is twittering on about, I have no idea, and I must have one of those bewildered looks on my face that tells the other person you haven't got a bloody clue what they are talking about.

'That's sorted then. Lovely.'

'Mum, I haven't got a clue what you're talking about,' I admit.

'Oh, Sammy, you are funny sometimes, love.' My mum laughs as she makes her way to the phone in the hallway.

'Missy! Missy!' I yell into the garden in a bid to persuade my cat that she cannot live on love alone. I know that falling in love is supposed to do funny things to your eating habits, but this is ridiculous. Missy has never been known to turn down a tin of salmon. To echo the words of Madness, 'It Must Be Love'. 'Yes, yes, Marjorie. It's all booked. You can officially let the other members know that Samantha will be available on Halloween to conduct the séance. Yes, yes, she's really looking forward to it. No, I don't think Princess Di will come through, but then you never know, she's really very good.'

Hang on a cotton-picking minute!

'Mum!'

CHAPTER FOUR

Oh my! You should see the cottage! Crystal Cottage. Our new home! After I picked up the keys from the solicitor's office, I literally ran up the tiny cobbled path that leads to the emerald green front door. Despite being autumn the front garden is still full of flowers and it looks like a scene from a picture postcard or a box of fudge. I've never owned my own home before and it's a fabulous feeling!

Our new home is situated in the tiny village of Castle Combe, twelve miles from Bath city centre. It's one of five Cotswold cottages at the top of Market Cross Road. From my kitchen window I can see the old village water pump, which provided water to the entire village in days gone by. Castle Combe has been hailed by the British Tourist Board as the prettiest village in England and it doesn't disappoint. The whole village is typically quaint. Despite there only being a population of around three hundred and fifty, the village has a museum, its own school, a pub and even a hotel, not to mention the famous Castle Combe racetrack.

A babbling brook runs right through the centre of the village and I've been informed by Mrs Jackson from the Old Post Office that the village is in much demand from film producers. Not only was *Dr Doolittle* filmed here, but more recently, the fantasy film *Stardust* was shot here too. The Old Post Office was originally a fifteenth century weavers' cottage and is no longer a post office, but a rather dainty little gift shop. Mrs Jackson has told me to make sure that we put net curtains up in the cottage as soon as possible. Apparently, thanks to the British film industry, the village attracts a large number of tourists who think it's quite acceptable to walk up people's garden paths and peep through their windows.

According to Mrs Jackson, this sixty-something lady who has

lived in the village all her life, someone, they're not quite sure who, told the British Tourist Board that magical pixies once occupied the cottages that dot the village. The tourists think nothing of knocking on the doors and asking to see the little village sprites. Poor Mr Brent, who lives in Brook Cottage, has even had people camping out on his front lawn in a bid to catch a lucky pixie. Don't people have better things to do with themselves? Obviously not.

So, here I am: keys in hand, standing in the small hallway of our new home, which echoes with every step I take. There's a slight chill in the air but once I discover where the electric supply is and turn on some lights, a warm glow is cast over the three-bedroom cottage, making it feel like home. Jack is going to love this place. There's even enough room for his guitars and train set. What is it with men and train sets? Not only have I discovered that Jack is a secret fan of Garfield the cat but it also transpires he's a closet Hornby enthusiast and has boxes upon boxes of 'N' gauge rail track, miniature engines and a vast number of what look like miniature shrubs, although they could be tiny trees; I'm not altogether sure, or that interested to be honest.

'Yoo-hoo! Are you in?' a voice calls from the hallway.

'Yes, in here!' I shout back from the living room, where I am in the middle of trying to reassemble an IKEA coffee table. Why I didn't just put it in the removal van as it was, instead of dismantling it in order to fit it into my little mini, I'll never know. And why have I still got six screws left over?

'I thought I would pop in to see how it's all going. I'm Gemma, by the way. Gem. I live in Rose Cottage, two doors down.' A petite young woman introduces herself.

'Oh, hi, Samantha, Sam,' I say, brushing my hair from my eyes and holding out my hand to her. Isn't it always the way? The minute you look like shit is the minute you will be introduced to someone new. I think it's one of those things that qualify as Sod's Law.

Gemma, an aromatherapist, is in her early thirties and married to Simon, who is serving in the army. They moved into the village last year and according to Mrs Jackson, my reliable source of village gossip, Gemma is very proactive in the village. If a problem needs sorting, it's Gemma who people generally turn to. And also according to Mrs Jackson, it's not been unknown to see Gemma running down Market Cross Road, chasing tourists down the hill, in a bid to stop them bothering the neighbours. She's a one woman neighbourhood watch.

'I thought you might need this,' Gem says, handing me a bottle of red wine. 'I remember when we moved in. Oh, what a nightmare! There always seem to be more boxes than you originally packed, doesn't there?' She smiles at the sight of the many storage boxes that litter every room in the house.

'Oh, you are a life saver, thank you!'

'Don't mind if I don't join you. I'll stick to the orange juice,' Gemma says, waving a bottle of orange juice in the air.

'No, not at all, although it could be a while before I locate the …'

Out of her back jeans pocket Gemma produces a bottle opener in the shape of a naked man. I think me and Gemma are going to get along just fine.

'*Ooh, I like her. Can I join you? Can I? Can I? She's preggers too!*' Ange, my spirit guide, says and I hear her clapping her hands in glee. Trust me to get a spirit guide who likes a drink or two. I do my best to ignore her.

'So, it looks like Si is going to have to serve out in Afghanistan,' Gemma says as I follow her up the stairs with a box marked 'bedroom stuff' on it.

'Oh no. When is he going?'

'Probably by the weekend.' Gemma shrugs. 'That's the chance you take when you marry into the army. We've spent three years in army accommodation and I wanted a nice place for us to settle down, especially with this little one on the way.' Gemma pats her stomach.

'What, you're pregnant?' I stare at her stomach, which shows no visible signs of a baby.

'Ha, told you. And you call yourself a psychic!' Ange laughs.

'Oh, shut up you!'

'Pardon?' Gemma says.

'Oh no, not you. Sorry ... I was just ...'

'Talking to someone on the other side?'

'How ...?'

'Mrs Jackson told me... Well she told the whole village actually that *the* Crystal Ball was moving here. So don't be surprised if you get more visitors than the rest of us. Mrs Jackson claims she doesn't like the intrusion of tourists, but between you and me, I think she loves it. Especially as she is the only gift supplier in the area. It does wonders for her business. I wouldn't be surprised if she starts selling crystal balls soon.'

'Well, if you see me talking to myself, you'll know why.'

By the time Gem leaves it's gone seven and the majority of boxes have been unpacked; those that haven't, have gone into the cupboard under the stairs. Having moved two flats' worth of furniture into a three-bedroom house, I think we are going to have to sell what I've got left in storage, including Jack's beloved retro beanbag in the shape of a giant Rubik's Cube.

'Have you moved everything in then?'

This is Jack's first question when he phones me an hour later.

'Well, almost. Unfortunately we don't have enough room for your beanbag, or the hanging wicker chair, or the didgeridoo you insisted on bringing back from Australia.'

'You haven't sold them? Oh, dear God, tell me you haven't sold them!' Panic rises in Jack's voice.

'No, I haven't sold them...'

'Phew, thank God. You never know when a didgeridoo will come in handy.'

You know, I think Jack is serious. I daren't tell him that I'm planning to donate his beloved objects to the local charity shop. I'm just hoping that he forgets about them when he sees how fabulous his train set looks in the 'train room', as the spare bedroom has now become. I've spent the past hour and a half hooking pocket-size sections of track together and sticking tiny trees down with Blu-Tack in an attempt to make it look like a miniature landscape. I've even put in some little figures to look like they are waiting on the platform for a train to come – I say figures; they're actually Santa and two snowmen from Mum's Christmas cake last year.

'So what are your plans for tonight?' Jack asks.

I look out of the kitchen window and down the dark road.

'Well, apart from sorting out where I'm going to put everything, I'm waiting for Colin to turn up with Missy – again. That stupid cat! I brought her with me this morning in the cat basket and as soon as my back was turned, she escaped and managed to walk the twelve miles back to Mum's house.'

'How do you know she walked? She might have caught the bus. Or hitched a lift.'

'Very funny. I don't know what's wrong with her. Mum's going to send Colin over with her in a bit.'

'There's nothing wrong with her. She's in love, that's all. And so am I,' Jack says in a mushy voice.

'Me too, but I wish you were here, Jack. It's a lovely place, but it's, well…it's just not the same without you. It's too quiet here on my own.'

'Well, only a few more weeks and then I'm all yours. Oh, I've just had a thought; you can put the didgeridoo on display in the living room. It'll look nice in there. Oh, and don't forget we've got that boomerang too that your brother gave us; you could put the two together, make a kind of Aussie theme.'

Oh crap!

As I wait for Missy to make her return with Colin, I pack away the multitude of cosmetics that promise to make me look younger, more beautiful and glossier, into the bathroom cupboard.

Screech!

The trees outside scratch against the bathroom window, making me jump. I know it's only the wind, but I feel really nervous being here on my own. It's cold in the cottage too. I've managed to locate the heating switch, but I think the radiators need bleeding, or something.

As I close the bathroom cabinet, I notice that the mirror has misted up and I rip a piece of tissue from the tissue holder and begin to wipe the condensation that has built up on the glass. All of a sudden the lights begin to flicker. I look up at the ancient light fitting and memo myself to get it checked out.

'Holy shit!'

As I turn back to the mirror I see a face staring back at me – and unfortunately it's not my own reflection, or if it is, then I'm in trouble and the face creams do not do what they say on the packet. The image is grey and hazy and only remains for a few seconds, but it is definitely not me looking back at myself. I can't even tell if it's a man or a woman. It's kind of grey and wrinkly. Oh shit! What with seeing the woman at the radio station and now this!

I'm still not totally comfortable with the fact that I can hear dead people. I certainly don't wish to see them as well, thank you very much! I must phone Miracle.

Before I get the chance to go downstairs and find my mobile, the bathroom door swings shut and a cold breeze brushes past my face.

'Ange,' I say out loud, 'now would be a really good time to help me out here, please! What's going on?'

'Oh, piss off!' Ange snaps.

Oh, just brilliant! Miracle did tell me that if I ever have any questions or need help then I should call on my spirit guide. Trust me to get a spirit with an attitude!

'Ange! I'm sorry. I didn't mean to tell you to shut up earlier.'

'Whatever!'

The small room is like an icebox and I can hear a buzzing noise coming from the spare bedroom. As I pull on the door handle, the door opens as suddenly as it had shut. I walk gingerly across the wooden landing and slowly push open the door to the spare room.

'What the …?'

My gaze is directed to Jack's train set and the small locomotive that is whizzing round and round the track at high speed. The tiny carriages and freight wagons being towed by the engine are on the verge of flying off the tracks. The icy breeze I felt in the bathroom has followed me and blows at my hair. Inside the front carriage are Mr Snowman and Santa.

'Oh shit! Ange? Dad? Anyone?' I scream, but it falls on deaf ears. Oh, I do not like this one little bit. This is way too supernatural and too far out of my comfort zone.

Since my dad made contact with me last year for the first time since he died, I haven't been able to make contact with him again. Miracle says it was because at the time he knew that I was in trouble and that he's probably been busy since then learning the ropes up there. Busy? Learning the ropes? I mean, what is there up there to learn that is more important than helping me out right now? It's not like I'm used to all of this and automatically know what to do, you know!

I slowly back out of the room and shut the bedroom door quietly.

'Aghhhh!' I scream as I feel a cold hand tap me on the shoulder, and I spin round.

There's nothing there.

Suddenly Missy sprints up the stairs and stops abruptly, hissing at the space between her and me. She jumps straight into my arms and purrs as if to tell me she is sorry for staying out so late.

'Sam?' Mum's boyfriend Colin comes running up the stairs.

I suddenly notice that the sound from the train in the bedroom has stopped. I must have a look of utter bewilderment on my face.

'Sam? Are you OK?' Colin asks. 'I just brought Missy back and heard you scream.'

My heart is still thumping loudly in my chest.

'I ... um ... yes. Yes, I'm fine, Colin. Thank you for bringing her home again.'

'You sure you're alright? You look like you've seen a ghost.'

Oh, the irony of it all.

'No, I'm fine. Just feels a bit odd being on my own. Don't worry, I'll be fine now Missy's home. Tell Mum I'll give her a call tomorrow and thanks again for bringing Missy back.'

'My pleasure. See you tomorrow,' Colin says as he skips back down the stairs.

'What was all that about, Ange?'

'*Piss off,*' my spirit guide says again.

Great, now I have a spirit guide nursing a grudge.

CHAPTER FIVE

'Well, you're a psychic now, what did you expect?'

This was Miracle's response when I phoned her immediately upon locating my mobile phone.

'Well, I didn't expect to see dead people in my bathroom mirror or for Jack's train set to become possessed by Santa and a frigging snowman!'

Well I didn't!

I didn't think it was part of the deal. I mean, if we're honest here, I didn't grow up thinking, 'Oh I know, when I grow up I want to talk to dead people. What fun that will be! No. I grew up thinking, Oh, I know, when I grow up I want to be Madonna and warble for a living. Later on I realised that there is and only ever will be one Madonna and, besides, leather trousers have a tendency to make me come out in a rash. Oh, and I can't sing, so I decided I would become a therapist instead.

And I would have made a very good therapist had there been enough Lachanophobes on planet Earth to enable me to earn a living from it. But there aren't.

'I don't want to actually *see* dead people!' I whine.

'Look, sweetie, for whatever reason, you've been given this gift, so get used to it. Did you ask your spirit guide to help you?' Miracle asks.

'Yes I did - and she told me to piss off.'

'Why on earth did she do that?'

'Because I told her to shut up.'

Now this *is* one of the most bizarre conversations that I have had to date.

'Ah well, she'll probably come back in a few days, if I know anything about Ange,' Miracle surmises.

'What, you know her?'

'Durh, yes. Who do you think assigned her to you?'

'Well, I don't know really. This is still all new to me, you know! I just thought they popped up when you needed them, and besides, couldn't you have given me someone nice like an old Native American or even a wise African witchdoctor, instead of someone who thinks she's an extra from *TOWIE*, just wants to get pissed, read *Heat* and go out on the town all the time?'

'I just asked the higher plane to assign someone to help you because I knew you were developing faster than you could cope with. It's not up to me who they give you, hun. You're still a bit sceptical about all this, Sammy, and I feel that you don't truly understand it all just yet.'

Yer think, Miss Marple?

'So you give me someone who has a permanent hangover and spends most of her time trying to get an eyeful of Peter Andre in the buff! Smashing!'

Part of me thinks this is just too bizarre for words. I mean, I'm twenty-eight years old, for goodness sake! I should be chatting to living friends about whether Revlon is better than Rimmel, or whether Kate Moss will ever get back with Pete Doherty one day, *not* talking about Mr Andre's peachy bum with dead people!

'Ange is learning too, Sam. She hasn't been in the spirit world for long. You have to understand her death was traumatic for her. She's bound to have a few issues. Give it time and the two of you will be just fine. Now, can I please finish my dinner?'

'Hum, I suppose so, but it was you who got me into all of this in the first place, so don't be surprised if I call you in the middle of dessert to tell you that Missy has become possessed!'

Thankfully, Missy hasn't become possessed – well, not that I can tell. The only thing that Missy is suffering from is lovesickness, poor thing. Since we moved in she's been pining for Spencer the tomcat. Maybe I should invite him over for tea or something. Although he's a bit of a free-spirit, is Spence. He doesn't have a home as such, and by all accounts he roams the city at night. See, Alexandra Burke was right: bad boys are good;

even cats are attracted to the bad boys. Missy wouldn't even touch her dinner tonight.

Since my ghost-in-the-spare-room/bathroom incident the other night, I haven't heard any more bumps in the night or seen any more dead people, thankfully. Mind you, that could be because I've remained permanently attached to my iPhone and avoided looking into any reflective surfaces. Bit of a problem when doing my hair and make-up and I've kind of had to rely on other people's reactions when they see me to really judge whether I've managed successfully to apply my mascara and eyeliner in the right places, or whether I've managed to make myself look like Alice Cooper – again.

'Oh, Samantha, is there something wrong with your left eye?' Mrs Jackson said yesterday when I popped into her shop – this was a clue to let me know that applying my make-up without the aid of a mirror hadn't in this case been successful. I did, however, notice that her gift shop has a rather mystical air about it now. Among the home-made greeting cards and postcards depicting scenes of the village, objects including a wrought iron cauldron and some specially designed tarot cards with 'Greetings from Castle Combe' written on the front of the box have appeared on the shelves. There was also a distinct smell of incense in the air. I think Gem was right.

My mobile rings; it's Annette.

'How's my little psychic friend?'

'Oh, not too bad, considering.'

'Considering what?'

Considering I have a trainspotting ghost and a spirit guide who still won't do her job and thinks guiding me involves guiding me in the direction of New Look!

'Oh, it doesn't matter,' I say instead. 'What can I do for you?'

'Well, two things really. You know that woman who phoned in the other day and you told her to ask for an inquiry into how her mum died?' Annette says.

'Humm … Petra?'

'That's her. Well, she phoned to say that when she told the nursing home that she wanted an inquiry, they got really funny about it with her. Anyway, some researcher from Living Today TV was listening to the show and contacted me to see if I could contact Petra, which I did, and they want to use her story in a new psychic detective programme *and* they want you to be part of it. They've heard good things about you and want to know if you might be able to dig up more about this lady's death.'

I feel myself going hot and cold at the same time.

'Oh, Annette, I really don't know …'

'I know, I know. I told them that you hadn't had a great experience of being on TV and that you would probably refuse anyway, but I thought I'd let you know. I've got the number of the researcher for you here in the studio. I didn't know whether to bother you with it or pass it on to your agent Larry, but you know what he's like. The mere mention of a TV show and he's off. Anyway, have a think about it.'

'OK, I will. Thanks, Annette. What was the second thing?'

It's then that Annette suddenly and without notice bursts into tears.

'I think I might be pregnant!'

'Oh,' is all I can stutter.

'You knew, didn't you?' Annette says quietly after about five minutes of sobbing into the phone.

'I … well … I …' I don't quite know what to say. 'How long?'

'Call yourself a psychic?' she half laughs. 'Four and a half months,' Annette says, her voice breaking with emotion.

'What are you going to do?'

'What can I do, Sam? I have two teenage sons, no husband since Mark decided to sod off to Amsterdam with that tart from office supplies and no support whatsoever. What choice do I have? Shit! Fuck! Shit, Sam! What am I going to do?'

'She's going to have a beautiful little girl.' A woman's voice comes into my head and I remember it's the same voice that told me to tell Annette to get her brakes checked on her car – which incidentally she didn't and ended up with a broken arm and in a neck brace for four weeks!

'Well, it's your decision, of course it is, and you have me for support ... but ...'

'But... what?'

'No, it doesn't matter,' I say. I don't want to be the person who has an influence on Annette's decision.

'No, tell me, Sam. What were you going to say?' Annette persists.

'I don't want to, because it's your decision and I should just be here as your friend, to support you, no matter what you decide.'

'But as a friend you should also be advising me as to what I should be doing,' Annette adds.

Touché!

I sigh.

'If you decide to keep the baby, it will be a beautiful little girl,' I tell her.

Annette gasps and then cries – a lot.

Oh shit, I didn't mean to upset her.

'Annette? Are you still there?'

'Yes,' she sniffs. 'I'm still here. I'm sorry, Sam. I ... I've always wanted a little girl.'

'I know you have, darling, but don't let that be the deciding factor here,' I say, trying to be logical about all of this. At the end of the day Annette has no support for her and her boys, let alone another child, and as far as I know, the father of this child is nowhere in sight either.

'It's Jeff's,' Annette says, as if reading my thoughts.

Oh blimey!

Don't get me wrong, Jeff is lovely. He's middle-aged and the kindest and funniest radio newsreader you are ever likely to meet. I don't even know if he already has a family of his own. I know I should, being a psychic and all that, but I don't. Jeff is a lone island, or at least that's what I thought – obviously not.

'What, Jeff at the radio station?'

'Uh-huh. He doesn't know yet though, so don't say anything.'

'Discretion is my middle name.' I laugh, and for the first time in this conversation Annette laughs too.

'But I didn't know you and Jeff liked each other, you know, in *that* way.'

'Neither did we!' Annette laughs. 'It just sort of happened by accident one night. Afterwards we agreed it wouldn't be wise to have a relationship in work and left it at that. I didn't think for one minute that I would get pregnant! Oh, Sam! You're the fortune teller. Tell me what I should do.' Annette sighs.

'I can't tell you what you should do, Annette; all I'm getting is that you will have a baby daughter, if you decide to go ahead with this.'

'Well then, it's settled,' Annette says assertively. 'I've always wanted a daughter. I mean, I love Tom and Jake to bits, but it's all Transformers and Play Stations with them. I want someone to go clothes shopping with, without them grumbling outside the changing room. And besides, I've managed to bring two up practically on my own, so another one isn't going to make much difference, is it?'

'Apart from the stinky nappies, sleepless nights, endless hours of watching Pepper Pig ...'

'Not to mention my age,' Annette adds.

I hadn't even thought about Annette's age. Besides, forty-four isn't *that* old, is it?

'Age is just a number, Annette. If you think you can handle it all over again, then I say go for it.'

'Yes, I will!'

'Now, I think you had better go and phone Jeff, don't you?'

CHAPTER SIX

'...my mother is still running around in a tizz because she can't find a hat for the wedding. Speaking of which, we really do need to sort out who we're going to invite from your side of the family, hun.'

Jack sighs as he wraps his arms around me.

'Let's talk about that later. I've missed you so much ...' He pulls me in close and starts kissing my neck again.

For the first time in weeks we've managed to get a whole weekend together, completely on our own – well, I say completely on our own, but that's if you don't count the hundred or so voices that keep talking in my head!

No sooner had I checked into the hotel than a dead lady by the name of Joan came into my head when I was in the lift and asked if I would please tell the porter – her son – that she loved him, and to ask him to do something with his hair. Following that a young man by the name of Jon came through and proceeded to tell me all about when he worked at the hotel as a barman. He wanted me to pass on his regards to a waitress called Sarah-Louise, who he always thought was "well fit" – his words, not mine – and he regretted not having the courage to ask her out. Oh, and then just as I was making my way to the room that Jack's management company had kindly booked and paid for, so that we could get some time alone together, an elderly gentleman decided it was a good time to tell me all about his honeymoon adventures in room twenty-eight – our room.

In the end I had to beg and plead with Ange to ask them to give us some privacy. Ange had refused to speak to me for the past two weeks, which also meant that I had no help whatsoever every time my unwanted house guest decided to pay a visit and play at being a train driver – which has been four times now. It took a lot of grovelling and a promise that I would take Ange shopping in Harvey Nicks before she would help me out and stop the lovely dead people from talking to me at some very inappropriate moments.

Having spent the past month rehearsing for the Vibe Awards and putting together a new album with the band, Jack is exhausted and he looks it. His baby-smooth chin is covered in stubble where he didn't have time to shave this morning, but it definitely suits him. He looks more handsome than the last time I saw him – which was fifty-seven days and five hours ago, to be precise. Not that I'm counting or anything.

We spent a wonderful day in London, taking in the sights and generally getting up to no good. Whenever we visit London, Jack goes into challenge mode and tries to find the most outrageous dare to inflict upon me. Knowing that I will do almost anything in order to prevent myself from getting a double dare, Jack was in his element as we made our way round Harrods.

'Double dare!' Jack said excitedly at the prospect of me failing the first dare, which was to hop on one leg all around the first floor of Harrods. I fell over, flat on my face, within ten seconds. He then spent the next hour thinking up more ridiculous dares for me to do. He really is a child sometimes, you know.

By the time we got back to the hotel I had completed a total of five dares and two double dares but Jack hadn't managed to complete even one dare, and it wasn't *that* hard – all he had to do was climb over the rails of Buckingham Palace, but would he do it? No, the big wimp! He said he was afraid of being shot by one her majesty's guards, or some other feeble excuse.

'Jack! We need to discuss this,' I say as I wriggle free from his clutches in bed, despite not wanting to. 'We've only got a few more hours and I don't want to continue planning our wedding by text message, thank you very much.'

'Well, I don't have any family, you know that. Your family are my only real family.'

'What about your Uncle Dave and Auntie Maureen? Don't you want them to come?'

Jack's Uncle Dave and Auntie Maureen are the only people I know who have anything remotely to do with Jack - they're not actually his uncle and auntie, so he's not biologically related to them. Dave and Maureen took Jack under their wing when he was fourteen; they gave him a part-time job in their fancy dress shop in Bristol when he ran away from the care home he was in. They generally helped him out by providing him with a roof over his head until he was sixteen and got his own flat. Having been dragged up in a care home from the age of one, Jack doesn't know any members of his family.

'Yeah, maybe...' Jack shrugs.

'Well, I'm sure they would want to be there.'

I've had the pleasure of meeting Dave on several occasions and was very grateful to him for providing me with a very realistic Scooby-Doo costume when the press were after me after my best friend Amy sold a made-up story about me, but I find it strange that Jack never wants to talk about his past.

'Well, I'll get hold of them and check that they will be able to come. You never know, they might be able to shed some light on your parents, seeing as how they were made your official guardians. I mean, someone somewhere must have agreed to them bringing you up. You never know, we might be able to track them down in time for the wedding...'

'For Christ's sake, Sam, just leave it, will you! My parents never wanted me, OK? And Dave and Maureen aren't even related to me; they're just some couple who took me under their fucking wing when no one else cared!' Jack snaps.

'*Leave it now, Sam,*' Ange whispers in my ear.

'But...'

'But what?' Jack says.

'Nothing. I'm sorry. Look, if you don't want any of your family to be there, we won't have any of them there,' I say quietly, and snuggle back into him. I have to say I'm a little worried about Jack. Whenever I mention his mum and dad, he clams up. He has no interest in knowing who his real parents are, which I find incredibly strange. Surely you would want to know where you came from?

After another hour of snuggling up in bed, I suddenly realise that I must hurry up if I'm to get to Harvey Nicks with Ange and back to Bath in time for my mother's séance at the WI tonight.

How I managed to get talked into that I will never know. Somewhere between worrying about the sale of the cottage going through, worrying about Missy settling in, talking to the dead, that kind of thing, I somehow managed to agree to conduct a séance for the local WI. Not content with shocking the nation with their nude calendars, the Women's Institute is now set on introducing 'new and modern interests' to the members of the hundred year-old institution, including dipping into the paranormal, apparently. Whatever happened to learning how to do macramé or filling shoe boxes for third world countries?

I mean, I've never had to conduct a séance before. In fact, I've only just got used to being able to speak to people who are, how shall we say, well ... dead as dodos. I've watched every episode of *Ghost Whisperer* and searched everything from Doris Stokes to Colin Fry on the internet, but I'm still not a hundred per cent sure of what I am supposed to be doing.

'Just make sure that you close the circle when you finish, especially considering you're doing it on All Hallows' Eve. The veil between the two worlds is more transparent,' Miracle warned me when I phoned her with my concerns.

'Oh, and don't forget to ask Ange to help you,' she added. Fat chance of that; she's been too busy flicking through a *What's Happening in London* brochure I picked up at the tube station.

I asked Gem if she would like to come along for the fun of it. With her husband Si duly despatched to Afghanistan, she needs something to take her mind off things. No sooner had I asked Gem than Mrs Jackson phoned me to ask if she could come along too. Then Mr Brent from Brooke Cottage said he would like to come along for the ride. I'm not altogether sure if men are allowed to WI functions, but it looks like I'm going to have a car full of enthusiastic amateur ghost hunters anyway!

'You'd better go,' Jack says as he reaches over and looks at his watch, and then kisses me on the nose. 'I wish you didn't have to.'

'Me too, but who else is going to get this house sorted, run a séance, plan a wedding and sort out the lovelorn Missy? Besides, I don't really fancy spending the week in this hotel room on my own while you rehearse.'

'You could always be our backing singer.' Jack smiles.

'Have you heard me sing?'

'Oh yeah, I have. Strike that thought then.' Jack laughs.

'You cheeky sod!'

I jump on top of Jack and hold him down. Jack's mouth twitches.

'So, what are you going to do with me now then, Miss Ball?'

'Well ...'

Ange will just have to wait a little bit longer to go shopping...

CHAPTER SEVEN

'No, Mum, I won't be late and yes, Mum, I will drive carefully,' I shout into the speaker on my phone as I wash the shampoo from my hair. 'I'm just getting ready now then I'm picking up Gem and Mrs Jackson. Oh, and can Mr Brent come too? I think he's interested in getting a spirit to help him scare the tourists off his garden!'

'Yes, I'm sure that will be OK, love. Now what time will you be here?'

'We should be with you by about nine thirty.'

'Oh, that's a bit late, Sammy. Mrs Horsham likes to be in bed before ten if she can. Poor Mr Horsham sleepwalks, you see, and if she doesn't get an early night, she will be murder tomorrow morning at the Save the Children coffee morning. She's an absolute saint, is Mrs Horsham. Every time her husband gets out of bed she has to go and find him and bring him back again. She found him in the neighbours' shed the other night. Trying to start their strimmer of all things. Thankfully it was an electric one and not petrol. The neighbour's don't have electricity in their shed, not like the Webbers, two doors down. They've got one of those fancy shed office type things, with computers, printers, electric and everything in there. I'm sure they're running some illegal dealings there you know. It wouldn't surprise me if they've got some illegal immigrants stashed away, two a piece in those fancy filing cabinets of theirs.'

'Mum, Mr Webber is a business consultant who just happens to work from home.'

'Exactly!' my mum says. You know, I do wonder about my mother's state of mind sometimes and this conversation is making me late. I haven't even stepped out of the shower!

'...and Mrs Samuels – she's the one with one leg shorter than the other, although you'd never guess; it's amazing what they can do with shoes these days. Anyway, she says she must take her medication at quarter to ten promptly, otherwise it puts her all out of sorts and if she takes her tablets at the meeting, she's likely to go giddy. That won't affect the séance, will it, Sammy?'

'Look, Mum, it was you and Marjorie who asked if I could make it as late as possible because, if you remember, you wanted to give the ghosts, as you like to call them, a chance to get out to trick or treat first, being as it's Halloween, remember? If Mrs Horsham has to get an early night, then she will have to miss it and Mrs Samuels will just have to be giddy!' I snap. God, my mum could talk for England if you let her! 'Now my hair is rapidly drying itself into tumbleweed and I'm freezing my butt off in here!'

'Why on earth is your bottom cold? I hope you're wearing something appropriate, Sammy! You're not wearing some skimpy little leather number, are you?'

'Mum, I am freezing my bottom off because I am trying to have a shower! And I have never worn a skimpy little leather number in my life – that's of course if we're not counting the time you made me dress up as Freddie Mercury for the St Martin's primary school fancy dress parade.'

'Oh, that's right! Oh, you did look cute. I think you would have won first prize had your moustache not got stuck to your bottom.'

'Yes, and thanks to that I was known as Freddie Hairy Bottom for the rest of my time at St Martin's.' I cringe at the thought. Kids can be so childish sometimes!

'Well, you'd better get a move on, Sammy. You're going to be late if you keep me chatting, dear.'

Grrrrr! This is where I hang up on my mother, before I scream at her.

'Now are you sure you have everything?' Gem asks, as she carries my CD player out to the car.

'I think so. Thanks for your help, Gem.'

'No problem. I'd only be sitting at home on my own watching re-runs of *Casualty* and getting up and down to answer the door to trick or treaters all night. Now, are you *really* sure you have everything?'

'Yes, I am *really* sure.' At least, I think I have everything. I've spent a great deal of time quizzing Miracle about what I should be equipped with to conduct a successful séance – you'd think by now they would have a Dummies Guide to Séances, wouldn't you? I have a list as long as my arm of things I must remember to do, say and take with me. Gem takes the list from my hand.

'Candles – purple and white?'

'Check.'

'Incense – two sticks?'

'Check.'

'Music?'

'Check.'

'Full moon?'

I look out of the window. Yep, one full moon as requested.

'Check.'

'One medium psychic?'

'Damn, I knew there was something I'd forgotten.'

'Come on, or Mrs Jackson and Mr Brent will wonder where we've got to,' Gem says as she hurries me out of the door.

The thirty minute journey into Bath is nothing if not an interesting one. Mrs Jackson spent the entire trip grumbling with Mr Brent about the recent influx of tourists during the summer months and how you never see a police officer in villages these days.

'In the good old days you'd see PC Drummer walking his beat up and down the village every day. PC Drummer wouldn't have put up with those blooming people trampling their way up and down the village, taking photographs of people's houses and gardens as if they owned them. I blame that Dr Doolittle myself. We even had a police house back then, didn't we Mr Brent?'

'That we did, Mrs Jackson,' Mr Brent muttered in the back.

Gem and I try not to laugh at the double act in the back of my mini, moaning and groaning about the modern world.

'I'm hoping Samantha's little meeting might bring about a solution for us,' Mr Brent muses. I do hope that Gem has told him that it is actually a séance that we are attending and not a parish council meeting, otherwise he's going to have one hell of a shock when he gets there.

By the time we reach the memorial hall that is home to the Bath Women's Institute, it is almost nine thirty and my mother is pacing up and down outside the building.

'Oh Sammy, there you are!' she exclaims breathlessly. 'Now, everyone who has been invited is here, apart from Mrs Landsbury. She's on her way, but said she will be ten minutes late because she's just washed her poodle and has to blow dry it.'

I do hope my mother is talking about Mrs Landsbury's dog.

'Now,' my mother continues, 'we thought it best to put the table in the centre of the room, to enable everyone enough room to get up to spend a penny if they need to.'

'Mum, they can't just get up and break the circle,' I say as we unload neighbours and boxes out of the car and onto the pavement. 'Once we're sitting down, we all have to stay put, so you'd better tell anyone who has a weak bladder to go to the bathroom before we open the circle.'

'I wonder why it's called a circle and not a square,' my mother muses as she takes a box from me.

The memorial hall looks as though it's about to fall down around our ears. Cheap paint is peeling off the walls and many of the wooden beams in the ceiling look as though they have been eaten away by some kind of creature that likes nothing more than munching its way through wooden beams. I hope they don't fall on someone. Still, I suppose it all adds to the authenticity for a séance on Halloween. Along with the natural cobwebs in the main hall, there are numerous spooky things dangling from the ceiling and adorning the breeze block walls, left over from a children's Halloween party earlier this evening.

As I carry all my 'ghost hunting' equipment into the main hall I find myself being accosted by a six-foot, glow-in-the-dark skeleton. It reminds me a little of Clive and a shudder goes down my back. Oh, I do hope this goes OK and Clive doesn't make another appearance.

'Right, I've told everyone to go and spend a penny – there's a bit of a queue forming out there now,' my mum says with concern. 'I've told Mrs Samuels just to take her medicine and if she feels giddy we've always got Marjorie on hand for first aid. She's a fully qualified first-aider, you know,' my mum continues as Gem and I throw a dark blue satin sheet over the large oval table, which is placed in the centre of the room.

'How many are coming, Mum?' I ask.

'Oh well now, let me think. There's me, obviously. Marjorie is here – I think she's on bathroom duties at the moment. There's Mrs Horsham. Mrs Samuels is here – the one with one leg shorter than the other, but you'd never guess. You've got Mrs Jackson and Mr Brent, so that makes six, and then there's Gemma, that's seven…' my mum counts on her fingers.

'The number has to be divisible by three,' I say, as I try mentally to count how many people are coming and whether a) we're going to have enough room around the table and b) we're going to have the right number of people.

'Three? Oh no, Sammy, we've got more than three.'

'No, the number of participants has to be divisible by three for a séance.'

'Why's that then?'

'Um … something to do with the number three being a magical number,' I say quickly.

To be honest, I haven't the foggiest idea why the circle has to be a circle and not a square or why the number of people has to be divisible by three, but if Derek Acorah insists on it, then that's good enough for me.

My hands shake as I try to light the twelve purple and white candles – again, the number of candles has to be divisible by three. I get Gem to light the incense sticks, which fill the room with a hint of frankincense.

'A bit nervous?' Gem asks with a smile.

'Does it show?'

'Nah, you'll be fine,' Gem assures me.

I mentally ask for Ange to come and help me.

'Oh, sorry, I was just admiring that lady's bag. Is that a Lulu Guinness?' Ange asks.

I have no idea, Ange. I do hope that Ange is concentrating on this. We had words earlier about her being here to protect me and make sure that nothing goes wrong, but at the moment I'm not altogether sure her mind is on the job.

'Ask her, ask her, Sam. I'm sure it's a Lulu.'

'No Ange, I am not going to ask that woman if her handbag is an authentic Lulu Guinness. Now, please concentrate on the job. You're supposed to be helping me here, not admiring other people's handbags.'

'Oh, sorry. Did you get this week's copy of Heat *for me?'*

Oh boy, I can already see this could all go horribly wrong at any given moment! When did someone write this in my life's grand plan, I wonder? Who thought, I know what we'll do, we'll make Samantha hear dead peeps and instead of, oh I don't know, working in an insurance office or a bank, like other twenty-somethings, we'll give her a job as a psychic and she can run séances for the Women's Institute; oh, and she can have a spirit guide who is as mad as a box of badgers as well. Everyone in favour say 'Aye'.

CHAPTER EIGHT

Having established that we have fifteen people in total to sit around the table, Marjorie, who as well as being on every committee known to Bath is also the Bath Women's Institute ring leader, or whatever they call themselves, jingles a small brass bell to signal that the meeting has commenced and, well, basically to tell everyone to shut up and listen to her.

'Welcome, welcome, one and all on this very special night,' Marjorie, who is dressed in a sensible beige Marks and Spencer suit begins. 'Now, as you are aware, tonight is All Hallows' Eve, otherwise known as Halloween, and we are truly honoured this evening to have a very special guest in our presence. Miss Samantha Ball, also known as Crystal Ball, psychic to the stars, has very kindly offered to perform a special Halloween séance for us.' A cheer goes up from the back of the hall. It's coming from an over-enthusiastic member who has already got her flask of tea out of her bag and is offering a cup to Mr Brent – at least, I think it's tea.

'Now, as anyone who has watched *Most Haunted* will know,' Marjorie continues as if she has taken on the presenting role of Yvette Fielding, 'one can often feel a bit funny if it's one's first time, so if anyone feels a bit giddy, just put your hand up and Samantha will stop the circle.'

Stop the circle? I don't know if you can just stop the circle once it's started. I make a mental note to ask Ange about that in a minute. I wonder how many séances Marjorie has actually attended. She certainly sounds as though she's an authority on the subject, or perhaps, like me, she's just researched it all on the internet.

I think I'm looking suitably mystical tonight in a full-length, black velvet dress with very tiny silver stars hand embroidered on it. Valerie made it for me, and I have teamed it with a black pashmina draped over my shoulders, making me looking appropriately mystical, if somewhat a bit black widowish. Unlike Gem, I decided not to complement the outfit with a pointed black hat, thinking that it would look a bit too over the top. Gem, on the other hand, has gone for the full monty witch effect and has even got a realistic wart on her petite nose. I'm sure it must be stuck on, unless the mere mention of Halloween has made her come out in lumps and bumps.

'Now, before we get on with this evening's entertainment, can I please remind those of you who are members that fees are due in and must be paid by the end of the week,' Marjorie says, 'and can I finally say congratulations to Mrs Bannerman for coming second in the Bath Horticultural Society's competition with her home-made green tomato marmalade? Very well done, Hilary.' A round of applause rings around the hall for Mrs Bannerman's attempts at making the most unusual conserve. I wonder what was awarded the first prize? Sprout jam?

'Now, if everyone is comfortable, then we will begin. Over to you, Samantha,' my immaculately dressed host says from the stage.

I stand up and make my way nervously to the stage.

'Um … hello,' I stutter, and wave for those who are hard of hearing. You would think with all the readings I've given, I would be used to speaking in public by now, but I'm not. In fact I'm a big bag of bloody nerves. 'Thank you for coming this evening. Now, I can't promise that anyone will receive any messages tonight, but I will certainly try my best to contact your loved ones.' I can see my mum, sitting next to Marjorie and smiling in an approving manner. 'Now, if you would all like to choose a seat at the table in the middle of the room, we will get started.' I signal to Gem to press play on the CD player and the haunting sounds of dolphin/Enya type music wash around the room. Incidentally, this was one of the many CDs that my agent Larry asked me to endorse for a new age music production company, meaning that I could have as many free CDs as I wished. Not that I'm a great fan of singing dolphins, but it's an improvement on the pan pipe drivel I was also asked to put my name to.

Gem lights the candles for me and orders my mum to dim the lights. In no time at all the hall is transformed from a draughty old memorial hall into an appropriate place in which to conduct a séance – it's still draughty, but at least it has a realistically spooky atmosphere.

As I take my place at the head of the table I hear the sound of clattering and I look over in the darkness to where the kitchen hatch is, to see my mother placing cups upside down upon saucers.

'Mum!' I hiss. 'We're about to start. Can you please do that later and come and sit down!'

'Oh, sorry dear, I thought while you got yourself prepared I would make sure we had enough cups and saucers for the break,' my mother whispers back. She scuttles back into the main hall.

'Um, Mum?'

'Yes dear?'

'Lights?'

'Oh, sorry, silly me.' My mum goes back to the kitchen and switches off the bright fluorescent kitchen light that has bathed the hall in artificial light, promptly bangs into something, shouts "Ouch! Who put that stupid tea urn there?" and eventually joins us at the table.

'I wonder if my John will come through tonight?' she whispers excitedly to Mrs Samuels – the one with one leg shorter than the other, not that you can tell – who is sitting to her right. Mrs Samuels burps her reply.

'Ooo, excuse me, dears, I have trouble digesting my tablets sometimes.'

Oh God, give me strength.

'Right, is everyone ready now?' I ask impatiently. I could really do without this tonight. I've still got loads of boxes to unpack at home and with Missy deciding to go AWOL *again*, I should really be at home to see if she's turned up for her dinner. I wonder what Jack is doing right now? Not entertaining members of the Women's Institute by holding a séance, I'm sure. I expect he's at some swanky club, schmoozing with celebrities in preparation for the band's up and coming performance.

'Make everyone link hands, Sam,' Ange instructs me, shaking me out of my domestic worries and reminding me why we are here. *'Now, I'm told you might feel funny to start with, but just keep with it and don't break the circle.'*

'What do you mean, you're told?' I ask out loud. All faces turn to me.

'Oh, don't worry, she often talks to herself,' Gem says with a smile.

'Look, I'm new to all this too you know!' Ange reminds me. *'How many séances do you think I've done? Just cos I'm dead doesn't mean I spend my days conducting séances, you know!'* she tuts.

'Right, if everyone can hold hands with the person next to them and please do not break the link,' I instruct, as I close my eyes and pray that this will go well.

'Ooo, isn't this exciting?' I hear my mother say excitedly. I open one eye and stare at her.

'By the power of the Almighty Spirit, we ask that you allow us to connect with you on this special night of All Hallows' Eve. We ask that you will come forth and allow our two worlds to become as one this evening. We come in peace and …'

'Oh crap, they're coming!' Ange whispers nervously in my ear.

'… allow your loved ones to …'

Holy shit! As Batman said to Robin, or at least he would have if they were holding a séance and he could see what I can see right now.

As I open my eyes the room is full of people. Not just the

people around the table, but *other* people. Now, I know I'm no Carol Vorderman, but the fact that there were originally only fifteen people in the room when I shut my eyes and now there is something like thirty-five people in the room, leads me to believe that there are an extra twenty people in this room. And I have a feeling that they are all dead. I deduce this from the fact that the extra guests all look as though they have been put on a hot wash for far too long and the colour has been washed out of them – in other words, they all look like ghosts, which suggests to me that my unexpected guests are not of the living variety. Like I said, holy shit!

CHAPTER NINE

OK, now this is way outside of my comfort zone! Last year, when I discovered quite by accident that I had this ability to hear voices 'from beyond the grave' and that I could make a substantial living from this unusual occupation, I thought, okay, this is a little odd, but at least I can provide a roof over my head. Which is more than I could do with a degree in psychotherapy treating people with unusual phobias. I have to say I have, over time, got used to it.

However, it's quite a different kettle of fish when you suddenly discover that you can not only hear them but can also see the dead buggers – and you're the only one who can. If other normal people could see them too it wouldn't be so bad, but as I look around the room at the members of my circle who have a pulse, they are either looking at the bad décor or have their eyes tightly shut. Gem still has her eyes closed and is swinging her head gently in time with the dolphin music. My mum is smiling contentedly to herself. Marjorie, who still has her eyes tightly shut, has a look of firm concentration on her face as if she is summoning up something sinister. There are no visible signs to say that anyone else in the room can see what I can see – which is pretty nerve racking, to be honest.

OK, Sam, deep breath. I close my eyes again and hope that when I open them there will be nothing but the bad interior design to distract me. Not so. As I gingerly open one eye, I notice that the greyish people are still standing behind the living people in the room. Maybe I should have put more chairs out.

I'm not quite sure what to do now. I mean, I've done the initiation bit and requested that someone show themselves, but I don't know what the protocol is now that they are here and Ange doesn't seem to be helping much. The only thing I've heard from her is, *'Bloody hell!'* when she too noticed the increase in party numbers, which wasn't very helpful if the truth be told.

OK, so what to do now? Um … right. Maybe I should just speak to one of them. I look around at the new guests. There is a pretty young woman standing behind Mrs Jackson. I wonder if she knows her. An Afro Caribbean man with a personal stereo with headphones attached to his head is dancing behind my mother, and bugger me, if I'm not mistaken, that's a Viking looking very Vikingish in all his furs and pointy horned hat, standing behind Mrs Horsham. That will please her. I understand from my mother that Mrs Horsham is very fond of history and belongs to the Bath Historical Society. As I look around the room I notice a little boy dressed in a grey flat cap, short trousers, and with a cheeky smile on his face. He wouldn't look out of place in a scene from *Oliver!* He stands behind Marjorie and winks at me. I take this to be my cue to ask him a question.

'Right, please don't be alarmed,' I begin, as I look at the members around the table. Some have dared to open their eyes; others have decided to keep them permanently shut tight. 'It looks as though we have some … some um … extra guests here.' All eyes open as the WI members look around the hall, obviously unable to see what I can see.

'Now, I'm going to ask one of them a question to see why they are here,' I say. My voice must sound like Minnie Mouse. It's risen by at least two octaves.

'Um … hello little boy. I'm Samantha. What's your name?' I ask the little boy who is standing behind Marjorie. Marjorie, who has now opened her eyes, is wondering why I'm looking straight through her.

'You've got a little boy standing behind you, Marjorie,' I say by way of explanation as to why I'm looking at her like a mad woman. Marjorie looks behind her and then back at me.

'*Alright missus,*' the little boy says in a cheeky Cockney accent. '*Me name's Tom. She's a nice lady, ain't she? I likes her clothes,*' Tom says with a twinkle in his eye.

'Marjorie, do you know a little boy called Tom?'

Marjorie, who actually looks a little bit terrified right now, shakes her head.

'Well, he's standing behind you and he says you're a nice lady,' I add.

Marjorie smiles nervously.

'She ain't related to me, or nuffin. I just like her. I used to live 'ere, you know.' Tom looks around the big hall. *'It weren't like this when I were a lad, mind you. It were me 'ouse once.'*

'Is there anyone you would like to talk to here, Tom?' I ask.

'Nah, I just thought I'd drop in, tis all.'

'OK, well, you're very welcome to stay with us, Tom, and it's very nice to talk to you,' I say, giving him a smile.

'Cheers, missus.'

My eyes are directed to the Afro Caribbean man who is still dancing behind my mum.

'Hello,' I venture.

The man is dressed in a shirt that would be in keeping with something that you would probably wear on a holiday to Hawaii – in other words, it's very loud! In fact, it's something my brother Paul would love. The man takes his headphones out of his ears and waves at me.

'Yo baby! How's it hanging?'

I've never been referred to as 'Yo baby' before and certainly not by a ghost. I stifle a laugh.

'Umm, fine, thank you. Are you here to talk to anyone in particular?'

'Nah, am just chillin, man. You know, man.'

OK then. Moving on quickly, I decide to pass on the Viking for a moment as I see the pretty young woman who was standing behind Mrs Jackson. She is now in the corner of the room. As I look at her, she looks away.

'Are you here to talk to someone?' I ask her.

She points to herself and I nod.

'*My name is Alice,*' the young woman says quietly.

'Does anyone know a young woman by the name of Alice?' I ask the members.

Mrs Jackson gasps.

'Mrs Jackson, do you know a young lady called Alice?'

'*She's my mum,*' Alice confirms.

Oh, my goodness. I didn't realise that Mrs Jackson had any children. Despite her being the main source of information and gossip in Castle Combe, no one seems to know much about Mrs Jackson's history.

Mrs Jackson shakes her head then looks down at the table.

'*I died when I was four. I drowned. But I've grown up now, look,*' Alice informs me and does a little spin, making her floral dress float around her legs.

'Um … Mrs Jackson, are you OK? If you don't feel comfortable with this I can tell Alice to come another time?'

Mrs Jackson has tears in her eyes.

'No, I'm fine. I don't know of any Alice,' she says, still avoiding my eyes.

'*She does know me! She's my mummy,*' Alice says, obviously upset.

'She's a grown woman now. She told me that she passed when she was four years old. She drowned, she tells me. But she's grown up now. She looks very pretty. She looks like you.'

'*Tell mummy I'm fine, really, and that I'm always around her. I like what she's done with the shop.*'

I relay the message to Mrs Jackson, who still won't confirm that the young woman is in fact her daughter.

'*She still has the last picture I drew, on her fridge. It's supposed to be the Tower of London, but it looks more like the Leaning Tower of Pisa – I was only four at the time though!*' Alice giggles.

'Alice is telling me about the picture you saved. The last one she drew for you. You still keep it on your fridge. She says it was supposed to be the Tower of London, but it looks more like the

Leaning Tower of Pisa.'

Mrs Jackson looks up. Tears are rolling down her cheeks.

'Tell her I love her and always will. It wasn't her fault and she must stop blaming herself for what was an accident,' Alice says quietly.

'Mrs Jackson, Alice says she loves you and always will. You have to stop blaming yourself. She says it wasn't your fault.'

'Thank you, thank you,' is all Mrs Jackson can say.

CHAPTER TEN

'Well this is bloody depressing!' A man's voice booms out around the room and I see that it's coming from the Viking. As Vikings go he's pretty much in keeping with what the historians say they looked like. Hum, I know, bizarre, hey?

'It's like a bloody morgue in here! Where's the bloody banquet?' he shouts, and then laughs a hearty laugh.

Dressed in his Viking costume with a fur cloak tied with rope around his neck, a hat with two great horns coming out of it and a huge, bushy ginger beard, he looks every inch the Viking. He's a large man with a booming voice and I wouldn't like to be the one who got on the wrong side of him. I hope he doesn't start raping and pillaging any time soon.

'Um...hello...sir...' I stutter. 'Mrs Horsham, I don't want to alarm you but you have a rather large Viking standing behind you.'

'Oh, my goodness!' Mrs Horsham swivels round to see him – and obviously she can't.

'Is he handsome?' she asks.

'I like her. She can be my wife!' the Viking says in a Scandinavian accent, and roars with laughter.

'He says he likes you and wants you to be his wife,' I say to Mrs Horsham, who blushes slightly.

'What's she doing with that blithering idiot husband of hers anyway?' the Viking bellows.

I can't say that!

'Well, that's what he is, a blithering idiot! She would have made a fine wife of mine.'

'What else does he say?' an excited Mrs Horsham asks me.

'Um...he says you would have made him a good wife,' I add cautiously, although I don't think I would have wanted to be a wife of a Viking. Can you imagine it? The minute you had a disagreement about what to have for tea he'd be shouting and waving his axe about at you.

'Ooh, how lovely!' Mrs Horsham says, a smile spreading across her face. Well, at least someone here in the room is happy!

In the past hour I have managed to give most of the members of the Women's Institute a message from someone they either know or may possibly have heard of. Unfortunately, my dad didn't come through for my mum; despite my best efforts to ask him to come and join us, I was informed that he was out. Out? I mean, where do they go? Out to the Heaven Pub? Out spiritual shopping? I did, however, manage to get my Aunt Rosy, my mum's sister, to come through and they ended up bickering with each other over the new title of Mum's book. My mum and my Auntie Rosy were always bickering, so it was nice to know that they would continue to do so in the afterlife.

My little Cockney boy, Tom, spent most of the time running around the hall or standing next to Marjorie and smiling up at her in awe, and well he might. I understand, again from my mother, that Marjorie is a very respectable pillar of society. She is not only on every committee in the South West, but is also one of those women, a bit like Joanna Lumley, who could do a twelve hour shift down a coal mine and still come out looking immaculate.

The Viking kept trying to interrupt me to ask me to ask Mrs Horsham if she would marry him and in the end I had to risk a beheading and politely tell him to wait his turn. Actually he was quite accommodating – between you and me I think the man is in love.

Mr Brent had a message from his late father. Mrs Samuels – the one with the medication and one leg shorter than the other, although I have to say, Mum's right, you can't tell; it's amazing what they can do with shoes nowadays – received a message from her mother. Mrs Bannerman, the lady who won the coveted second prize for her unusual preserve, received a message from an ex-lover! To look at her you would never imagine that the sixty-year-old woman could possibly have had a love affair. Her grey hair is tied neatly into a bun and she's not what you might call a fashion queen. Rather, her chosen attire is more suited to Ann Widdecombe than Nicole Scherzinger. She blushes when I tell her who I have with us in the room – a very charming, middle-aged French man by the name of Stephan.

'Oh my!' Mrs Samuels says. 'I feel quite faint.'

'Do you think it's her medication?' my mum whispers to Marjorie.

'I think it's more to do with Stephan,' Gem giggles to me.

Ange has been no help whatsoever and the only time she has spoken to me is to ask again if I can find out if it really is a Lulu Guinness handbag or if it's a fake from the market, as the fakes are so good nowadays, you can hardly tell they're fakes.

'Er, a little bit busy here right now, Ange,' I remind her, and then predictably she goes off in a sulk again. Grrr, damn spirits!

'You're doing just fine, Sammy Puddleduck,' I hear my dad say. *'Just remember to close down properly when you've finished,'* he advises. I look at my mum who is whispering something to Marjorie and decide not to tell her that I have just heard from Dad. I feel all warm inside and yet sad at the same time. *'Don't worry, Sammy, I'll be there. And tell your mum I love her,'* my dad says, as if reading my thoughts.

Before I can ask him anything else I suddenly see a ghostly figure standing directly behind Gem. I look at Gem and then at the grey figure behind her. I can't make out whether it's a man or a woman and with all the dead people bustling about in the room right now, it's a bit difficult to concentrate. The person stretches an arm out and touches Gem on the head, making her turn round.

'Did something just touch me then?' Gem asks.

I nod. 'I can't make out who it is though, Gem,' I whisper, still staring intently just above her head. I close my eyes for a moment and when I open them again there is nothing there. Nothing but a ghostly, grey figure.

'*I'm so sorry ...*' the voice whispers. I still can't make out whether the person is a man or a woman, young or old. I just don't know.

Sam, are you OK? Gem asks. 'Do you know who it is?'

I look at Gem and then back to where the hazy image was. It has gone and in its place is the regulation fire extinguisher on the wall. For a moment I have a really uneasy feeling.

'Um ... no, I couldn't get anything for you, Gem, sorry.' I mentally ask Ange if she can work out who it was, but Ange is subtly moving handbags around the room.

Can you stop that and concentrate please, Ange! I say in my head.

'*Oh, sorry, sweetie. I just wondered what she had in her handbag. I reckon it's a fake meself,*' Ange muses. '*I can't see a genuine label on it.*'

Trust me to get a fashion-conscious spirit!

'OK,' I say, as I break hands with Gem and a woman on my left who I don't know at all, 'I think that's about all we have time for tonight, I'm afraid.' I rub my eyes. 'I hope you have all felt that it was an interesting demonstration and thank you for coming tonight.' I nod to my mum to give her the cue to go and pop the kettle on for refreshments.

The members all let go of each other's hands and stretch, yawn and chatter to their neighbour.

'Oh, wasn't she good?' I hear one say.

'And what about you and the Viking chap!' another giggles with Mrs Horsham.

'Fascinating stuff. Fascinating. I thought the community officer was coming tonight. I wanted to have a word about those damn tourists trampling all over my begonias,' Mr Brent says to Mrs Jackson, who still refuses to acknowledge that her daughter has visited her.

Marjorie stands up and cautiously looks behind her.

'It's OK, Marjorie, they've all gone now.' I smile.

'Even the little boy?'

'Even the little boy,' I confirm.

'Right then, very good! Well done, Samantha. Very well done, dear.' Marjorie starts clapping her hands together and before you know it, the entire hall is singing 'For She's a Jolly Good Fellow'!

'Now, Cathy is about to serve refreshments in the kitchen if anyone is thirsty and if anyone would like to ask Samantha any questions, please feel free to ask her,' Marjorie says.

I smile politely but all I can think of right now is Gem. She is standing listening to Mrs Samuels talking about her mother and how accurate I was in my information. Gem looks as though she doesn't have a care in the world. I really hope that's true.

CHAPTER ELEVEN

By the time I get home it's past midnight and I am exhausted. All I want to do is collapse into bed and I really hope that my unwanted house guest is not up tonight of all nights. I have to say, having initially been scared silly at the sight of real dead people, it kind of feels more real to me now. When I could only hear dead people in my head, I would still wonder if it was just me going mad. I mean, I did train as a psychologist, so if anyone knows anything about the symptoms of going mad, it's me. However, the fact that I can now see who I'm talking to proves to me that I am not mental; I just have this unusual ability to connect with people who are…well, without a pulse.

My answer phone flashes to tell me that I have three messages. One is from Jack, telling me that he hopes the evening went well, the second is from Miracle, saying much the same and the third is from…well, I don't quite know who it is from, actually. All that is on the machine is a crackly whisper saying 'Jack, Jack' over and over again. When I try to replay the messages, the third message has been wiped from the machine. I quickly hit speed dial on my mobile.

'Hey,' Jack says sleepily.

'Jack, it's me, are you OK?'

'Yeah, just asleep, that's all. Are you OK?'

I don't know. Am I?

'Yes, just got in and there was a message on the phone. Someone was saying your name over and over again. I was worried about you,' I say, trying to justify why I was calling him at some ungodly hour.

'Yeah, I'm fine, honey. You sure you're OK? Did the séance thingy go well?'

'Yes, fine. Look, I'll let you get some sleep. I'll call you tomorrow. I love you.'

'I love me too. Sleep well, darling.'

No sooner do I hang up on Jack than I hear a thump on the upstairs landing, then the train set starts up again. Oh, just bloody great. 'What do you want from me?' I scream up at the ceiling. The sound of the engine whizzing around the track stops as suddenly as it had started.

I decided to sleep on the sofa and I wake up feeling as though I've been trodden on by a herd of wildebeest in the night. Not that I've ever been trodden on by a herd of wildebeest, but if I had, then I think I would feel very similar to how I feel now. My head aches, my back aches and I think at some point in the night I must have rolled off the sofa and banged my head on the coffee table because when I look in the mirror I notice that I have a huge bump on my forehead. It was either that or my house guest came along in the night and clonked me on the head while I was sleeping. I pray it was just my lack of ability to sleep on a sofa properly and not the doings of an attention seeking ghost!

'Hiya! OK if I come in?' Gem calls from the front door. She is looking particularly gorgeous in her white uniform. I on the other hand am looking particularly crap, in my attire of Winnie the Pooh pyjama bottoms and one of Jack's one-size-fits-all promotional t-shirts for the band. Why they decided on olive green for a colour is beyond me. It's not at all flattering, you know. In fact, I've a good mind to design a new range of Otherwise t-shirts for the girls as well as the boys, if only to prevent people looking like complete morons when their neighbour pops round unannounced.

'Yes, come on in, Gem. You'll have to excuse the state of me; long night last night and I seem to have an unwanted house guest in the house at the moment.'

Gem swivels round.

'Oh, right. I thought you might be a bit the worse for wear this morning, so I brought you this to help,' Gem says, handing me a small brown bottle, with what smells like a mixture of vanilla, jasmine, lavender and lots of other yummy stuff inside it. 'Just put a couple of drops on your temples and you'll have a spring back in your step in no time!'

'Oh, thank you. You are a life saver. I've got to go and see the producers at Living Today TV later and last night drained the life out of me,' I say, as I attempt mentally to give my naturally unruly hair a good talking to in the mirror. As I glace at Gem's reflection in the mirror I suddenly notice a grey shadowy figure standing behind her. It is the same figure that was standing behind her last night. I spin round quickly but the image disappears again.

'Are you OK?' Gem asks, as I look right through her.

'Um…yes…sorry…slept on the sofa last night and I feel as though I've gone ten rounds with Rocky Balboa.'

'You should never sleep on your sofa, you know. That's why in this oh so modern world we have things called beds. Now, if you're aching, I've got just the thing. Call in tomorrow and I'll make something up for you. Now, I must go, I've got Mrs Bramley coming for a head to toe in fifteen minutes.'

'OK and thanks, Gem. Have you heard from Simon yet?'

'Not yet, but I expect they're still settling in. He said they have internet access but it's as and when they can get on to it.' Gem smiles. 'By the time he comes back, this little one will be born!' She taps her tummy.

'Well, just you look after yourself and thanks for this,' I say, waving my bottle of magic potion at her as she heads out of the front door.

I wish I could work out who it is that keeps appearing whenever I see Gem. Oh well, this is not getting my hair brushed, nor is it getting me to work.

Having managed to make myself look more like a living human being rather than resembling the living dead and doused myself in Gem's magical potion, I make my way into Bristol to meet up with the producers from Living Today TV in the Marriot Hotel. I'm no longer nervous at meeting TV producers. After my brush with the media last year, a meeting with Living Today TV to talk about a new psychic detective programme is going to be a walk in the park.

'Hi, Sam, lovely to meet you,' a young woman by the name of Georgia greets me at reception. 'I've booked us into the Pascoe suite, if you'd like to follow me.'

I do as I'm told and follow the woman up several flights of stairs – memo to self: get fit before the wedding Samantha. I'm tempted to suggest we use the lift but Georgia, who incidentally oozes sex appeal and looks as though she spends every waking hour at the gym, thinks nothing of climbing ten flights of stairs and she bounds up them like Tigger on speed.

'Here we are,' Georgia says with a brilliant white smile and not so much as a hair out of place. Whereas me, well, my hair is stuck to my face, I have sweat pouring down my tights and I really think I'm about to have a heart attack.

Georgia opens the door to the Pascoe suite where there are three people sitting drinking coffee. Having mulled over the idea of this psychic detective thing with Larry, I came to the conclusion that it might be interesting. Larry, my agent, came to the conclusion that being paid five thousand pounds for each episode would bring him in a tidy bit of commission.

The first person I look at in the room is a middle-aged woman and I instantly know who she is.

'Petra?'

The lady stands up and reaches her hand out to me. She's as nervous as I am and her hand shakes.

'Hello,' she says shyly.

'Have you two met before?' a handsome man dressed in casual clothes asks as he makes his way over to introduce himself to me. 'Mark. Mark Parker, producer for Living Today TV.'

I look at Petra for a moment.

'No, we've never met, well, apart from on the radio,' I say, returning Mark's handshake. 'I just had a feeling, that's all.'

'See, I told you she was good.' Georgia giggles.

The third person in the room is a woman called Maria who has the title of programme manager.

'Sit down, sit down, Samantha, you look exhausted,' Maria says.

'Thanks, not as fit as I thought I was,' I laugh as I flump down into one of the black leather armchairs.

'Now, you know why we are here,' Maria begins in a whisper. 'We're running a new programme called *The Psychic Detective*. One of our researchers heard you and Petra on the radio the other week and she was so impressed that we managed to track down Petra and ask her if she would like us to investigate her mother's untimely death at the nursing home.'

'Have you spoken to the home's manager?' I ask.

'Our research team tried but they won't speak to us,' Mark says.

I look at Petra again. I really don't want to get into another media fight, which is what could happen if I agree to help her, but I feel certain that Petra's mother wasn't meant to die when she did.

'And how do you feel about this, Petra?' I ask. This is going to open some very sore wounds for her and if I'm right, it is going to upset her.

'I just want to know what happened to my mum,' Petra says quietly. 'I need to know what happened to her, however upsetting it might be. I think Samantha is right. Something happened to my mum and I want to find out what.'

'And what does your brother think of this?' I ask, remembering that it was Petra's brother who insisted their mother go into a nursing home.

'He's not happy about it and doesn't want any part of this,'

Petra says, waving her arms around.

'Do you think he'll cause trouble?' Mark asks nervously.

'No, I don't think so. I think it's more out of guilt than anything else.' Petra smiles. She's a pretty woman, but looks tired, as if she hasn't had a good night's sleep in ages.

'So,' Maria asks, 'do you think it's something you would like to work on, Samantha? We have other cases lined up, including a child who went missing in 1963 and a man who mysteriously disappeared. Your agent said you were the best in the business.'

Well, Larry would say that, wouldn't he? I mean, he's not going to say I'm crap when he's getting twenty per cent in commission from TV rights, is he? Larry wasn't able to attend the meeting due to trying to sweet-talk a publisher into signing me for an autobiography. I keep telling him I'm not old enough to have an autobiography, but will he listen?

'I think this is something I *have* to work on,' I find myself saying, and I think it is. I can't let this one go. I feel as though I owe it not only to Petra, but to her mum too. Despite the fact that I am trying to organise my wedding, am missing Jack like mad and have more than enough work on my plate, when I look at Petra I just feel so sad and I think her mum would at least like to know I've tried.

'*Thank you,*' a woman's voice whispers in my ear, and I take that as my confirmation to go ahead with this.

CHAPTER TWELVE

It's gone six when I get home from Bristol. I throw my bag onto the kitchen counter and open the back door. It is so nice to have a home of my very own and it's looking more and more like a home as the weeks go by. Vases of fresh cut flowers are in every room and it's now got my personal stamp on it. I love it. I could do without the ghost in the house, but …

'Missy! Missy!' I shout into the small but perfectly formed garden. You know, if I put one of those cast-iron bistro tables and a couple of matching chairs just to the left and then create one of those arches with some rambling roses, it would be like having our very own secret garden. Our very own secret place, just for Jack and me to sit and relax in.

'Missy!'

Where is that bloody cat? This is the fourth time this week that she's been late for her dinner. I bet she's over at Mum's again with that tomcat Spencer. Will that girl ever learn that it pays to play 'hard to get' sometimes? The moment you let your guard down, it all goes downhill from there. I know from previous experience – start running after them and they will break your heart. Of course, now I'm with Jack, my soul mate, it's all very different, and I don't mind telling you, a little bit scary. I mean we're going to be pledging to spend the rest of our lives together. To have and to hold, till death do us whatsit, no holds barred, for better for worse, and I don't mind admitting that I do worry that once the novelty of knowing another person inside out wears off, Jack just might break my heart. Especially now he's a heartthrob in his own right. Oh God, what if he runs off with a groupie? Now that he's a gorgeous pop star, he will have women throwing themselves at him all the time. His management company have already told him they don't want the fans to know anything about us getting married.

'Missy!' I shout again, not sure if I'm more annoyed that she hasn't come home when I've bought her fresh salmon for dinner, or about the fact that I'm now worrying that I'm not good enough for Jack. I mean, Jack and I know each other inside out. We were friends for years prior to actually getting together as boyfriend and girlfriend. What if he gets bored with me? What if he meets some gorgeous young teenybopper who has posters of him adorning her bedroom walls? What if he decides it's not very good for his image to be a married man when in a pop group? Oh bollocks! I wish my brain would stop thinking for just one minute!

I decide that Missy must still be at Mum's house. I don't know quite how she manages it. I mean, Mum's house is a good twelve miles away from my cottage and despite dragging her home she still manages to make her way back to the love of her life. Her poor little paws must be worn out. Unless of course she takes the bus, as Jack suggested.

I close the back door, pick up my phone and speed dial my mum's number.

'Boomchakawahwah!' someone who sounds not too dissimilar to my mother says on the other end of the line.

'Hello, Mum? Is that you?' I look at my phone, just to check that I've got the right number.

'Hey! It's mama's baby girl!' the voice says loudly. The reason the voice is loud is due to the Eddie Grant music playing in the background.

'I'm gonna rock down to the electric avenue and then we'll take it higher. Oh no!' My mother, or at least I think it's my mother, sings into the mouthpiece.

'Mum? Is that you?' I ask again.

'Yo, baby girl! How's it hanging?'

'Mum, are you OK?'

'Never better, man!' my mother says.

Oh God, I hope Mum hasn't been taking those pills again that the doctor prescribed for her when Dad died four years ago. They will be out of date by now and who knows what they might do to her. Oh, Christ, I hope she hasn't been trying to grow cannabis again.

'Have you been smoking something, Mum?'

'Nah, not yet,' my mother says, as casual as you like. 'I'm gonna rock down to the electric avenue and then we'll take it higher. Oh no!' she sings again.

'Okay, um…Mum…um, I was just phoning to see if Missy was at your place. She hasn't come home for her dinner again and the only place I can think that she would be is round yours, looking for Spencer again.'

The background music stops for a moment.

'Mum?'

'Yes, love?' my mother says in her normal telephone voice.

'Um … Missy. Have you seen her?'

'Yes, dear, she's here. I gave her and Spencer some semi-skimmed outside just now. You know you're spoiling that cat, Samantha. She's getting a right little fatty-bum-bum,' my mother warns. Yep, this is more like the mother I know and love.

'OK, well, I'll be over in a minute to pick her up. Are you sure you're OK?'

'Yes, fine dear, just fine. Boomchakawahwah!'

Unfortunately all is not fine when I get to my mum's house. As I walk up the path to the front door I can hear Bob Marley blaring out from the house. I look at the next door neighbours' house, thinking it might be Mr and Mrs Gale having a party, but nope, it's not coming from their house, and besides Mr and Mrs Gale are more likely to be listening to Classic FM than the king of reggae. Yep, it's definitely coming from my mum's house.

As I open the front door with my key I stand in the hallway for a moment, unable to move in disbelief at what is in front of me.

My mother, dressed in a flowing kaftan, which resembles

something out of *Joseph and his Amazing Technicolour Dreamcoat*, and with a multicoloured, woolly tea cosy/hat/thing on top of her head, is expressing herself through the medium of dance to 'Buffalo Soldier', with Missy hanging on for dear life in her arms. Missy looks bemused by it all, as well she might. I look equally bemused by it all. I mean, it's not every day that you see your mother singing and dancing to Bob Marley, is it? Before I know it, she'll be refusing to wash her hair, allowing it to form into manky dreadlocks.

'Mum!' I shout above the music. She can't hear a word I'm saying, so I walk over to the CD player and turn it off.

'Buffalo soldier, in the heart of the Caribbean...hey, I was listening to that!' My mum turns round to see who might have interrupted Bob and his Wailers.

'Oh, hello love. Just having a little dance with Missy here.'

I don't know whether to burst out laughing or tell her off.

'Mum, what are you doing? What do you look like?'

My mum looks down at her unflattering smock.

'Oh, this, I just thought it would be fun. God, Sammy, chill out a bit, love.'

Chill out a bit? Chill out a bit? My mother, who normally favours fashion that Margaret Thatcher would approve of, is dressed as if she is going to the Notting Hill Carnival and she wants me to chill out!

'*Uh-oh,*' I hear Ange say in my ear.

Uh-oh? Uh-oh? What do you mean, uh-oh? Ange just giggles to herself.

'We're just having a bit of fun, aren't we Missy, man!' my mum squeals as she sashays her way to the CD player and presses play again. I shake my head in disbelief as I take Missy from her. I sniff the air, which smells of incense, or at least I think it's incense – oh my God, I hope my mother hasn't been smoking dope. I wonder if Colin is having this effect on my mother. Or maybe she's just decided to recapture her youth. Goodness knows. Since my dad passed away, my mother constantly surprises me.

Maybe that's what it is – it's a coping mechanism over my dad's death. Yes, that's what it must be. I mean, we all cope in different ways, don't we? Mine was to slob out, eating too many Kit Kats and watch daytime TV for a year. My older brother, Paul, coped by waging a one-man war on the hospital that, as he says, "killed our dad". My younger brother Matt's way of coping was just not to talk about it – ever. Mum's coping mechanism is obviously one of having fun and living life to the full, even if it does mean dressing up in ridiculous gear and shouting out boomchakawahwah every five minutes!

'Come on, Sammy, get in the groove!' my mum sings as she dances towards me in a funny fashion – yikes!

'I'd love to, Mum,' I shout above the music, 'but I've got to get home. I'm on call tonight and I want to get Missy settled, and I have to phone Jack and sort out where we are going to have the reception.'

'You do too much, Sammy. You need to chill a bit, man,' my mother advises.

Yeah, OK, well, I think I'll just be going now.

'Oh well, I'll just have to get Colin in the groove,' my mum says as she twirls round and turns the CD player up more.

'OK Mum, but don't play that too loud. You don't want Mr and Mrs Gale banging on the walls.' God, I sound like my mother, or at least I would if I knew which planet she was on at the moment! 'I love you!' I shout as she turns the music up another notch and accompanies Bob to 'One Love'.

As I walk back down the drive to my car with Missy in my arms saying thank God you came when you did, that woman's bloody mad – or at least this is what she would be saying if cats could talk – Colin pulls up in the drive. I have to do a double take because in the passenger seat is someone who looks like his cousin Clive – his dead cousin Clive. They both wave to me and

Colin winds down his window.

'Evening Sammy, how are you? Haven't seen you for a while, love.'

I look into the car. The only item in the passenger seat is a box of old military magazines. I really like Colin and he's come out of his shell since he met my mother – I think my mother could persuade a snail out of its shell. He will never replace my dad and he would never want to; and despite looking like Jasper Carrott, he's really very nice and seems to be keeping my mum grounded. Boy, is he going to get a shock when he walks in the house.

'Oh, I'm fine, it's my mother you need to worry about,' I laugh, picturing Colin walking in to find my mother has suddenly become a fan of reggae music.

Between you and me I think they are a match made in heaven. Colin is good for my mum and I think she's good for him.

'Right then, must get on, things to do and all that,' I say quickly, remembering that I have to work tonight.

'Now then, young Missy, what's the matter with you today?' I pick up the bowl of salmon that Missy hasn't touched and kiss her little pink nose. She mews and then rubs her head on my cheek. She's not right, you know. 'Maybe you're coming down with something,' I surmise. She responds with another mew, which I take to mean yes. 'Well, let's make you up a little bed on the sofa, and no more running off to see that fella of yours, young lady. I've told you before it won't hurt him to wait around for you. If you keep chasing after him he will only take advantage of you. You mark my words,' I advise like any good mother. 'You know, your grandma's right, you are getting a bit chubby, young lady.'

I momentarily wonder whether I will make a good mother. I can't wait to marry Jack and make him a proud father. I think it's even more important to Jack to have a family of his own because he's never known what normal family life is like. Having spent the majority of his childhood in one care home after another, Jack wants more than anything to be settled with a family and I can't wait until the day when I tell him we're pregnant. Which reminds me: I must contact my brother Paul to see if he can find out some information about Jack's family. Jack has no idea what happened to his parents and I think deep down he would like to know where his mum and dad are. Maybe I will be able to trace them in time for the wedding.

'Of course you'll make a good mother, Sammy Puddleduck,' I hear my dad whisper in my ear. My stomach does one of those contented flips and I lie next to Missy, smoothing her silky tummy. Together we drift off to sleep for an hour before work begins again.

CHAPTER THIRTEEN

I took a total of forty-five calls last night and my head is hurting again this morning. I know I should be grateful for the work; I mean, if I hadn't phoned Miracle in the first place, I wouldn't be where I am today, but sometimes, particularly now, I wish I could just switch myself off from it all for a while. Jack and I still haven't decided where we are going to have our wedding reception and every time I think about it, something else comes up. Take last night, for instance: I was finishing a call to a young woman who had phoned the psychic line to try and get advice on whether or not she should quit her job and become a chef. Ange then warned me that she had a man in spirit for the next caller waiting to speak to me. Having already spoken to thirty odd people – some odder than others, I hasten to add – I had told Lynda our call centre manager that I wanted to wind the calls up for the night because I still had to phone Jack back.

'Oh, please take the next call,' Lynda said, 'he seems pretty desperate.'

And desperate he was. The poor man was heartbroken at the death of his son and needed to know that he was alright. I could tell initially that he didn't believe a word I was saying, but when I told him the exact spot where his son had died, what he was wearing and the circumstances surrounding his death, he was so pleased and couldn't thank me enough. I guess calls like that are what make people like me stay in this job rather than do something a bit easier with sociable working hours that would permit me to organise my wedding.

'Why don't we just get one of those wedding planners to organise it all? Or better still, why don't you agree to getting that okeydokey magazine to cover it and let them organise it all?' Jack said, when I eventually got round to phoning him in the middle of the night.

'No! I want to do this myself, Jack! And besides, your manager would kill you if we had a big media wedding. Think of how disappointed all your adoring fans will be,' I laugh.

'I just don't want you to get so stressed out that you don't enjoy your big day,' Jack says. 'Why don't we just bugger off somewhere and do it quietly?'

'Because, my darling, I hope I'm only going to do this once and I want it to be the best day of our lives. I don't want to run off and have a quickie wedding. And besides, my mother would kill the pair of us!'

'And how is the delectable Mrs Ball these days?'

'Oh, you know, as mad as ever. I caught her listening to Bob Marley this evening. I think she's finally cracked.'

'If she was a decent future mother-in-law she would be listening to my music.' Jack laughs. 'Look, don't worry, it will be the best day of our lives.'

Yes, it will, if I have five minutes to spare to actually concentrate on it and a fiancée who wasn't a rock and roll star and currently living in a hotel in London.

'I want you to come home, Jack, I'm lonely,' I whisper to him.

'I want to come home too, baby. It won't be long now. Another few weeks and we should have finished the first six tracks on the album. I tell you what, why don't you come and see me on Friday? I've got the day off because the sound engineers just want to record the bass guitarist, so they don't need me. We could go shopping in Covent Garden if you like,' Jack tempts me. He knows how much I love Covent Garden.

'I would love to, but I've got to go to Bristol to check out the nursing home for that psychic detective show for Living Today TV.' All in a day's work, hey?

To add to my stress levels the sound of that damn train whizzing round and round in the spare bedroom meant I didn't sleep very well and I still can't work out who it is that is trying to get my attention. I've tried asking Ange to find out, but she's more concerned at the moment with when Kerry Katona is going to announce she's getting married for the umpteenth time than with spooks in my house.

Still stiff from sleeping on the sofa the other night, I decide to go and pay Gem a visit for one of her cure-all miracle mixtures. As I walk down the hill towards her house/treatment room I notice Mr Brent in his garden. I stop for a moment, wondering what on earth he is doing. The dry stone wall that surrounds his garden has been covered with barbed wire and as I look closer Mr Brent is erecting a set of wooden stocks where his wishing well used to be.

'Hello Mr Brent,' I call out.

Mr Brent looks up and scowls at me.

'This will keep the bastards out!' he shouts back.

'Yes,' I say quickly, walking down the hill and into Gem's gate – ouch!

'Only me!' I call out as I open the front door to Gem's cottage. The smell in the cottage is wonderful. You only have to walk into Gem's house and you're cured, I'm sure of it.

'Be with you in a minute!' Gem calls out from the spare room that is her clinic.

'Okay, I'll wait in the lounge.'

It's nice to have a new friend in my life. After the episode with Amy, who I had known practically all my life, I've been a bit wary of letting new people into my life, and even more so now that I have a whole new career that is in the media spotlight. I mean, it's not every day that you're chatting to someone new and they ask you what you do for a living and you have tell them that you're a professional speaker to the dead, is it? And it takes a pretty open-minded person to accept that apart from talking to the dead, you're really quite normal and not a complete nut job. Gem did just that. She doesn't understand it all, but then neither do I, and I'm the one who hears voices all the time, but she does accept it, which is more than some I can think of. Like the ones who recognise me, take one look and run as fast as they can across the road, taking the chance that there is no traffic coming.

I make myself comfortable on Gem's sofa and look around the room. The air is filled with the fragrance of lavender coming from a small oil burner on the coffee table. Black and white photographs adorn the otherwise plain white walls and I immediately recognise Gem with her husband Simon. They look so happy together. There's one of them at their wedding; another of them on a beach somewhere hot and sunny. There's a photo of Gem with her mum, standing outside a museum, and another of Simon looking incredibly smart in his uniform. As I pick up the picture and look at the handsome soldier, the image begins to fade before my eyes.

'Right, sorry about that, Sam,' Gem says as she comes into the living room. 'I had to mix up a quick pick-me-up for Mrs Ashton down the road. She's a bit of an odd one, I have to say, but she's one of my regulars and always pays on time, unlike some I could mention.'

I quickly put the photo back in its place on the mantelpiece.

'So, what can I do for you?'

'Err, the magic potion for my aches and pains?' I remind Gem.

'Oh, of course, sorry, my head's all over the place today. Must be the hormones,' Gem laughs. 'Come on, I'll make it up for you now.'

I follow Gem into her clinic. It's spotlessly clean and very white. The stainless steel shelves are awash with bottles of all shapes and sizes, full of delicious essential oils, and the smell is wonderful! I could sit in here all day and just sniff.

'So, have you recovered from Halloween?' Gem asks as she dispenses several secret ingredients known only to her into a small silver measuring jug.

'I think so. I think everyone enjoyed it. Have you spoken to Mr Brent lately?'

'No, why?'

'Oh, nothing. I just saw him in his garden. He was acting a bit odd actually.'

'Odd?'

'Well, I mean, I don't know him that well, but when I walked past just now I couldn't help but notice that he's put barbed wire all around his garden and is replacing the wishing well with wooden stocks. I mean, that's a bit odd in anyone's books, don't you think?'

'Maybe he's just had enough of people walking all over his garden,' Gem says, as she pokes her tongue out in careful concentration so that she doesn't spill a drop.

'Maybe.'

As Gem concentrates on adding single drops of rose oil to my magic solution, I notice the ghostly grey figure that I saw in the hall the other night and in the mirror yesterday, standing beside her. Who are you? I ask in my head. Show yourself to me. Please let me know who you are.

'Oh, this is mine and Simon's song!' Gem suddenly says as Take That's 'Back For Good' comes on the radio. 'We had a Take That tribute band at our wedding – couldn't afford the real thing, but they were really good.'

As Gem walks across the room to turn the music up, I notice that the shadow follows her. Who are you? And how are you connected to Gem?

All of a sudden the grey hazy shape begins to form into something recognisable. As Gem sings along with Gary, Mark, Robbie, Jason and the other one whose name always escapes me, I stare at the shape forming behind her. Slowly it forms into a human. A man. A handsome young man dressed in uniform. Oh, my God! Fuck, shit and bollocks. No! It's Simon!

'Oh my God,' I whisper.

'Want you back, want you back, want you back for good...' Gem sings along to the music. The image of Simon puts his finger to his lips as if to tell me to keep quiet. I put my hand over my mouth as tears build up in my eyes.

'*She doesn't know yet,*' Simon says, looking at Gem, who's lost in her own little Take That world.

You mean?

'*I'm dead,*' Simon confirms. '*I died three days ago. They set us up at a road block.*'

No! This can't be happening.

'You know,' Gem says, as she places a top on a brown glass bottle and shakes it vigorously, 'it was so funny the night before we got married. Si was so wracked with nerves that he spent his stag night being sick and then passed out in the toilet.' She laughs. I notice Simon smiling at the memory of it. 'I thought he'd had too much to drink, when in fact he hadn't touched a drop.'

'*Yeah, she gave me grief all morning. She went mental at me!*' Simon says. I can't take all of this in. This cannot be happening. I look to where Simon is standing. His face is serious.

'*They will be coming to tell her soon,*' he whispers. '*Tell her I am so sorry. All I wanted was for us to be a happy little family. Tell her I love her and I always will. I don't want to be here, Sam. This is so unfair to Gemma. I will always be looking out for her and our baby boy.*'

Oh God, no! Don't go!

Simon's image disappears as Gem spins round.

'Here you go, sweetheart. Sam?'

I look at Gem.

'Um...yes, sorry...um ...'

'Are you OK?'

'Um...yes...no... I...I've got to go. I'm so sorry Gem,' I say, as tears roll down my face. Gem looks at me with concern on her face.

As I leave Gem's house a black car with blacked-out windows pulls up slowly and comes to a halt outside her house. I wait as I watch two officers in uniform, one male and one female, approach Gem's front door. I collapse on the small lovers' bench that Simon and Gem bought together to sit on in their garden, and I wait. I wait for the anguished cry to ring out. Sure enough it does.

CHAPTER FOURTEEN

As I hold Gem in my arms and let her cry, I see Simon standing in the corner of her living room. I can barely look at him. The anguished look on his face says it all. As I hug Gem tightly to me, Simon walks toward us. He strokes the back of Gem's long brown hair and kisses her head. Through sore red eyes Gem looks up at me.

'You knew, didn't you?' she whispers.

'I...' I begin. What can I say? I didn't know for sure that it was Simon trying to come through to Gem at the séance, but I knew it was Simon in the kitchen. I knew Simon had died three days before the army had sent their officers to tell his wife the bad news. Shit! I hate the fact that I knew Gem's husband had died before she knew. I hate this. I hate it! I wish I never had this stupid, crappy gift or whatever they bloody call it! I wish I had never accepted the stupid job in the first place and had persevered in my search to cure vegetable fearing folk, instead of having to know when someone has died before their loved ones know.

'When did you know?'

'Not until today,' I whisper. You would think that by now I would be used to this death thing, but I'm not. Not at all. It all seems so unfair and I am constantly asking the question, why? Why, when Gem and Simon had their whole lives ahead of them, was Simon suddenly taken away from her? Why, when Simon was about to become a father, was he suddenly snatched away? What did they ever do to deserve this?

'Why Simon, Sam?' Gem asks, as if reading my thoughts.

I take a deep breath and pause for a moment.

'Because it was just my time to go, tell her,' Simon whispers. *'I never wanted to leave her, but we don't have a choice in the matter. If more people realised that, then they would cherish every moment they*

did have on earth.'

'I don't know, Gem, I just don't know,' is all I can manage to say.

'Is he here? Now?'

I nod. Gem nods too.

'I can feel him here. I can smell his aftershave. Can you smell it?' she says, before dissolving into floods of tears. 'What are we going to do without him, Sam? How am I going to cope without Simon? How am I going to bring up a baby on my own? A baby who will never know his or her dad. I love him so much. It's so unfair!'

It's another three hours before I get back to my house. I wanted to stay with Gem for as long as she needed me, but naturally all she wanted was her mum. Having phoned her I waited with Gem while she drove the forty miles to be with her daughter, and we sat in almost silence, punctuated only by the occasional blow of a nose on a Kleenex.

'I must phone my next client, she'll be wondering why I can't make her appointment,' Gem said all of a sudden. She jumped up and started rummaging around in the sideboard drawer for her client address book. It would make no difference whatsoever if I tried to make her sit down with another cup of rose hip tea, she wouldn't listen. I know, because this is how some people react when they hear the news that someone they love so much that it hurts has died. I know this, because this is exactly how I reacted when my dad died.

Having spent the whole day at the hospital, watching and waiting for any slight sign of improvement in my dad, I'd driven home to get a quick shower before going back to give my mum a break for the evening. As I was unemployed at the time and still living at home with my parents, it was only natural for me to share the role of caring for my dad while he was in hospital, fighting prostate cancer. For eight weeks I was at his bedside: reading out the news headlines in the paper for him; doing the crossword in the *Daily Express* with him; and popping down to the lobby where the drinks machines were kept to get him a hot, milky coffee and a small packet of three custard creams from the vending machine for his supper.

Although he was having morphine pumped into him morning, noon and night, to ease the pain, he still had the energy to voice his opinions on the crap daytime programmes they would show on the small hospital TV monitor just above his bed. He would insist I topped his TV card up with five pounds every day, even though he would watch every programme that came on with a critical eye and moan about it.

We would religiously watch *Countdown* every afternoon at four o'clock and guess whether the contestant would ask Carol Vorderman for a vowel or a consonant, invariably guessing the wrong one. Then we would try to form a word from the chosen letters and get that wrong too.

As I'd stepped out of the shower, my mobile began to ring and I knew that it was my mum – maybe I had psychic skills back then and just didn't know it. 'Sammy, get here now, your dad's going,' my mother shouted down the phone. Going? Going where? The logical part of me had wanted to ask.

By the time I got to the hospital he was no longer with us. He had gone to wherever he was going. Where? I didn't know. Why? I didn't know that either. And do you know what the first thing I did was after I saw my dad for the last time? I started tidying up the area around his bed. While my mum was crying her heart out on my dad's chest and pleading with him to wake up again, I was busy brushing up biscuit crumbs from under his bed with a dustpan and brush, cursing whoever it was who invented custard creams. How stupid was that?

I don't even remember how I got home that night. Mum refused to leave dad alone, but insisted I drove home to put the lights on in the house so that we didn't get burgled. All I remember is texting Jack and Amy as I walked out of the hospital, with a simple message that read, my dad is dead.

I sit on my sofa, cradling Missy on my lap, and I cry and cry. I don't know whether I'm crying for Gem or for myself. It's a close call really.

'She'll be fine, Sam,' I hear Ange whisper in my ear.

'But it is so unfair, Ange!' I scream out loud, disturbing Missy from her sleep.

'No shit,' Ange says, *'you don't think I don't know that? One minute you're having an awesome time and the next, poof! Gone!'* Ange puts it so eloquently. *'Still, it's not so bad once you get used to it,'* she muses. *'I can get as pissed as a fart here and I never get a hangover. And you do get to listen in on all the best gossip!'* Ange continues. *'I saw that tart from that talk show, you know, the one who tried to stitch you up last year. She was in the bathroom at The Ivy the other night and you should have seen the amount of powder she was putting up her nose!'* Ange informs me. I smile at the thought of Miss-too-much-make-up's secret. *'And you know that Jeremy Brown? The host on* Other People's Lives? *Well, I bet you didn't know that he's gay. He is, you know. All that wife and three happy kids crap is a cover-up. I've seen him with his lover, you know – a lad aged about eighteen. They meet at The Arosfa every weekend. He claims he goes there to lean his lines. Learn his lines, my arse!'*

God, I could get a lot of people into trouble if I wanted to, couldn't I?

'But it doesn't make any sense to me, Ange,' I whisper. 'I mean, why do good people have to die?' This is the one question I am asked the most when someone who is recently bereaved phones me up and I always have a problem answering it. It just seems so unfair all the time. The most wonderful people are suddenly snatched from this world, just like that. No warning. No nothing. Just gone. And yet other people, vile people who should be hanged get to live long lives. I am so pissed off about it right now.

'Like your dad told you, sometimes it's just their time, hun,' Ange

says kindly. *'We don't have a choice in the matter. You think I prefer to be up here than down there with you? When people realise that we don't actually have a choice in this game, only then will they bloody well learn to really live every day of their lives. Most people take it all for granted, Sam. I know I did. You don't ever think that today could be your very last one on earth, do you? No one does. If they did, then they wouldn't spend so much time being petty with each other and arguing over stupid things.'*

You know, I'm learning that for someone who is usually brash, loud and more than a little bit bonkers, my little spirit friend can be quite philosophical when she wants to be.

'Now, enough of this bollocks, let's go shopping tomorrow to cheer ourselves up, shall we?' Ange finishes in typical Ange fashion as only she can.

CHAPTER FIFTEEN

It's after lunchtime before I finally manage to pull myself together again to drive into Bristol to meet the team from Living Today TV. As I stop at the traffic lights in the centre of Bath to turn off to the main road to Bristol, I fiddle with the radio to try to find something to cheer me up. Ironically the old eighties song 'The Only Way is Up' by Yazz comes on. Oh well, it's a good tune I guess, although the only reason I remember it is because my mum used to sing it to me in the bath when I was eight years old – my mum was a bit of an eighties fashion victim at the time. She even sported one of those big hair hairstyles, all backcombed, and vivid blue eyeshadow, if I remember rightly.

As Yazz tells me to hold on, hold, on, hold on, I look down the high street and notice the HMV store where Jack used to work. It seems a million years ago now since we used to meet up at lunchtimes in Royal Park; Jack filling me in on the latest tracks to hit the store; me telling him about my attempts at finding meaningful employment. Now look at us – one a successful psychic and the other a successful rock star. Don't get me wrong, I'm truly grateful for the success and I am so proud of how Jack is doing, but sometimes, just sometimes, I long for the good old days when I had nothing more to worry about than making sure Valerie got her rent on time and deciding whether a Pot Noodle could be considered a nutritional lunch or not.

I look at the entrance to McDonalds and do one of those double takes one does when they think their eyes are playing tricks on them.

'Spare change, luv?' a voice from the pavement shouts to a passer-by. There was a time when Bath City Council introduced a no tolerance policy about begging on the streets, but no one really bothered about it. Of course, for a few weeks the police community officers would walk the streets and move people on, but after that, no one would bother calling them out, or if they did, the police would fail to turn up due to understaffing or something. Since then the beggars of Bath have come out in force so it's not unusual to hear the familiar request for small change coming from the pavement.

What is unusual, in this case, is the voice in which it comes. It doesn't sound like your usual street beggar. In fact, the voice I hear is very middle class, which is why it caught my attention in the first place.

'Change? You got any spare change?'

'Marjorie?' I mutter to myself. The woman dressed in a red Marks and Spencer wool suit, sitting cross-legged on a tartan picnic blanket on the cold pavement outside the fast-food establishment, certainly looks like my mum's friend Marjorie. A passer-by tosses the woman fifty pence to which she responds, 'Cheers, darling.'

It can't be Marjorie, but it certainly looks very much like her. OK, so she hasn't got her half-moon glasses on and her usually immaculately tight-permed hair is hidden beneath a red felt hat that would be better suited to Paddington Bear, but I'm sure it's Marjorie from the WI. As Yazz warbles on about the only way being up, I sit in my car, open-mouthed and staring at her – I swear if it's not Marjorie, it's her double.

The car behind me sounds its horn to tell me to get a bloody move on as the lights have turned green and I quickly pull away, looking over my shoulder at the posh beggar woman.

I hit the speed dial on my hands-free and pray that my mum is no longer worshipping Bob Marley and can hear the phone ringing.

'Hello? Cathy Ball speaking.'

'Mum, it's me. Are you OK now?' I ask nervously.

'OK? Of course I'm OK. Why?'

'Oh, nothing. Listen, can you get down to the high street. I think Marjorie is ... well, I'm not quite sure what she is, but I'm certain it's her sitting outside McDonalds begging for money,' I whisper into the speaker.

'What? Marjorie? Oh don't be silly, Sammy. Marjorie wouldn't be begging, for goodness sake! Malcolm, her husband, is an investment banker!'

'Mum! I'm sure it's her. She's got the same features *and* she's wearing Marks and Sparks!'

'Oh, Sammy, you are funny sometimes.'

'Mum, I just saw her. She was sitting on the pavement asking for spare change.'

'Who was?'

'Marjorie, Mum! Marjorie was sitting outside McDonalds.' God, keep up mother!

'No, it wouldn't be Marjorie, she doesn't like McDonalds, love. She makes her own mince, you know. It's so much better than anything you can buy at a supermarket. She often adds mint to it. Anyway, what would Marjorie be doing outside McDonalds? She doesn't go to town on a Tuesday. If she's going into town it would be on a Thursday or a Friday, not a Tuesday; that's when she usually does her chores.'

'Well, how the hell should I know?'

'Well, there's no need to shout, Samantha,' my mum scolds. 'You're very stressed lately, aren't you dear? You have to stop getting yourself so worked up, you know, it's no good for you. Oh, Missy's turned up here again by the way.'

That damn cat! I take a deep breath.

'Mum, will you just pop down to the high street and take a look, please!'

'Oh very well, Sammy.'

'Look, I'm on my way to Bristol at the moment, so you'll have to keep Missy at yours until I get home. Oh, and can you phone the Abbey back and tell them that we definitely want to book 21st December?'

'Yes sweetheart. Now you drive carefully.

Boomchacawahwah!' my mother finishes.

Boomchaka what? God, I despair sometimes, I really do.

Due to being temporarily delayed by why my mum's best friend was sitting in Bath high street, begging for money, I am now running late. I eventually arrive at a small hotel on the outskirts of Bristol twenty minutes late to find Georgia, Maria and Mark waiting for me in the car park – not a good start.

'Sorry, sorry, sorry,' I pant as I lock my car and rush over to the patient trio. 'Got a bit delayed, in traffic.'

'Oh, don't worry. It happens to the best of us,' Mark says and smiles. I notice that Georgia's smart dress she wore to the first meeting has been replaced by SAS combat-style gear. Even covered from head to toe in black, she manages to look as though she's about to step out on the catwalk and I wouldn't be surprised if she told me it was Stella McCartney.

'Right, Sam, if you follow me inside, we'll get you miked up,' Maria says efficiently. 'Now, as planned, you and Mark are going to go into the nursing home just round the corner, posing as Mr and Mrs Spears looking for a home for your mother.' Now there's an idea.

'Mark is going to have a hidden camera on him in his holdall and we will be recording everything in there.' Maria points to a black van with blacked-out windows that is sitting discreetly behind some trees that line the public car park. It's all very CSI-esque.

'All we want to do is to see what you get, if anything. Don't worry if you don't feel anything. Now, remember, we don't want to give away the fact that we are investigating them, so don't mention Petra or her mother Pearl to anyone. We're just there to see if you get anything. Any questions?'

I raise my hand as we walk to the entrance of the hotel.

'Just the one. What if these people recognise me? I mean, they might have seen me on the TV or in the magazines I write for,' I add, panicking that I'm not at all prepared for this.

'This is why we have these.' Maria produces a bright pink headscarf and a pair of sunglasses that wouldn't be out of place on Victoria Beckham.

'*Oo, nice,*' Ange says.

'You don't think they will think I'm trying to disguise myself then?' I say, looking at the two items in her hands.

'When Mark phoned up to make the appointment he gave the owners the impression that the two of you were famous actors from America. They will expect you to turn up in some form of disguise,' Maria explains.

'Hang on a minute; you mean I have to put on an American accent?'

'Hell, it's real easy,' Georgia says in a Texan drawl – at least I think it's a Texan drawl. My own American accent leaves a lot to be desired and sounds more like Justin Lee Collins than Jerry Hall.

'Hell, it's real easy,' I try to copy Georgia's accent, but it comes out more like a Bristolian Minnie Mouse.

'Tell you what, I'll be the American, you can be the Brit. I'll be Michael Douglas to your Catherine Zeta-Jones,' Mark says, although it has to be said that Mark looks nothing like Michael Douglas, however much you squint your eyes. Whereas Mr D is middle-aged and somewhat wrinkled, Mark is in his mid thirties, with blonde floppy hair and darned good looking to boot!

'But she's Welsh!' Oh, I'm worried now. My Welsh accent is marginally better than my American accent, but not a patch on Catherine Zeta-Jones's.

'No, I don't mean you have to be Welsh, just be yourself. Tell you what, how about I just do the talking, OK?' Mark winks at me – ooh boyo!

'OK,' I stutter. I've come over all girly and weak – not a good look on any woman.

'You're blushing!' Ange teases.

Maria escorts me to a private room to get miked up and ready to enter the nursing home where Petra's mum ended her days.

To make it look more authentic, it's been decided that Mark and I will drive from the car park, round the block and into the nursing home car park in his silver BMW.

'Now, remember, just leave the talking to me,' Mark advises as I tie the pink headscarf under my chin and put my big sunglasses on.

'Ooh, you look like a movie star!' I hear Ange squeal in my ears. *'Just like Angelina Jolie!'* she says as she starts clapping with joy. Well, at least one of us is happy with the outfit.

Mark holds the door open for me, and then taking me by surprise he holds my hand as I get out of the car and kisses it tenderly. I peer at him from underneath my shades.

'Just trying to make it look authentic,' he smirks.

Hum, so long as that's all he's doing.

CHAPTER SIXTEEN

As we make our way to the front door of We Care Nursing Home – *The Home From Home* – Mark switches on the camera in his holdall and it beeps, signalling that it is now recording. He rings the brass doorbell and we wait for someone to answer. I nervously push a stray curl of hair back underneath my headscarf and take a deep breath.

The house is huge and is set in acres of land. From the outside it looks like one of those houses that feature in *Country Homes*. The sheer elegance of it makes me feel quite small.

A young girl in a nurse's uniform comes to the door.

'Yes? May I help you?'

'Hello Mam, we've come to have a look at your lovely home as a possibility for my darling wife's mother,' Mark drawls, in what has to be said is a very convincing American accent. He flashes a smile at the young girl, who smiles back.

'Have you got an appointment?' the girl asks.

'Yes, mam, it's Mr and Mrs Spears. We just saw your darling little home the other day on our way through and thought, that's the place for us, didn't we, darling?' Mark looks at me. I nod, unsure whether the girl might think it a bit strange that so far I haven't uttered a word. Maybe she thinks I'm the mute wife of the charming American? And who came up with Spears for the name? I'm thinking that it was probably Georgia's idea. I just hope Britney doesn't find out and try to sue us.

'Oh, right, well, if you would like to follow me,' the girl opens the door wider and we follow her down a long, narrow hallway that is tastefully decorated in several shades of lemon.

'If you take a seat there, I'll just let Mrs Lance know that you're here,' the girl says.

'Why, thank you, mam. This is just charming, darling, isn't it?'

I nod again. OK, don't go over the top, Mark.

'*I don't like it in here,*' Ange whispers in my ear. '*Old people give me the willies.*'

'So what do you think? Have you got anything yet?' Mark whispers to me as we wait for the owner to show us around. Blimey, give me a chance!

'Nothing yet,' I say. For once, aside from Ange declaring how much the home gives her the willies, my mind is completely quiet and peaceful, which is a bit of a rarity for me.

Within minutes I notice a large woman walking towards us from the end of the hallway and I immediately have a feeling of nervousness in the pit of my stomach. The woman, who I assume to be Mrs Lance, barks an order at a young nurse in an adjacent room and then walks faster towards us. Mark and I stand up. Oh my God, she knows who we are.

'Mr and Mrs Spears?' the supersized woman asks.

We both nod. I suspect Mark is as nervous of this woman as I am. She looks like Miss Trunchball from Matilda, but on a bad day – the hair on her top lip is quite scary too.

'Welcome to We Care Nursing Home. If you would like to follow me this way into my office, I will explain what our home can offer your mother. Sandra, get Mr Salmon off the commode, will you!' she bellows to another nurse who is passing by in the corridor.

'Of course, Mrs Lance,' the nurse says as she scuttles away down another corridor. My eyes follow the nurse and I feel as though I should be following her.

'Charming, utterly charming, and so quaint,' Mark drawls as we follow the old dragon to her dungeon – the dungeon being a small office off to the right of the hallway. Two chairs have been placed in front of a desk and Mrs Lance waves her arm dismissively for us to sit in them. No amount of American charm is going to win this woman over, methinks.

Right, what can I do for you, Mr and Mrs Spears?' Mrs Lance puts on a pair of glasses and clasps her hands in front of her.

'Well, as I was saying to the lovely nurse who answered the door, we saw your charming little nursing home when we were passing through and thought, that's the ideal place for my wife's mother. She already lives in England, but is finding it hard to walk now, isn't she, honey?' Mark says. I nod.

Mrs Lance grunts as though she has heard this story a thousand times before, opens a drawer and pulls out a blue folder. She flicks through a few pages until she comes to the relevant form, unclips it from the folder and hands Mark a copy of the home's terms and conditions. As I look at the woman's gnarled hands, I suddenly get a vision flashing through my mind. I can see the same hands and then I smell something sweet, but I'm not altogether sure what it is. I sniff the air.

'Isn't that right, darling?' Mark says. I haven't a clue what Mark has just said to me, so I nod enthusiastically. As Mrs Lance goes to the adjoining office to photocopy some paperwork, Mark mouths, Are you OK?

'I've got something,' I whisper, 'but it's not ...'

'Here you are. This tells you a bit about the home and the care of our residents and these are our rates.' Mrs Lance leans over Mark, almost smothering him with her ample bosom in the process, and places several sheets of paper in front of us.

'Thank you mam.' Mark mumbles while being suffocated. 'May we have a look around you wonderful home?'

'Of course. I'll get one of the nursing staff to escort you.' Mrs Lance presses some buttons on her phone and requests a member of staff to come to her office immediately.

Within seconds the young nurse who opened the front door to us is at Mark's side, ready to escort us around We Care Nursing Home.

The grand home is spread over four floors. I am desperate to go down the corridor where I saw the other nurse go earlier, but the nurse accompanying us takes us up the stairs and to the first floor.

I can feel many old spirits around me up here and a great deal of sadness. I can't of course tell Mark any of this because he's too busy, three steps ahead of me, chatting up the bloody nurse – see, I told you all men had a thing about nurses! As they turn left into another corridor, I take my chance and run back the way we came, down the stairs, into the hallway, and turn down the corridor I've been drawn to since we came here.

No sooner do I start walking down this corridor than I start to feel very distressed indeed.

'*Sam, I don't think this is a good idea,*' Ange says.

She's right. I feel as though I want to run back up the corridor and out of the house again. OK, keep calm, Sam, I tell myself over and over again, like a mantra. Just keep on walking. There's a reason why I'm feeling like this and I need to get to the bottom of it. I just wish Mark was with me, because he's the one with the flipping camera. Never mind, I'll just have to talk into the microphone and hope that Maria and Georgia pick it up at the other end.

As I approach a row of doors to my right, I feel compelled to open the second one, with the number four marked on it. I look over my shoulder to make sure no one is coming and gingerly turn the brass door knob. I open the door and I feel as though I shouldn't be entering this particular room, and yet I know that something in there holds the key to Petra's mum's death. I don't know how I know, I just do.

I peer in through the gap in the door to make sure no one is in there. The room is dark and I notice that the curtains are closed. The bed is neatly made and yet the feeling I get from standing in this room is one of horror.

'Pearl, are you here?' I whisper.

'*This was my room. I can't...*' a voice replies. It's Petra's mum, Pearl.

I suddenly get an overwhelming feeling as though I can't quite catch my breath, as though something is preventing me from doing so. I can't breathe and I struggle like a fish to gulp air into my lungs, but no matter how hard I try I can't get any. I have crippling pains in my stomach and feel dizzy all at the same time. I feel as though I'm suffocating.

'Help me, Ange!' I gasp as I collapse by the bed on the floor.

'I can't help you until you can get out of that room!' Ange says. *'Sam, get out of the room!'*

I still can't breathe, I feel so sick and dizzy. The room spins above my head, but I use every ounce of strength in me to get to the gap in the door. As I crawl along the brown cord carpet, in my mind I can see Pearl doing exactly the same thing. She's in a white nightdress and is desperately trying to get out of the room. She is desperately trying to get out so that she can scream and get someone's attention. This is how she died. This is how Petra's mum died. She couldn't catch her breath. I can feel Pearl struggling to breathe and clutching at her throat and stomach.

The open door seems so far away and I don't think I can make it. Oh shit!

'Sam? Are you OK?' I hear Maria ask in my earpiece. I desperately want to scream for help, but I can't even breathe let alone say anything. As I make one final attempt to reach the door, I suddenly smell something familiar on the brown carpet and it is then that things start to click into place. Pearl didn't die naturally. Something was preventing her from breathing properly. The sweet aroma I smelt in Mrs Lance's office is the same smell that I can smell in this room. In room four. Pearl's room. As I crawl back out of the room it's like a rush of fresh air is filling my lungs. I can breathe again! Bloody hell! I've never been so grateful for that rush of air in my life.

I shove my sunglasses back up on to my nose, straighten my headscarf and look back at the carpet in the bedroom. Without really thinking about it I rummage about in my handbag for something I can use to cut the carpet. Pen, nope; collapsible hairbrush, nope; a packet of Wrigleys chewing gum, hardly a suitable cutting tool; Ruby Rush nail polish, no. It's then that I find the tiny pair of silver nail scissors at the bottom of my bag. It was from one of last year's Christmas crackers. In fact it originally belonged to my brother Matt who swapped it for the silver bookmark that I had won, on the basis that Matt bites his fingernails and would have no use whatsoever for a pair of nail scissors. I doubt very much that he will find a use for the silver bookmark either, as I've never seen him read an actual book, unless it contains the words C++ programming in it.

I get on to my hands and knees and crawl back just inside the bedroom door and sniff the carpet until I find the spot where I smelt the strange odour. As I puncture a hole in the carpet and begin to cut roughly at the carpet, I hear Mark's voice coming down the corridor. Oh bollocks! Quick, Sam! I snip as fast as I can and have to rip the final threads, ending up with a two-inch sample of brown cord carpet and a hole in the bedroom floor to boot - oh crikey, I hope they don't notice.

'Well, I'm sure she...' I hear Mark's voice as I back out of the bedroom on my hands and knees. 'Honey?' Mark, who is standing outside the bedroom door with Mrs Lance in tow, looks down at me. 'What on earth are you doing down there, honey?' Mark says, remembering his American accent just in the nick of time.

I look up at both him and the Trunchball and blush from head to toe. I wink at Mark in my best Velma Dinkley impression to give him a clue that I indeed have a clue to this mystery, and then I remember that unlike Velma my glasses are in fact shades and he can't actually see me winking at him.

'I ...'

'Oh, honey, have you had one of your funny turns again?' Mark says, as he hooks his arms under my armpits and awkwardly pulls me to my feet. One of my funny turns?

'I....'

'I'm so sorry, mam,' Mark says to Mrs Lance, who looks at me as though I should be committed - and she would be only too happy to oblige. 'My wife loses her balance every now and again. The doctors have no idea what it might be; they think it could be all in the mind,' Mark whispers, and winks at the old battleaxe. I steady myself under Mark's grip and stamp on his left foot as I regain my 'balance' – good job I'm wearing my pointy heels, eh?

'Ouch! Oops, now let's get you back to the hotel, honey,' Mark winces. 'I'm sorry about this, mam. Perhaps we could make another appointment to see you. I will call you to arrange a more convenient time,' Mark says, as he ushers me down the corridor and into the hallway. Mrs Lance just looks at the two of us. I can feel her eyes penetrating into my back. Oh dear God, please don't let her notice the hole in the carpet until we get out of here!

'Mr and Mrs Spears!' Mrs Lance bellows from the corridor. Oh shit, oh shit. She's noticed.

Mark turns round.

'Mrs Spears left her handbag on the floor.' Mrs Lance grunts and hands Mark my bag, which is a good job because it has my only piece of evidence in it.

'Ah, thank you, mam,' Mark says, and winks at her as the two of us hobble out of the nursing home – him from having a four-inch heel dug in his foot, me from having one of my 'funny turns'.

CHAPTER SEVENTEEN

'What did you stand on my foot for?' Mark says as he quickly bundles me into the car and hops into the driver's seat.

'Oh, did I stand on your foot? Sorry,' I smile sweetly at him.

'Yes, you did and it bloody well hurt,' Mark winces.

'Oh, it must have been when I had one of my 'funny turns'.'

'Well, I had to think of something. What on earth were you doing on the floor anyway?' Mark says as we pull out of the car park.

'As a matter of fact, I was getting evidence.' I pull out the small sample of carpet and show Mark.

'A piece of carpet. You ripped up their carpet?'

'Not just any old piece of carpet. Smell.' I shove my carpet sample under Mark's nose. He sniffs it.

'What's that?'

'Does it smell familiar?'

Mark nods.

'I'm not sure what it is though,'

'Neither am I but I smelt the same smell when we were in Mrs Lance's office. This carpet came from room number four – Pearl's room.'

'How do you know it was her room?'

'She told me. You can check it out with Petra if you like, but I bet you anything room four was Pearl's room. I think that whatever it was that was spilt on the carpet in her room was what killed her. If you get this checked out by a chemical lab, they will be able to tell us what the chemical on it is.' Ooh, the Scooby Gang would be proud of me.

'Right. I'll get someone on to this and we hope to begin recording next week if you're free?' Mark says, looking at the carpet sample.

'Yes, no problem, as long as I don't have to go into that bloody home again.'

As I head back home I can't help but glance at the high street to see if Marjorie or Marjorie's double is still begging outside McDonalds. Nope, the street is deserted, free from beggars and vagrants. Maybe it was just my imagination.

I drive back home and as I drive up the hill to my house I look at Gem's house, which is in complete darkness. The curtains are closed and I guess that Gem must still be staying with her mum.

'Go on, off with you, or I'll skin your hide, so I will!'

The sudden shouting from Mr Brent's house stops me in my tracks and I slam on my brakes.

'Go on, get out of here!' I hear Mr Brent shout.

As I step out of my car to see what on earth is going on, I see Mr Brent, dressed in what looks like a brown skirt and a pair of rope sandals, swinging a mace around his head and chasing a middle-aged couple down his garden path. The woman with a backpack on her shoulders looks absolutely petrified and screams for someone to call the police. Her husband, also sporting a backpack and interestingly dressed in an anorak that matches the woman's - please shoot me the day me and Jack start wearing matching anoraks – shouts back at Mr Brent, but thinks better of it when he sees him bend down to pick up a rock from his ornamental rockery and set about putting it into a makeshift slingshot to throw after the couple. It's not long before he's outrunning his wife, leaving her running after him, screaming, Brian, wait for me!

'Go on your bastards! You'll be skinned alive! You mark my words you will!' Mr Brent shouts, opening his garden gate and starting to run down the hill in hot pursuit of the couple.

Oh my God!

'Mr Brent!' I shout after him. It's no good; I'm going to have to go after him.

'Mr Brent! Stop!' I wail as I try to run after the old-age

pensioner in my high heels. I knew it was a mistake to wear these today, but Ange insisted, saying my legs look like tree trunks when I wear flatties – who does she think she is, bloody Gok Wan?

'Mr Brent!' I shout again as he turns the corner, armed to the teeth and still in hot pursuit of the couple. Blimey, I am so unfit it's unreal! I can't even keep up with a bloody pensioner.

By the time I round the corner, the couple are nowhere to be seen. Mr Brent turns and walks towards me. Oh crikey, I hope he's not as cross with me as he was with that couple.

'Afternoon Samantha,' Mr Brent smiles. 'Lovely day,' he says as he strolls back up the hill, slingshot slung casually over his shoulder as though he was just returning from a long day on the battlefield.

'Er, afternoon Mr Brent,' I say cautiously and watch him walk back to his cottage as though nothing has happened. I look around to see if I can see any evidence of bloodshed, but the couple are nowhere to be seen. Mr Brent obviously drove them out of the village – big time!

'*Uh-oh! Something's not right here!*' I hear Ange sing in my head. And I think she might just have a point.

As soon as I get in to the safety of my own cottage I flop down on the sofa. It's been a long day, what with one thing and another, and I forgot to switch the timer on the heating system to on, so it's bloody freezing in the house. Before I go upstairs to switch the heating and the hot water on I must phone my mum to see if she has tracked down Marjorie – I'm sure there must be some good explanation as to why she was begging in the high street. Maybe she was doing it for charity? You hear of middle class people doing this sort of thing, don't you? I also want to see if Missy has wandered back to the love of her life again because she isn't in her cat bed. She's become a feline aborigine and I do wish she wouldn't keep going walkabout all the time. One of these days she is going to get herself lost and then who will she come meowing to, huh?

'It's only me,' I say cautiously as my mum answers the phone, thankfully in her normal telephone voice.

'Oh, hello darling, how are you? How did the TV thing go?' My mum sounds very cheerful today.

'Oh, good, yes, very good. Are you OK? Did you go to the high street?' I venture.

'Well I did, but I couldn't see Marjorie. I phoned her when I got home and she didn't have a clue what I was talking about. Are you sure it was her you saw?'

'Yes, I'm sure, Mum. It was Marjorie, I'm positive.'

'Oh well, perhaps it was just someone who looked like her. One of those double clangers, dear.'

'A what?'

'You know, a double clanger, someone who looks just like another person,' my mum says.

'You mean a doppelganger, Mum.'

'Whatever. Anyway, come to think of it, I was walking by Marjorie's house the other day and you wouldn't believe the number of wine bottles that were on her doorstep! Hundreds of them. Maybe she's having a clear out,' my mum muses. 'Oh, and you'll never guess what…' she begins again.

'Go on.' I hate my mum's guessing games. No sooner do I start guessing than she gets excitable and says things like, "No, guess again." This time, however, she doesn't ask me to play the guessing game, so it must be some good newsworthy gossip.

'Well, you know Mrs Horsham – the one who came to the séance the other week?'

'The one with one leg shorter than the other?'

'No, that's Mrs Samuels. No, Mrs Horsham, you know, short brown hair, has one of those funny gold clips in the side all the time. The one whose husband goes sleepwalking at night.'

'Oh, yes, I know,' I say, wondering what gossip my mum has been told about sleep-deprived Mrs Horsham.

'Well, you are never going to believe this, Sammy,' my mum starts and lowers her voice just in case our phones are being tapped, 'but she's only booted him out.'

'Booted who out?' I'm already confused by which one has the wonky leg.

'Mr Horsham. She's booted her husband out and made him sleep in the shed at the bottom of the garden. She said she'd had enough of him getting her up at all hours of the night, and she finally snapped. One night last week Mr Horsham went sleep-walking down the garden, so she got up, locked the back door and went back to bed. Poor old Mr Horsham ended up sleeping on next door's sofa. They found him wandering around their back garden and thought he was a burglar, until Mr Lawrence recognised who it was.'

Oh dear, poor Mr Horsham, but then I suppose if I'd been deprived of sleep for thirty-odd years I think I might be tempted to do the same thing.

'And that's not all,' my mum continues. 'Mrs Landsbury, you know, the one with that horrible poodle – bloody horrible dog it is, does nothing but snap at you - well, she said that she popped round to Mrs Horsham's the other day and discovered a family photo of Mrs Landsbury and Mr Landsbury on Mrs Horsham's mantelpiece!'

'What's Mrs Horsham doing with a photo of Mr and Mrs Landsbury on her mantelpiece?'

'Who knows?' my mum says. 'And that's not all,' my mum continues in hushed tones. 'She told Mrs Landsbury she went out on one of those speedy dating things the other night in town. She's been dating all sorts of men! She told Veronica, who told Joan, who told me, that she's never been so popular! She's thinking of getting her boobs done.' My mother gasps.

'*Uh-oh,*' Ange says again.

'It's speed dating, Mum. Anyway, maybe she's having a midlife crisis, you know, recapturing her youth. Where's Mr

Horsham now? He's not still living in the shed, is he?'

'Oh no, the Lawrences felt sorry for him and are letting him stay with them for the time being, but I think between you and me that Mrs Lawrence is finding it a bit of a problem, with his nocturnal wanderings and all that, and has told Mr Lawrence that he will have to go soon because he can't keep coming into their room in the middle of the night and getting into bed with them.'

Well, it all happens in my mum's street, doesn't it?

'Well, I'm sure they will sort it out eventually. Oh, while I think about it, have you got Missy with you? She's gone missing again.'

'No, love, I haven't seen her all day. Come to think of it, I haven't seen that tomcat of hers either.'

My stomach does one of those sickening flips. I hope they haven't eloped to Gretna Green or whatever the feline equivalent is.

'Well, where is she then? She isn't here. Oh God, you don't think she's been run over, do you?' Tears sting my eyes. I have visions of putting up those 'Missing Cat' posters all over the town, requesting people to please look in their sheds. I wonder if Mrs Horsham has had to do that to find her missing husband before now. It's my own fault for leaving her on her own for so long. If I had been here to keep an eye on her, she wouldn't have wandered off again in search of Spencer – bloody men cats!

'Well, don't worry, love, I'm sure she'll be home soon. I'll ask Colin to have a run out in the car when he gets home. Now I must go, there's a documentary on Nelson Mandela I want to watch,' my mother says and abruptly ends our conversation.

Nelson Mandela? Since when was my mother a fan of Nelson Mandela? Oh well. I sigh, suddenly feeling very cold and remembering that I still haven't switched the heating or the water on so it's going to be another hour before I get a hot bath. That's the problem with old houses, they're very beautiful but boy are they cold!

As I climb the stairs I'm a bit apprehensive that the train room will suddenly come alive again. There is no set pattern to when my mysterious ghost shows itself and I still have no idea why it comes when it does or even what it wants. Ange is as flummoxed as I am and no one seems to be able to give me any clues and the bugger always takes me by surprise. I might be brushing my teeth and suddenly the train set comes alive again, or I might be having my supper and it starts. Some days nothing happens at all and those are my favourite days. Other times my ghost will be banging doors and playing with the train set all day. I need to get to the bottom of this and make a mental note to ask Miracle to come over and see what she makes of it all.

As I cautiously open the airing cupboard and reach into it to turn on the switch and get a couple of towels ready, I look down and see two pairs of green eyes looking back at me.

'Meaow!'

'Missy? Spencer?' I bend down to see Missy and Spencer, her tomcat boyfriend, all snuggled up together inside my yellow bathrobe.

'What are you doing in here, you silly pair? I thought you'd gone out again.' The relief of seeing her looking up at me makes me feel like crying. As I reach down to pick her up, Missy meows again. I look down and, oh my goodness! Snuggled up against her furry little tummy are eight tiny balls of fluff. Missy has had kittens! Oh my God, Missy is a mummy!

CHAPTER EIGHTEEN

'Want to talk about it?' Miracle asks when I arrive at the academy. Due to my new duties as a result of becoming a grandmother to eight adorable kittens, she's already had to cover my class entitled 'So You Think You Can Hear Voices That Are Not Your Own?', and has just sent everyone off for refreshments, including my A star student Alistair, aka Elvis, who has just gone past us, thrusting his pelvis and singing 'Jail House Rock', in a very un-Elvis style.

'God, where do I start?' I sigh, as I throw my bag to the floor and slump down in the chair beside her. Miracle hands me a much appreciated cup of hot chocolate.

'The beginning is always the best place, I find.' She smiles her wonderful kind smile, the smile that makes you want to tell her all your troubles. You know, Miracle would be perfect as an interrogator. She would sit a suspect down, hand them a cup of her famous hot chocolate, smile her warm smile and bingo, they would spill the beans in an instant.

'Well, I've just become a grandmother to eight for starters – Missy had kittens last night. Lord knows what I'm going to do with them all. I don't suppose you and Max want a cat do you?'

'Can't I'm afraid. Max is allergic to them.'

'Oh well. Just one more thing I have to sort out. We can't keep them all, as much as I love them,' I sigh.

'So what else is bothering you?' Miracle asks, handing me a chocolate digestive to dunk – oh this woman knows me too well.

'My friend Gem, you remember I spoke to you about her?'

Miracle nods.

'Her husband, Simon, he's been killed in Afghanistan. A car bomb.'

'And you've seen him?'

Damn, she's good.

I nod.

'And?'

'And I wish I hadn't. She is distraught, Miracle. The pain that poor girl is going through ...'

'And you can't understand why, when they had so much to live for, he was taken away from her.'

I nod again. Is Miracle a mind reader as well as a psychic?

'Ange said what my dad said, that when it's our time, it's our time, and there is nothing we can do about it.'

'That is true,' Miracle confirms.

'But it's just so unfair, Miracle. It's just so unfair. That girl is left with a baby to bring up all on her own.'

Miracle holds my hand.

'Darling, it's not for us to decode when and why things happen when they do. All we can do is help to mend those broken hearts, my love. Imagine how you would feel if it was suddenly your time. That's why we get so many distressed spirits coming through. They all say it's not fair; even the suicides. They may think they want out of this world, but when they're successful, they want nothing more than to be back here on the earth plane. You will send yourself mad if you try to question why all the time, Sammy. We're just the messengers; remember that.'

'Hum, I guess. Oh, and if that isn't bad enough, I've got my mother acting all weird on me, deciding to play homage to Bob Marley and the Wailers by dancing around in a frigging reggae hat; my ghostly guest won't tell me what he wants from me; and would you believe I saw my mum's friend Marjorie begging for money on the street yesterday. I mean, she's the Chair of the WI for goodness sake! Then there's Mr Brent. You know, the old man who lives down the road from me. I caught him running after a couple of tourists yesterday, wielding a slingshot at them. It's like the world has gone mad. Mum was saying that a neighbour of hers, Mrs Horsham, who is usually such a nice woman, has turned into a kleptomaniac and is looking at having a boob job;

she's in her seventies! And now I've gone and got myself involved with this psychic detective thing, as if I don't have enough on my plate. I'm a hundred per cent sure that Petra's mother, Pearl, was poisoned. They're going to start filming next week. So besides all that, trying to organise my wedding by text message and missing Jack like crazy, I'm fine! We can't even decide on where to have the bloody reception and time is running out!' I take a deep breath, realising I sound like a woman on the verge of being committed to the loony bin.

Miracle looks at me for a moment.

'Hang on a minute. You said your mum was acting all weird. What do you mean by weird?'

'Oh, just putting on this Jamaican voice whenever I phone up and playing reggae music at full volume. I mean, she doesn't even like reggae music!'

'So she's never listened to it before then?'

I shake my head.

'Not to my knowledge. She's more of a Shirley Bassey kind of girl, is my mum. Me and Jack can't decide on whether to have the reception at the Royal Hotel or have a marquee in Mum's back garden or have it at our local. I mean it's big enough ...' I twitter on.

Miracle looks at me seriously for a moment.

'Sammy, hang on a minute; did your mum attend the séance by any chance?'

'*Uh-oh,*' Ange says. What do you keep saying that for?

I nod, as I sip my wonderful hot chocolate. Oh, that tastes so good.

'And this other woman, Marjorie? You say she's the chair of the WI?'

I nod again. Was Miracle not listening to my wedding dilemma?

'I'm assuming she doesn't usually have to beg for a living?' Miracle asks.

'What, Marjorie? Oh God no! She lives in the Crescent, the posh part of Bath. Marjorie's middle name is posh,' I laugh, and I'm sure it is. Marjorie only ever shops at the most exclusive boutiques in town; Marjorie has two cleaners in every week to keep her grand Georgian house spotless and she even has someone in just to do her laundry, which is why I was shocked to see her sitting looking like a vagrant outside McDonalds.

'I think she must have been doing something for charity,' I muse, as I nurse my drink and soggy digestive in my hands. 'She's always involved in some sort of charity work.'

'Wasn't this lady the one who organised the séance? Did she attend it too?' Miracle asks.

'Oh yes, it was quite funny, there was a little Cockney boy there called Tom who came through from the spirit world. He took quite a shine to her,' I chuckle, as I remember the look on Marjorie's face when I told her she had a little friend standing next to her.

Miracle looks seriously at me for a moment.

'Sam, now I want you to think very carefully when you answer this question.'

I nod and laugh nervously. What is up with Miracle today?

'Uh-oh.'

'Sam, the man you saw running down the street, Mr Brent? Did he by any chance attend the séance too?'

I nod.

'He and Mrs Jackson, the woman from the gift shop, wanted to come along. I think they thought it was going to be a run of the mill WI meeting. But I did get Mrs Jackson's daughter come through. She didn't seem very happy about it though.'

Miracle frowns.

'Right, and this Mrs Horsham, the one you said is the klepto-maniac and is going to get a boob job, was she there too?'

'Yes.' I'm not sure where this conversation is going, but I don't like it one bit.

'Sam, I want you to tell me something. Did you remember to close down the circle on Halloween? Think carefully, Sam. Did you close the circle?'

I think for a moment.

'Of course I closed the circle down. I mean, I'm not that stup...' I hesitate. Did I? I hear Ange laughing hysterically. You know, I honestly can't remember if I did or not. Yes, of course I would have. I mean I wouldn't have just ...

'Sam, this is very important.' Miracle speaks very slowly, so that I get the gist of just how important this is.

'You need to think what you did. Tell me exactly how you closed the circle,' Miracle urges. I've never seen her this serious before.

'Well, we had lots of people come through – Tom, the little boy I told you about; Mrs Jackson's daughter, and nobody knew she even had one; um...oh, and would you believe it, a Viking came through! He took a shine to one of the ladies there. I couldn't believe my eyes! Oh, and my dad helped me a bit. I couldn't rely on Ange to guide me because she was too busy helping herself to other people's handbags. Um...oh, there were lots of people in the background wandering around.'

'*Cow!*' Ange says.

'Did a Jamaican person come through too, by any chance?' Miracle asks. I can sense her disappointment.

'What?'

Miracle shakes her head.

'Tell me who you saw, Sam, just before you closed the circle. Think. This is very important.'

And she does look serious this time.

'Um...oh well...oh, that's right. Well, I was looking at Gem for a moment and there was this grey shadow behind her. I couldn't make it out at the time, but I now know it was her husband, Simon, coming through. He had died that day, but he was obviously having trouble coming through to us.'

'Uh-huh,' Miracle nods, 'and then what?' She grabs a pencil and starts jotting down things on a notepad in front of her.

'Well, I was a bit shocked because I couldn't make out who it was and I was tired too, so I ended the séance then,' I say, trying to think what I did next.

'And exactly *how* did you end the séance, Sam?'

'I broke hands with Gem and told the table that was all I could do tonight and...'

'So you didn't close the circle properly?' Miracle says.

'And I...oh crap, I don't know if I did or didn't.'

'Right, let me put it this way. Sam,' Miracle talks very, very slowly now, 'did you thank your spirits for coming and ask them to go back into the light?'

'Ha! No she didn't,' Ange teases.

Err, no. I don't remember doing that bit. It was more of blow the candles out and say goodnight.

'Um...' is all I can mutter.

Miracle puts her pencil down and holds her head in her hands.

'Um...is that bad?' I squeak. I feel like I'm back at school and about to be reprimanded for copying Amy's answers in our maths test.

'Ha, ha!'

Miracle looks at me.

'You let spirits come into this world on All Hallows' Eve, Sam. The one night in the year when they can physically enter our realm and you forgot to send them back.'

'And that's bad because?' I ask, all wide-eyed.

'And that's bad, Sam, because they are now still inhabiting our world. All the spirits that came through to you on Halloween are now in our world, because you didn't send them back to their realm. Which means, Sam, that whoever attended that séance could easily become possessed by any one of them.'

Oh shit. That is bad.

CHAPTER NINETEEN

Before I have time to digest just how bad the situation is, my mobile rings. It's Mark from Living Today TV.

'*Ooo, I like him!*' Ange says as I pick up the phone.

'Mark, hi.'

'Hey, Sam, I thought I would let you know we got the results back from the lab this morning,' Mark says.

'And?'

'It was ethylene glycol on the carpet – commonly known as antifreeze to you and me.'

'What do you mean, antifreeze?'

'That was what you could smell; that sweet smell you recognised? It was antifreeze.'

'And?'

'And my dear, do you know what happens if you drink it?' Mark says.

'No.'

'Breathlessness, stomach pains, dizziness and eventual liver and kidney failure, among other things. Apparently it contains…hang on, let me find the notes…ah, here we are, it contains lots of nasty things including ethylene glycol, methanol and propylene glycol, all things we shouldn't have in our bodies. When ethylene glycol is oxidised to glycolic acid which in turn oxidises to oxalic acid, it becomes toxic, according to St. James's Hospital.'

'So that's what happened,' I gasp. 'I told you I couldn't breathe in that room. Well, Pearl told me that was her room. Oh my God, Mark, that's it! They poisoned her. The home poisoned Petra's mum with antifreeze!' The same image I had of an elderly woman comes into my mind and she's nodding in agreement.

'*I told you!*' Ange says.

No, you didn't!

'I did so. Anyway, is Mark married?'

I have no idea, Ange.

I wish she would shut up for a minute.

'Now he is someone I could seriously haunt!' she giggles. Don't even think about it, Ange.

'And he wears purple boxer shorts! I love the colour purple!' my mad spirit guide informs me.

'So Georgia has contacted the police and they are talking about requesting an inquest and post-mortem into Pearl's death. The reason they never suspected anything was because of her age – and the fact that that trout of a matron is very convincing. They will want to interview you at some point, Sam,' Mark adds, 'and we are going to have to recreate the footage for the programme because I had the camera when you went off in search of Petra's mum, so all we have is the recording of you saying you couldn't breathe.'

'Fine, but I don't think we are going to achieve quite the same effect as if you had actually been there on the day,' I say, recalling the reason why Mark was in another corridor.

'Ah you'll be great,' Mark assures me.

'So what happens next? I mean, how many other pensioners are they poisoning at that home?'

'I guess the police will want to talk to that old dragon, Mrs Lance, and there will be a full investigation.'

'Right, well, let me know when you need me next. Oh, and Mark?'

'Yes?'

'Have you by any chance got purple boxer shorts on?'

'Erm…yes. Why?'

'Oh, no reason,' I say smiling to myself.

'So it looks as though Petra's mum was poisoned' I say as I relay the story to Miracle.

'Well hopefully they will do a full investigation and justice will be served. Now, about this séance, Sam,' she continues. 'It sounds to me as though we have a few unwanted party guests left over from Halloween, so what I need you to do is to try and work out who they are and just how many have escaped into our world.'

'And I'm going to do this how?' I have enough trouble playing hide and seek with my mother, let alone dead peeps!

'You need to see all the people who came to the séance and see if they act out of character again.'

'You mean like my mother.'

'Yep, your mother, Mr Brent, Mrs Horsham, anyone and everyone who came to the séance,' Miracle says.

'And then what? Douse them in salty water and say three hail Marys?'

'No, Sam. We will need to get them all together again and do another séance so that we can send all the spirits back.'

'But what if I can't get them all together again? Mrs Horsham's thinking of going to Spain to have a boob job!' I cry. Oh great, now I'm going to have to fly out to Spain and track down a middle-aged woman who is about to have her boobs enhanced!

'You'll just have to try and do your best, Sam, and it's probably best not to tell anyone what has happened. We have enough trouble as it is convincing people we're for real without word getting around that we let dead people roam the earth, possessing village folk. The next thing you know they will be gathering firewood and looking for the biggest stake they can find to tie you to.'

Oh bloody marvellous!

Once I've finished working out with Miracle how I am going to track everyone who attended the séance, and then popped in to see Valerie about her designs for my wedding dress, I decide I've had enough excitement for one day and head home.

As I drive up the road I glance to the left, where I see Mr Brent in his garden in a passionate embrace with Mum's friend, Mrs Samuels - the one with one leg shorter than that other; not that you can tell.

Oh bloody hell! And what has he done to his garden? As I slow down – God, I must look like a right voyeuristic nutter – I look at the garden. Instead of the normal pretty, gnome-adorned picturesque cottage that Bath is used to, there is a four-foot wide moat, complete with drawbridge, surrounding his house. God knows how long it took him to dig that out! I mean, he's no spring chicken. Mr Brent, complete with axe, looks like he's smothering Mrs Samuels to death. The poor woman's legs are splayed all over the place. I wind down the window.

'Are you OK, Mrs Samuels?' I yell.

Mr Brent and Mrs Samuels look up from their cuddle against the wooden stocks. Mr Brent looks as startled as a rabbit caught in the headlights and promptly drops Mrs Samuels from his clutches.

'Agghh!'

Mrs Samuels loses her balance and clonks her head on the offending stocks, knocking herself out. Oh my goodness!

Before you can say, "The Vikings have landed" I'm out of the car, have jumped the moat – not easy in a pair of heels, I might add – and am administering first aid to Mrs Samuels. Since Jack's drowning-in-the-sea incident I'm a bit of a Florence Nightingale these days; I can spot a fractured fibula or a compressed coccyx at fifty paces.

With Mrs Samuels in the recovery position – see, I told you I knew what I was doing – she comes round after a few seconds.

'Oh my,' is all Mrs Samuels says.

'Are you OK?'

'Oh, yes dear. I don't know quite what happened there,' Mrs Samuels says. 'And who on earth is that?' she points at Mr Brent, who looks equally confused as to who he is and why he's dressed like a Viking. 'And where the hell is Henry?'

'Henry?' I ask, looking down at her.

'The king...my husband, Henry?'

'*Uh-oh*,' I hear Ange say.

Uh-oh indeed. Mrs Samuels thinks she's Anne Boleyn or one of the many wives of Henry the Eighth.

'*Maybe it's the bump to the head?*' Ange ventures.

Hum, maybe. Or maybe like Mr Brent and half the village, Mrs Samuels has also become possessed.

CHAPTER TWENTY

So then, what's a girl to do when faced with the prospect of a village half-possessed by the spirit world? Go home and sulk for a bit, that's what.

The kittens, who I have temporarily named after the characters in the *Wizard of Oz*,– my all-time favourite film – seem fine when I return home and Missy is completely smitten with every one of them and is proving to be a good mum, feeding and cleaning them all day long. Spencer is equally smitten and keeps bringing home little presents in the form of various rodents, by way of congratulations to his girlfriend – personally I'd prefer flowers. It's such a wondrous sight to see this little feline family together in their new home. Having vacated the airing cupboard on account of it being far too small for a family of ten, they have now relocated to the comfy armchair in the lounge.

I look at Missy and think how proud I am of her. She returns my look with the look of what a clever cat she is, as she expertly picks Scarecrow up by the scruff of the neck and jumps up on the chair with him.

One, two, three, four, five, six, seven...hang on, where's Dorothy? I look around the living room to see if she's fallen off the armchair, or is stuck in the litter tray again. Nope. Where is the little bugger? It's then that I hear a little mew from above and the train starting up again.

'Oh not again! Ange?' I say as I run up the stairs, two at a time.

I tend to keep the train room door closed and it's still shut when I reach the top of the stairs.

'Meow!'

The noise is coming from inside the room.

'Ange? I could do with a bit of help here, please?' I ask, and take a deep breath.

'*I don't know what to do!*' Ange cries, rather too quietly for

Ange.

'Oh, for God's sake!' I mutter as I quickly visualise a circle of white light surrounding me – a little trick that Miracle taught me for when I need to protect myself. As I open the bedroom door, I stare in astonishment at the site of Dorothy the kitten sitting in the middle of the train track with the express train going full pelt around the track, circling her over and over again. Dorothy mews at me.

'It's alright, darling,' I say, scooping her up into my arms. I look at the plug where the power is for the train and notice that it is turned off, which only means one thing.

'Right, I've had enough of this! If you've got something to say, then say it, otherwise piss off, you're not welcome here!' I shout above the rumbling of the train that is gathering momentum as it goes by. Suddenly it stops and I hear someone cough behind me.

'Clive?' I hold Dorothy closer to me.

Oh, this is not good. Standing at the top of the stairs is Colin's cousin Clive, looking more and more like an undertaker by the day, dressed from head to toe in black, and sporting a top hat. The big question is, what's he doing here – he's dead.

Clive smiles a rather sinister smile.

'I'm sorry, Samantha, I didn't mean to make you jump,' he says, staring past me at the train track.

'What are you doing here?'

I will not be scared by someone who is dead. I will not be scared by someone who is dead, I repeat in my head.

'I think we have some unfinished business, don't you? Nice train track, by the way.' Clive smiles again.

'No, we don't, Clive. Now go away please,' I say, trying not to sound as though I'm about to wet myself.

Dorothy meows at him and Missy runs up the stairs, hissing.

'I'll be back soon,' Clive says, and with that he is gone again.

I place Dorothy back with her mum, who licks her enthusiastically.

'Well thanks for the help, Ange,' I mutter. 'I thought my spirit guide was supposed to help me, not be a pain in the arse!' I snap angrily as I make my way to the kitchen.

'I'm sorry. I just don't know how to help you,' I hear Ange whisper.

'Yeah well, you're supposed to know, Ange! That's why you were assigned to me, wasn't it? To help me with all of this? I've got enough on my plate without having to deal with you all the time. I've a good mind to ask for a refund!' I snap, as I put two heaped teaspoons of hot chocolate powder into a mug.

It's then that I hear Ange starting to cry and I don't mean just a few tears because she's been told off, I mean huge, shoulder-heaving sobs, and now I feel really bad, but I'm right: why give me a spirit guide at all when she can't even help me in any way?

'Ange? I'm sorry. I didn't mean to have a go at you,' I say, pouring the hot water into the mug.

More sobs.

'Ange? What's wrong?' This isn't like Ange at all.

'I...I hate it here. I want to be down there with you. I don't want to be a bloody spirit guide! I want to be me – normal Ange. I want to be alive again!' Ange wails.

Oh crikey!

'You want to talk about it?' I say as I make my way back to the lounge. 'I've got the new copy of *Heat* in my bag for you.'

'I want to be able to actually read it, Sam, not just listen to you telling me who's hot and who's not. I want to be able to taste chips with loads of vinegar on them. I want...I want to be able to comfort my sister and my mum. I want to hug them and tell them that I'm OK. They're in bits, Sam. I...' Ange starts to cry again.

'Tell me all. In your own time,' I say comfortingly. Ange makes a huge blowing-your-nose sound.

'I had everything to live for. I was your all-time party girl. I had a good job as a receptionist for Pulse FM and I loved life. I really loved life, Sam. I was going to become a radio DJ and tour the world. I had a

good home life too – okay, so we might all seem a bit brash at times, but we always looked after each other.'

Ange goes quiet for a moment.

'Who's in your family, Ange?'

'Well, me dad left when I was thirteen, so it was just me, me mam Jackie -you'd like her – me sis, Ali, and me cousin, Pip; that's not his real name, he's actually called Michael, but we nicknamed him Pip on account that he used to like dressing up in me Auntie Sue's dresses, so we called him Pippa – Pip for short. He was on Jeremy Kyle once,' Ange adds proudly.

Right, OK then. I know from my therapy training that all Ange wants to do is talk, so I let her as I snuggle down on the sofa and just listen.

'And then there was this guy called Marcus – he was well lush.' Ange says.

Having spent half an hour sobbing about how much she missed her mum Jackie, her sister, Ali, and Pip and Auntie Sue, Ange has moved on to tell me all about her relationships, including Marcus, who was a bit of a ladies' man by all accounts.

'I really liked him: that was until I found out he was cheating on me with Stacey Fisher from the chippy – the bitch – and she stank of chip fat too,' Ange adds.

'Then, after him, I started seeing a guy called Dan, but he got a bit possessive – wanted to know where I was going, what I was doing all the time. He even tried to control what I was wearing.'

I can't imagine for one minute anyone trying to change Ange. She wouldn't change for any man.

'Now if I could just master how you haunt people, he is one person I would happily haunt, and that Marcus and Stacey bloody Fisher. Anyway, the night I had the fateful accident, I was out on the pull with Ali. I was looking well gorge, Sam.' Ange goes quiet again.

'Ali was mortified. I could see her face as I was lying on the pavement. She was desperately hitting me in the chest – you can't imagine how much my boobs wobbled! But I was already above her

looking down.'

I feel tears welling up in my eyes.

'I don't want to be here, Sam!' Ange wails again. *'It's not fair! I was only twenty-five! I want to see my family. I want to argue with Pip over why he's always borrowing my boob tubes. I want to go shopping in Primark with Ali. I want my mam to know I'm around her.'*

'Then we will tell her,' I say, without really thinking.

'You mean you will contact her for me?' Ange says, her voice like that of a small child.

'If you want me to contact your mum, I will, Ange.'

Ange brightens up a little.

'I haven't been able to see them since I...you know...I don't know what to do to make myself get there. I remember our phone number though,' Ange says excitedly. *'It's 020 192 6655.'*

I make a mental note.

'Can you phone her now?'

'What, now?'

'Please?' Ange begs. *'She'll be home now. She never misses EastEnders.'*

'Oh, for goodness sake, Ange!' I huff and grab my phone. 'Right, what's the number again? And just so you know, if your mum has a head fit on me, I will never speak to you again!' I snap as I punch in the number Ange dictates. The phone starts to ring.

'If that's you again, our Trevor, I'm going to bloody kill you; you know *EastEnders* is on!' a woman answers.

'That'll be our Dwayne,' Ange confirms. *'He always rings right in the middle of EastEnders. Drives Mam mad, it does.'*

Great, I bet Ange's Mum is in a bad mood now.

'Um...hello, is that Jackie, Ange's mum?' I ask nervously.

'Yeah, who's asking?' the woman replies. 'Pip, turn that bloody noise down!' she shouts above the *EastEnders* theme tune. She sounds cross.

'Um...Jackie, my name is Samantha Ball. Otherwise known as Crystal Ball.'

'What? Hang on a minute. Pip! Will you turn that frigging TV down, I can't hear meself think! Say again, love. You'll have to speak up; this idiot can't seem to work out how to operate the remote!'

Ange chuckles in my ear.

'Can you hear me now?' I shout into the mouthpiece.

'Yes, love, no need to shout, I ain't deaf yet yer know. What can I do for you and if you're selling anything I'm not interested,' Jackie says.

'I said my name is Samantha Ball, otherwise known as Crystal Ball. Psychic to the stars.' God, now I do sound as though I'm trying to sell her something. Before Jackie has time to slam the phone down, I add, 'It's about your daughter, Ange.'

'Ange? Are you taking the piss?' Jackie says angrily.

'*Quick, tell her you're a psychic!*' Ange says.

I just did that, Ange!

'No, Jackie. I'm not taking the piss, really I'm not. I have a message from Ange for you – well several messages actually,' I add.

'You sick bastard!' Jackie shouts. 'Who the hell do you think you are? Do you get some kind of kick out of phoning up bereaved people?'

'*Quick! Tell her she used to call me Angry Andy when I was little and threw a strop,*' Ange says.

'Jackie, I'm not playing a joke on you. Honestly. Listen, you used to call Ange Angry Andy when she was little.'

'*And tell her you know about the time I got a tampon stuck up my nose and she had to take me to A&E.*'

I quickly relay the message before Ange's mum can cut me off.

'Holy crap! I forgot all about that! Silly bugger thought it was one of those Vic inhalers,' Jackie laughs. 'How did you know about that? She was only three at the time.'

'I'm a psychic, Jackie. It's my job. Ange is my spirit guide. I have her here with me and she wanted me to contact you.'

'What? Ange? A spirit guide?' Jackie shrieks with laughter, 'Pip, Ali, you'll never believe this, our Ange is one of those spirit guides!'

'A what?' I hear someone say in the background.

'A spirit guide. I told you she would amount to something in the end. It's that Crystal whatsit on the phone. You know the psychic whatsit. Does that radio show for Town FM. Says our Ange is her spirit guide.' Jackie laughs again.

'*Gee, thanks Mum,*' Ange says.

'So, you're telling me that my baby is now your spirit guide?' Jackie says, not quite believing it.

'That's right, Jackie. Ange is now my spirit guide and a very good one at that,' I lie – well, no one wants to be told that their dead daughter is about as useful as a chocolate teapot, do they?

'Look, I know this is all a bit of a shock, but Ange desperately wants me to pass on some messages to you. She misses you, Pip, Ali and Auntie Sue very much.'

Once I manage to convince Jackie that I am for real and not someone trying to sell her something, I begin to relay everything Ange wants to say to her; from how she still craves her mum's home-made toad in the hole to how she's going to haunt all her exes and how she would like Pip to have all her frocks and to let Ali have her room now and to stop keeping it like a bloody shrine.

Jackie laughs and cries, and shouts out the occasional bit of information to her other daughter and to Pip, who are in the background asking questions.

It's a very emotional hour and I am exhausted, but Ange is one happy spirit as I retire to my bed – alone again.

CHAPTER TWENTY-ONE

I'm awake, much too early I hasten to add, but I've been woken by the sound of Ange impersonating Beyonce – badly.

'*If you like it then yer should have put a ring on it,*' she repeats in my ear. I still haven't got the hang of how to make her shut up without her getting in a grump.

'*Sammy! Are you awake yet? I've got something mega important to tell you. If you like it then you should have put a ring on it,*' she choruses, out of tune. Beyonce she ain't.

Oh God, make her shut up for five minutes.

I look bleary-eyed at my phone – 6.55 a.m. Aghh!

After I spent much of the previous night reuniting Ange with her family, Jack phoned just as I was climbing into bed. I miss him so much it hurts every time I think of him and I worry about the amount of time we are spending apart and that it's going to ruin our relationship before it's really got started. Warning girls: never marry a successful pop star. You will spend your days worrying that he's not getting fed properly and your nights worrying about where he's sleeping. I only have to look at the band's Facebook page to see that there are some pretty hot young things out there who all want to bed the band members. Jack's got fifteen thousand fans alone, for goodness sake! And there's one who just won't leave him alone. Her name's Bethany, or 'Busty Beth' as she likes to be called, and she is constantly messaging him through the band's Facebook page – *I'm sooo in lv with u Jack* and *I cn show u a gd time*, and the like. I have to stop logging on and just trust that Busty Beth will bugger off and get busty with someone else. Failing that, I could always get Ange to haunt her for me.

It doesn't help matters that the band's management team insist they keep girlfriends (and future wives) secret from the fans – they don't project the right image for the band, apparently.

Although most people in the media know that Jack and I are an item, the management don't make a song and dance about it, and whenever the band are interviewed the media are pre-warned not to ask questions about relationships and to avoid the subject at all costs.

It appears I have no need to worry though. Jack is as wonderful as ever and misses me as much, if not more, than I miss him, although I do wonder how this is affecting our sex life which has resorted to a lot of phone sex – more often than not resulting in mutual hilarity, rather than mutual orgasms. We tried text sex but that didn't go well. Because my nails are so long and it takes me ages to compile a sentence, poor old Jack was spending a lot of frustrating minutes awaiting my response to 'Wt r u wearing 2nt?' When half an hour later I'd eventually typed back 'Black silk kippers', it kind of killed the mood a bit.

Phone sex is not as easy as you may think either. For starters, it's virtually impossible to set the mood when you've got a spirit guide as mad as a box of frogs in your ear advising you what to say:

'Tell him you're wearing crotchless knickers! I had a gorgeous pair from Ann Summers; leopard skin they were. Really turned Marcus on, they did.'

'I'm not telling him that! And besides, I've never worn crotchless knickers in my life! Now sod off, Ange!' I repeat – out loud.

'You've never worn crotchless knickers?' was Jack's response.

'No! Have you?'

'Well no, but can you imagine it? Me, in a pair of crotchless knickers? Do they do those for men?'

Oh gawd! Then I have a mental image of Jack in a pair of leopard skin crotchless knickers and it's not an attractive image. So thanks to Ange's suggestions we end up debating the pros and cons of underwear, which then led to us discussing whether Y-fronts will ever make a comeback, which in turn led us to discussing Jack's band mate Dillon's filthy Y-fronts that he hung out on the hotel balcony in the rain to wash them. Romantic – not.

'If you like it then you shoulda put a ring on it!' Ange continues to serenade me as I hold the pillow over my head.

'Ah! Ange, can you please be quiet for five minutes? You sound nothing like Beyonce!'

'Ooo! And you do? I've heard you singing in the shower and you sound like Missy being strangled!' Ange snaps back. *'A bit narky this morning, aren't you?'*

'I'm sorry, Ange.' I don't want to make her angry so that she doesn't speak to me again; I've got a whole host of spirits wandering around the village, possessing the village folk at every given opportunity, and at some point I am going to need her help to get them all back to where they belong. 'I'm just tired, that's all, and I only have a few hours to sort out who, if anyone, from Jack's family is coming to the wedding and …'

'Oh, just chillax a bit will you! He said he doesn't want anyone to come; says he's got no family.'

'I know, but it's going to look a bit one-sided, don't you think – me with all my family and Jack with none.'

'You'd be wise to just leave it, Sam,' Ange says a little too seriously. *'Anyway, I've got something mega important to tell you!'*

'Go on,' I say, knowing full well that unless I let Ange tell me her important news, I will never shut her up.

'Well, you know we were talking last night about my exes?'

'Uh-huh,' I grunt from beneath the pillow.

'Well, I worked out how to visit them! You know, like, haunt them?'

I lift the pillow off my head.

'You did what?'

Ange giggles like a child.

'Haunt them. Sam, it was brilliant! You should have been there. First I mustered all my energy to visit Dan – you know the one who looks like a younger version of Gary Barlow. My God, he got the shock

of his life when I turned the taps on in his bathroom! Then I wrote 'bastard' on the mirror with his toothpaste. Oh, I did laugh!'

'Ange! You can't do that!'

'Why not? It's not like I'm not telling the truth; he was a bastard. Anyway, I then went to pay a visit to Marcus – you know, the lush one who two-timed me with Stacey Fisher. That was hilarious, Sam, you should have seen me! He was coming down the stairs, stark naked, to get a drink – he always did have a good bod –and I managed to get a box of fish fingers out of the freezer and whacked him on the arse with them! Hee, hee, he yelped like a puppy! Oh, it was so funny, Sam! You should have seen him run back up those stairs! I tried to make a wooing sound, you know, all ghost like, but I couldn't stop myself from laughing! Oh, I can't wait to haunt Fishy Fisher tonight!'

It's lovely to hear Ange so happy and I can't help but giggle at the thought of her ex being whacked on the bum with a packet of frozen fish fingers.

CHAPTER TWENTY-TWO

While Ange is on planet happy land today, I am walking around like a zombie. Not only did no one tell me quite how exhausting the life of a psychic could be, but also no one told me quite how exhausting organising a wedding could be either.

The idea of me and Jack just buggering off to Las Vegas and being married by Elvis Presley is very appealing right now, but it would upset my mum too much.

'And then there's Colin's family. Mum wants them to come. Then do I invite all of Dad's side of the family just because they're related to me, despite the fact that we haven't seen them since my dad's funeral?' I ask Annette as we prepare for the lunchtime radio show.

Poor Annette looks like a woman at breaking point. Poor love is in no way what you would call glowing not in any way, shape or form. Her ankles have swollen, she's permanently hot and has to stand, leaning on the desk, to do the show because the baby keeps lying on her sciatic nerve. And here I am worrying about place settings and table flowers.

'And what about Jack's family?' Annette asks as she winces in pain.

'He doesn't have any – well, apart from his uncle and auntie; you know, the ones who own the fancy dress shop in Bristol. But he isn't even actually related to them. He was put into care shortly after he was born and has no idea who his mum or dad are.'

'Ouch!' Annette looks very pale as she holds her hand to her stomach.

'Annette, are you OK?' Stupid question really.

The *Sixth Sense* theme tune is playing, which is the lead up to my programme, meaning that I am on in about thirty seconds, but I'm more concerned about Annette who is looking whiter by the second.

'Annette?'

Annette clutches her stomach and falls to the floor.

'Oh no! Jeff!' I shout through the mic to the booth next door.

Jeff looks up from his desk of switches that resembles the Starship Enterprise, but is in fact the sound system for Town FM.

'Oh shit!' he says, as he throws his headphones and latest travel report to the floor and rushes into our room.

'Annette? Are you OK?'

'Get her to the hospital, Sam, or she will lose the baby,' I hear Ange say.

I've never seen Jeff, who is very much a middle-aged man – pepper-grey hair, shirt, tie and dad-sweater – look so panic-stricken. Usually the only contact I have with Jeff is when he reads the news and travel report after me. He's just your typical dad-type figure. Never married, Jeff has always kept himself to himself – or so I thought. Obviously got that wrong.

'Sam, do something!' Jeff begs as he sits by Annette's side, holding her hand tightly as Annette doubles up in pain.

I quickly punch 999 into my mobile and request an ambulance, while simultaneously flicking some switches on Annette's desk and waving to Liam, the sound tech, to do something with the show.

'I'm going to lose the baby, aren't I, Sam?' Annette sobs between surges of pain.

'No, you're not, Annette. Not if we get you to hospital now.'

It seems as though I've been sitting in the hospital waiting room for hours, waiting to hear any news about Annette. They rushed her away on a trolley and Jeff has been wearing the floor out ever since she was admitted. Ironic really: when Annette told him about the baby, they both agreed that it was a one-night stand and that while Jeff would support her and the baby financially, neither of them had any intention of becoming a couple. Annette is off men since her husband decided life would be much better with a younger model in Amsterdam and Jeff is too stuck in his ways to start a family now. And yet here he is, pacing the floor and worrying about her.

'She's going to be OK,' a young nurse smiles as she comes through the door which leads to the theatre.

'And the baby? I'm...I'm the father.' Jeff says nervously, glancing at me.

'The baby is doing just fine. We will need to keep Annette in for a few weeks to settle things down. Baby was trying to make an early appearance, but she's not ready to come into the big wide world just yet,' the nurse says.

'Can we see her?' I ask.

'She's very tired at the moment, but you're more than welcome to wait, if you want?'

Jeff looks at me for some kind of decision.

'I tell you what, you stay and I'll go back to the studio and see if I can save the show,' I tell Jeff.

'Would you? Thanks, Sam.' Jeff looks relieved. 'And can you get Liam to do the news and weather reports? They're all on my desk in time slot order.'

'Of course. Give Annette my love and tell her I'll call in tonight to see how she is.'

I'm mulling over whether or not to go and see Dave and Maureen with an invitation to the wedding as I brush my teeth, when my mobile rings. It's Jack. Odd, he never usually rings in the middle of the day. He's usually rehearsing or sleeping off the night before.

'Hello, darling,' I answer with a mouthful of toothpaste.

'Alright,' Jack replies.

'*Uh-oh. He's not happy,*' Ange advises.

Uh-oh indeed. Jack only ever gives one-word answers when he's in a bad mood or there's something wrong. I spit toothpaste into the old enamel sink.

'Sorry about that. I was in the middle of brushing my teeth. Are you OK? Bad day?'

'Kind of.'

'What's up?'

'Nothing. I was just thinking about my mum, you know, with the wedding and all that. Just wondered what made them not want me. Anyway, what have you been up to today?' Jack feigns bravado

'Nothing much. My show got cancelled because Annette fell ill, so I had to go to the hospital with her, but she's going to be OK...'

I stop mid sentence because as I'm talking to Jack the mirror in the bathroom has misted up and writing is beginning to appear in the mist.

I'm no longer listening to a word Jack is saying. Instead, I'm looking at the words in the mirror.

I'm so sorry. I love you. The words form in the mirror.

It's then that I see the image of a young woman with big hair and Jack's eyes.

'It's Jack's mum, Sam,' Ange whispers to me. *'Her name's Marianne Lewis. She's just like me, Sam.'*

'I'm so sorry, Jack,' I whisper into the phone.

'What? Sam, are you OK?' Jack's voice softens.

How can I possibly tell him his mum is dead?

'Jack, I am so, so sorry, you know, about your mum,' I sniff, tears welling up in my eyes. Then the floodgates open and I can't stop crying.

'Sam? It's OK. Really. It doesn't matter. All that matters is that I've got you. Nothing else really matters to me. It's just...look, I've accepted that my parents, for whatever reason, didn't want me. Why else would they have put me into care?'

Why indeed?

'You're everything I want and will ever need. I don't need

anyone else, Sam.'

The writing and image I saw in the mirror have gone and I'm left staring at my own reflection – not a pretty sight considering I have black mascara tracks down my cheeks (that will teach me to buy waterproof mascara from the market because it's cheaper) and toothpaste dribble on my chin.

'Sam, don't cry.'

'I'm just so sorry, Jack, and I miss you so much.'

'Look, it doesn't matter. And hey?'

'Uh-huh.'

'You mean the whole world to me and I'll be home soon. I love you more than anything else on this planet, Samantha Ball.'

'I love me too,' I smile.

CHAPTER TWENTY-THREE

I know, I know, sometimes I just can't help myself, but on this occasion I am blaming Ange for this, because if you think I'm a nosey parker, then Ange is the epitome of nosiness. I can't tell Jack that I know that his mum is dead, but maybe I can find out what happened to her.

Someone, somewhere must know something and I intend to find out what, if only to satisfy Ange's curiosity and give her something to think about other than Brangelina and Big Brother.

I phone Paul in Australia and tell him the name of Jack's mother – Marianne Lewis.

'I thought you were the psychic,' Paul says between mouthfuls of something; I'm guessing Vegemite or kangaroo, or whatever it is they eat in Australia.

'I am.'

'In which case, did you not think to ask the woman in the mirror how she died and why she put Jack into care in the first place?'

'It doesn't work like that, Paul.'

'Well, why not? What's the point in having psychic powers if you can't solve mysteries?'

He's right of course. What is the point?

'Well, I don't know, but it just doesn't seem to work like that. Maybe it's so that people can have fun coming up with conspiracy theories. Imagine if all we had to do to find out who killed Marilyn Monroe or Princess Di or whoever, was just ask a psychic? Or maybe it keeps people like you in a job?'

My brother Paul is still part-time beach bum, part-time private investigator, and since coming to my rescue by uncovering the truth behind who sold a false story about me to the press, his 'agency' has been inundated with requests for work, much to Paul's annoyance. He'd much prefer to surf the waves and polish his surfboard than work any day of the week.

'Alright, leave it with me. I'll get one of the lads to look into it.'

'You mean one of your beach bum friends,' I laugh.

'I'll have you know I run a very reputable business. And I employ three staff now!'

'What, Mickey the Moaner, Cowboy Tony and Nine Fingers Nige?'

'Exactly!' Paul says 'Leave it with me, sis.'

'And not a word to Jack,' I warn him.

'Discretion is my middle name, sis. Discretion is my middle name.'

It's not, you know. It's John. Both of my brothers' middle names were named after our dad.

I can see Paul now: sitting in his 'office', which is in fact a bar stool at the surf bar, tapping his nose and winking into the phone.

Because my show has been cancelled for the day, I decide to go and see Valerie for a wedding dress fitting.

'Hi Donald!' I chirp as I approach the security gate.

'Miss Ball, good morning. And who might you wish to visit today?' Donald, in his lovely burgundy and gold uniform, asks.

'Hum, now let me think…' I say, looking up to the sky as if deep in thought.

Donald waits patiently.

'Donald! It's me! You know very well who I want to visit!'

'I'm sorry, Miss Ball. It's my job. Have you any ID?'

'Oh, for goodness sake! Yes, here it is. The same driving licence I gave you the other day and the day before that.' I hand over my ID and just like the last time Donald scrutinises it.

'Very good, Miss Ball, you may go up now.'

'One of these days I'm going to give him a fake driving licence, you know,' I tell Valerie, who is behind me, pinning the back of my wedding dress together.

'Ah, he's only doing his job, Sam. Think of the trouble he could get into if he didn't check everyone coming and going.' Valerie says through a mouthful of silver pins.

'I know, but come on, he knows who I am,' I say, slowly turning as she continues to pin my hem. I have to say, Valerie has done an amazing job. I look and feel like a real princess. She's created an amazing fitted dress from my description of, "think Kate Middleton, Victoria Beckham and Audrey Hepburn all rolled into one."

My wedding dress is cream silk. Hundreds of tiny crystals, hand sewn into the bodice, catch the light as I turn. Tears sting my eyes as I think of my dad and how proud he would be of me right now and how sad I am at the thought of him not being there.

'I am so proud and I will be there, Sammy Puddleduck. I promise,' I hear him whisper in my ear.

'... and I wasn't sure quite what to do,' Valerie says.

Whoops!

'Sorry, Valerie, I was miles away.'

Valerie goes quiet.

'Oh, it doesn't matter.'

'No, go on.'

'No, really. It's ...'

'She was telling you that Donald, that security guard downstairs, has asked her out for dinner and she doesn't know what to do.'

This time it's not my dad that I hear, it's Frank, Valerie's dead husband, and not only do I hear him, I can see him smiling back at me in the mirror that hangs over the mantelpiece in Valerie's living room. I recognise him from the many photos that Valerie has dotted around the place and he's smiling a kind, genuine smile as he looks down on her hemming my dress. I must be getting used to this because I no longer freak out at the thought of seeing dead people. They always look so serene, peaceful and worldly-wise to me.

'*She should go. She knows I'm always here for her, but she has to live her life and stop worrying about what I think,*' Frank says.

'Frank says you should go to dinner with Donald. He says he will always be here for you, but you have to live your life and stop worrying about him.' I look over my shoulder. Valerie just nods. She's pretending to concentrate on my hem, but I know she's secretly smiling to herself.

And who'd have thought it? Valerie and Donald!

As Frank's face fades from the mirror, I see my own reflection.

'*You look friggin amazing, hun!*' Ange says.

I do, don't I?

And I do.

CHAPTER TWENTY-FOUR

'I think you'd better come and see for yourself,' a very worried Colin says to me over the phone as I am just about to leave Valerie's apartment.

'OK, Colin, don't worry, I'll be there in a minute.'

The reason why my mother's boyfriend sounds so worried is because my mother is at this moment dressed in full Rastafarian costume and is entertaining the tourists as she bangs on a set of bongo drums, while sitting cross-legged on the steps of Bath Abbey.

'She appears to be in some kind of trance, Sam,' Colin said when he phoned me. 'I thought she was only going to the Abbey to sort out where the flowers were going to be placed for the wedding, but when she came down with fake tan on her face and a woolly hat on her head, asking if I could dreadlock her hair for her, I began to worry.'

Quite right, too!

'Oh my God, you didn't, did you?'

'Didn't what?'

'Dreadlock my mother's hair?'

I can imagine it now: my mother with dreads in her hair at my wedding. There is no way her hair will be back to normal in time!

'No, no, Sam. I told her I had to go and check on the carrots. Then she took off, saying something about how she would get someone called Germaine to do it,' Colin said.

This just gets worse by the day. The other day I caught her and Marjorie in town, outside HMV, singing and dancing to UB40's 'Kingston Town' that was blaring out of the shop, while trying to sell shell-rope bracelets to the tourists of Bath. I'm surprised they didn't get themselves arrested. Bath City Council doesn't take kindly to buskers at the best of times, let alone a pair of white middle-aged women dressed up like Eddy Grant.

Thankfully, one of Jack's ex-colleagues from HMV recognised my mother and persuaded them to pack up and go home before any police officers appeared.

'Boomchakawahwah!' was my mother's reply, followed by Marjorie's, 'It's cos we're black, innit!' before they ran up the road, looking, well, looking like two mad, middle-aged women with Rastafarian hats on.

On the scale of the most embarrassing things my mother has done, this moment has got to be one of her best. As I pull into the car park I can spot her a mile away. She's the one dressed from head to foot in multicoloured clothes with a tea cosy on her head, and dancing in a very odd fashion as she plays her drums, completely in the way of visitors trying to gain access to the Abbey. Thankfully, no one seems to think it slightly odd that this woman is there. Perhaps they think it's all part of the tourist attractions?

'Mum,' I prod her in the arm, 'what on earth are you doing?'

She doesn't reply, but simply smiles at me as she concentrates on pounding her drums. 'She's been like this for over an hour,' a worried Colin says. 'I've tried everything to move her.'

'We could always use a tow rope,' I mutter. Right, I've had enough of this. Is she trying to get me banned from having my wedding here?

'*This is brilliant!*' I hear Ange say.

This is not brilliant, Ange! This is a bloody nightmare!

'*One minute she's a normal woman and the next she's Rastamouse! Ha! Oh, you couldn't make it up, could you? I tell you what: you could earn a few quid selling your story to* Pick Me Up!' Ange laughs.

That's it! She's been possessed again. My God, my mother must be one of those people who are really easy to possess. I speed dial Miracle's number.

'Miracle, it's me. Look, my mother has become possessed again; she's playing drums outside the Abbey as if she's Bob Marley and refuses to be moved. What should I do?'

'OK, you're going to have to ask Ange to help you.' Miracle doesn't sound at all surprised by the fact that my mother has become possessed again.

'Ange? You're kidding, right? Do you know what her suggestion was? To sell my story to *Pick Me Up*!'

'Well, Sam, you need someone on the other side to persuade the other spirit to move on from your mum, Sam,' Miracle says.

'You hear that, Ange?' I say

'Me? I can't do that. I know nothing about it. I'm new to all of this, you know!'

'Hum, I thought as much. I'm going to have to think about getting a new spirit guide to help me, Miracle,' I say into the phone.

'What do you mean, a new spirit guide?' Ange asks.

'Well, you're no use, are you? I mean, it's all very well haunting your exes and getting me to read Cheryl Cole's latest celebrity tweets out to you, but in the grand scheme of things, you're not really helping me, Ange,' I say.

'You don't think I can do it? Well, I'll bloody show you!' Ange snaps.

The next thing I know my mother is lying on her back, arms and legs flailing in the air, looking rather like a fly that has been swatted.

'Now sod off and go and possess someone else, you stupid Rasta! Just cos you can play the drums, doesn't make you less of a pain in the ass, you know!' I hear Ange shout.

My mum sits upright and looks up at me and Colin.

'Sammy, what are you doing here, love? Have you come to talk to the reverend about the wedding too?' she asks. 'You should have said, we could have come together,' she adds, looking down at her unusual costume in puzzlement.

'Yes, that's right, Mum. I'm done now, so shall we go?' I offer her my hand and pull her up.

'Did you ask him if it's OK to have the congregation all sitting together?' my mum asks as we put her in Colin's car. I want to cry. As funny as it may look, to a passer-by my mum just looks like a confused and bewildered woman, and as Colin drives away, I burst into tears.

'Don't cry, Sam,' I hear Ange say in my ear. *'I got rid of him for you, didn't I?'*

'I know you did and thank you, Ange. I couldn't have done it without you and I'm sorry...it's just...it's all getting too much for me,' I sob in the car park.

Ironic really: my mum dresses up as a Rastafarian and no one bats an eyelid; I have a breakdown in the car park and all eyes are on me.

'I think it's time we had another séance, don't you?' Ange says. I agree.

CHAPTER TWENTY-FIVE

I haven't heard from Gem since she heard about Simon and she went to stay with her mum. Being back at the WI hall brings back the memories of her helping me out the last time we were here.

'Well, I don't think it's really affected anyone, do you, Sammy? I can't say I've noticed anyone acting strangely. Have you?' my mum says as she helps me to pull all the chairs round in a circle.

'Nothing strange? You are joking, Mum?'

My mum looks at me as if I'm the one that should be locked up.

'What about Marjorie begging on the streets, not to mention the two of you outside HMV? And Mrs Samuels and Mr Brent?'

'What, the one with one leg shorter than the other? Not that you can tell.'

'Yes, Mum. The one with one leg shorter than the other. Remember, I told you I caught them kissing outside Mr Brent's house?'

'Who was kissing who outside Mr Brent's house?' my mum asks as she moves another chair into the circle.

'Aggh! Mrs Samuels, Mum!'

'What, the one with ...'

'One leg shorter than the other, yes Mum!'

'Not that you can tell, mind you. Well, I can't see Mr Samuels agreeing to that, can you? You must have got your wires crossed, Sammy love. You are funny,' she muses to herself.

You know sometimes I could quite happily strangle my mother.

'Mum, do you know why we are here tonight?'

My mum is now waving a fire lighter around in the air as she attempts to light the nine tea light candles on the table.

'What's that, dear?'

'Oh, it doesn't matter. Just watch what you're doing with that thing, will you?' I dodge the flame thrower as she turns to wave to Mrs Bannerman who has just come through the doors.

Thankfully, Miracle and her motley crew have also arrived to help me; the motley crew consisting of a few select people from the psychic academy, including Alistair, aka Elvis, who insisted he knew how to make these spirits return to their rightful homes in the sky. The fact that he is dressed as Elvis is slightly unnerving, but then looking around at the odd combination of people here, he actually fits in quite nicely. We have Mr Brent, who is still dressed as a Viking and sporting a fully grown bushy beard, and I'm talking proper beard here. Not one of those little bits of fuzz on the chin ones. No, it's a real, heavyweight, fully fledged bushy beard. Mrs Samuels (yes, the one with one leg shorter than the other, although you would never tell) is standing by Mr Brent's side, looking longingly at him. Mrs Horsham – the one with the sleepwalking husband – is talking to Marjorie, telling her that she didn't realise there was an extra WI meeting this month.

We haven't told anyone the real reason we are here. Our explanation was that the last séance went so well that we are going to repeat the experience. Yeah, it went so well that half the village became possessed!

'So, are you ready?' Miracle asks.

'As ready as I will ever be, I guess,' I reply glumly. You know, all I want is to live a normal life, doing normal things. I want to be able to arrange my wedding with Jack, rather than by text message, and I want to go out to a club with friends of the living kind, rather than a deceased Essex girl who thinks she's a member of TOWIE. I just want to be normal!

'You've been given a special gift, Samantha,' Miracle says – I'm sure she's a mind reader as well as a psychic, you know. 'I know it's hard for you and it takes a lot of getting used to, my love.' She hugs me to her huge bosom.

Getting used to? I don't think I will ever get used to this.

'Come on, let's get this over and done with,' I sigh.

'Mind if I join you?'

Gem appears in the doorway.

'Gem! What are you doing here? I thought you were staying with your mum?'

Gem hugs me, bouncing me off her protruding stomach.

'I was. I am. I needed to check on the house; you know, post and stuff like that, and Mrs Jackson mentioned that you were having another séance, so I thought I would come along, if that's alright?'

'Alright? It's fantastic. And Gem? I am so, so sorry...you know, about Simon.'

Gem shrugs.

'I knew what could happen when I fell in love with him, Sam. I hope...well you know, I thought coming here tonight might ...'

This is why I'm doing this job; for people like Gem. I just hope that Simon does come through for her.

'Right, let's get this show on the road, shall we?' I say as my mum dims the harsh hall lights. I'm thankful that Miracle is here to oversee things and more importantly close the circle properly this time.

As we all settle down Miracle opens the circle and I can see all the spirits milling about in the hall. There's Marjorie's little urchin, Tom, who is busy playing tag with Mrs Jackson's daughter, Alice. There's Mum's Jamaican friend swaying his head in time to the music coming from his Walkman. The Viking is standing behind Mrs Samuels, stroking her hair. They're all here and quite a few new faces too.

'We are here this evening to send you home,' Miracle says, her eyes closed and in deep concentration. I wonder if I'm the only one who can see all these dead people. No one else seems to have a clue that they are here, aside from Mrs Samuels occasionally looking behind her and touching the back of her head.

'Send who home? Is Mrs Horsham not feeling well again?' my

mum says, looking bewildered out of one eye.

'Just close your eyes, Mum,' I hiss.

'Before I ask you to all walk back into the light, is there anybody here who would like to talk to our guests?'

The spirits all start shuffling around.

'I wanna stay wiv her,' Tom the urchin shouts as he stops playing tag with Alice and runs over to Marjorie's side.

'Marjorie, the little boy, Tom, who took a shine to you is back,' I say, smiling as Marjorie's head swivels from side to side, looking for him.

'He's to your left,' I instruct.

Marjorie looks down and to her left.

'Hello, my dear. How are you?' she says, looking at me to confirm she's facing him.

'I like her,' Tom says to me.

'She likes you too, Tom, but Marjorie has her own son,'

'Not that you'd know. Does he ever visit? He doesn't, does he, Cathy? How many times have I invited him and Fleur over for dinner?'

My mum opens her eyes.

'Many times, Marjorie, many times,' my mum sighs.

'I was only saying the other day, wasn't I Cathy, that Jonathon never comes over now he's got himself married,' Marjorie continues.

'Um...hello? Mum?' I interrupt the two women's chat.

'Excuse me a moment, Marjorie. Yes dear?'

'We are not here to have a good old chat about Jonathon's reluctance to visit Marjorie.'

'Are we not? What are we here for then?'

I give up!

'Mum, just close your eyes and concentrate. We are trying to persuade Tom and his friends to go back to where they came from.' I sigh – deeply.

'Uh-huh,' Alistair/Elvis agrees with me.

'Right, unless there is anyone here who has an urgent message for a loved one, could you all please leave,' I snap.

Mrs Horsham shuffles her chair backwards.

'No, not you, Mrs Horsham. I meant the spirits.'

'Oh, right you are, dear. I thought the meeting was a bit short.' She chuckles and sits back down again.

Oh, give me strength.

'I have a message for a loved one.'

I look to where the voice is coming from and see Simon standing behind Gem. Gem looks at me.

'He's here, isn't he?'

I nod.

'Hello Simon. What is it you want to say to Gem?'

The mindless chatter that is my mother ceases as all eyes are on Gem. Even the spirits have been good enough to shut up for five minutes.

'I am so sorry, Gemma. I love you and our unborn baby so very much and I'm sorry I had to go. You have to stop worrying about what to do with my things. They're only things, Gem. Let someone else enjoy them. I certainly don't need an iPad here. I can be with you whenever you need me now, just call my name.'

As I relay the words Simon says, tears are streaming down all our faces, even stony-faced Mrs Landsbury; you know, the one with the poodle.

Gem puts her head in her hands to hide her own tears.

'I...I wasn't sure what to do with...you know, with Si's stuff. All his CDs, his iPad, the...'

'Tell her to give the photo of me and my brother to Andy, if she wants. He'd like that.'

'...photo of him and his brother, Andy.' Gem laughs through her tears.

'I'll be back soon. I promise,' Simon whispers as he disappears and I am looking at the bare wall.

'He will be back soon, Gem,' I assure her. She nods and holds her hands to her eyes.

'OK, it looks as though that is the only message we have tonight.' Miracle takes over. She can see I'm not really up to the job this evening.

'Can we all close our eyes again and remain holding hands? Spirits, thank you for joining us. Could you please make your way back to your own world now?'

I peek out of one eye and see that they are all still here with us. I look at Miracle.

'Spirits,' she asks, 'please go back to your own world so that we can close the circle behind us.'

Again they are still here.

'Spirits, you must go back now, please,' Miracle instructs.

Nope, they are not going anywhere.

'Ange,' I whisper, 'what's going on?'

'Sorry, Sam, I was looking in that woman's handbag. She's got one of those new lip tint sticks I told you about. You should get one. She's got one in coral pearl.'

'Right, will do, but at the moment I'm a little busy. I need to know why the spirits aren't moving on.'

'No clue,' Ange mutters.

'Well, do you think you could ask one of them?'

Ange huffs to herself.

'Right, they're not going until they get an invite to your wedding,' she says.

'What?'

'They want to come to the wedding.'

'Ooo, a wedding! We're going to a wedding!' A woman dressed in typical ghostly attire like a white wedding dress, cries.

'A wedding! How wonderful! I've been to a few of those!' Another spirit roars with laughter.

'But they can't come to my wedding, Ange!'

'Well, they're not leaving until they get an invite. I can assure you of that,' Ange says.

'Miracle, they won't go because they want to come to my wedding,' I whisper.

'Well, it looks like you're going to have to extend your guest list then.' Miracle laughs her throaty laugh.

What? Oh bloody marvellous! Now I have dead people requesting to be put on the guest list. It's one way to make up the numbers, I suppose!

CHAPTER TWENTY-SIX

So just how do you explain to your fiancé that your wedding guest list has expanded tenfold?

'*Don't tell him,*' Ange advises.

'But why? We tell each other everything.'

'*You don't think it's a teensy-weensy bit strange to say to your future husband, Oh, and by the way, we have an additional two hundred guests coming, only they're all dead?*'

She has a point.

'*And besides, he won't be able to see them anyway, will he?*'

'I guess not.' Jack has never seen so much as a spooky shadow, let alone a dead person, which is probably a good thing really because he is such a baby at the best of times. He can't even watch Scooby-Doo without hiding behind a cushion – and this is the guy who is supposed to be looking after me until death do us part, forever and ever amen.

'So I won't tell him then.'

'*Correct. It will only unnerve him,*' my spirit guide says very sagely. '*Anyway, I've got a surprise for you, Sammy girl!*' Ange adds.

'Hang on one mo, Ange. Let me get the phone. Here, here's the latest copy of *Fate & Fortune* for you to read.' I leave the copy of Ange's second favourite mag on the armchair and watch in amusement as the pages turn as if by themselves.

'Hey Paul. How's it all going down under?'

'Sammy! How's things? It's ninety degrees in the shade here,' my brother gloats.

'How lovely for you, but don't you miss the wind and the rain of good old England?' I say to my lovely brother who is a gazillion miles away in sunny Australia right now.

'Hum, let me think for a second…no.'

'So why are you calling me at what must be an ungodly hour over there?'

'I've got some info for you, on Jack's mum,' Paul says.

Oh. Suddenly my stomach does one of those lurch things. Do I really want to know? I am the crappiest of crappiest people at keeping a secret.

'And?' I say apprehensively.

'Well,' Paul begins, 'I found a total of eight women called Marianne Lewis who would have been born around the same time as Jack's mum. Two were Nigerian and members of the same tribe, so I counted them out for obvious reasons – Jack's not black, is he?'

'No Paul, as far as I'm aware Jack is not black and never has been.'

'That's what I thought. One woman is married to a Scottish vicar and lives somewhere in the middle of nowhere. Another is living in Leicester, again married, kids in their twenties, etc. Another one…'

'Paul, just cut to the chase.'

'Yeah, well, you get the idea. Now, having had no luck on my list of eight, I thought she might have married, or that Lewis wasn't her original name, so I dug around a bit. Now, there was a woman born in 1963 by the name of Marianne Ranger who, according to my sources, had a relationship with a wealthy American entrepreneur by the name of Peter Lewis. Lewis was killed in a car crash in Florida in October 1984. When was Jack born?'

'On 18th February 1985.'

'Right. According to a newspaper report Lewis and Marianne were due to get married once the baby was born, but obviously that didn't happen. It looks like Marianne had Jack and gave him Peter's surname on the birth certificate, which was registered at York register office.'

Just talking about Jack makes my heart ache. I can't imagine how Gem feels, knowing that she will never see Simon, the love of her life, again.

'So why did she put him into care?' I ask. I really feel for Jack. We all want to know where we came from, right?

'That I have yet to find out. Can you not just ask the woman yourself?'

'I told you it doesn't work like that. All Jack has is a photo and note saying how sorry she is and that she will return to get him, but she never did.'

'Well, leave it with me. I'll see what else I can dig up, but Sam?'

'Yes?'

'This is *Jack's* business. You don't have to be the fixer of all problems, you know, and he might not even want to know,' Paul says quietly.

This takes me aback a bit. Paul is usually the one who goes in all guns blazing and thinks about the consequences later – usually much too much later – and here he is advising me to leave things alone.

'Perhaps you're right,' I say, and maybe he is; maybe Jack really is quite happy and doesn't need to know.

As I finish my call with Paul, I notice that the pages of the magazine I gave to Ange are still flicking over of their own accord.

'So, what's this surprise you have for me then, Ange?'

'Ange?'

There's no reply from my slightly wacky spirit guide, and yet the pages of the magazine I gave her are still flicking over and over. Does this mean she's not speaking to me again?

'Ange?'

Suddenly the outline of a figure emerges on my sofa – and unfortunately it's not Ange. It's Clive.

'Oh Jesus Christ!'

'Now, now Samantha. We should not use the Lord's name in vain, should we?' Clive says in his usual sinister manner.

'What are you doing here? What do you want?' I look around the room.

'There's no point looking for your little friend. She's not here. She's gone.' Clive sneers. My little kitten Dorothy hisses at him then runs away to the kitchen.

'Gone? What do you mean, she's gone? What have you done with Ange? Ange?' I find myself screaming into thin air for my spiritual buddy. Despite having been assigned the most useless spirit guide in the world, I feel an affinity with Ange and am quite protective of her.

Clive smiles at me. He looks just as I remembered him when he was alive – lanky with ill-fitting clothes and glasses that are far too big for him. I wonder if when we die we get to choose how we look? I make a mental note to ask Ange.

'I like how I look, actually,' Clive says, as if reading my mind.

'What do you want, Clive? Haven't you got something better to do than annoy me, like oh, I don't know, ghost train spotting?' I know, I know, but this guy is seriously pissing me off now. Not content with being a pain in the butt when he was alive, he has to be a pain in the butt in the afterlife too!

'We have unfinished business, remember?'

'What unfinished business?' I look at Clive with defiance. I will not be intimidated by a ghost.

'You were going to cure me of my phobia, remember?'

'And you became a weird pain in the butt, remember?' I retaliate. This is madness; I'm arguing with the ghost of someone who once had a crush on me and held a grudge because I wasn't interested. You'd think he'd let it go now, wouldn't you? I mean, don't dead people have better things to think about, like, oh I don't know, like comforting their loved ones? Mind you, Clive didn't really have any loved ones to comfort, being your stereotypical trainspotting loner.

'I'm here to stay,' Clive says as he settles back on my sofa and crosses his legs.

'Right, if that's the way you want to play it...' I snap. I will not be intimidated by a lanky ghost in bad clothes. I furiously stamp out to the kitchen, empty the veg rack and arm myself with enough varieties of vegetables to make Paul McCartney proud.

'Right, you want to play games, do you?' I shout as I return to the living room armed with my very own harvest festival.

'What are you doing?' Clive stutters, and despite him being somewhat washed out, I can still see the shocked look on his face.

'Come on then. You want me to cure you of your vegetable phobia, do you? Well, here have some carrots...' I throw a bunch of them at Clive, who visibly squirms, '...and how about a turnip? Do you like them too, Clive?' A turnip flies through the air. 'Or what about a...' I look at the strange orangey vegetable in my hand, trying to recall what it is, '...a squish, no a squash. Is that it? Do you like whatever these bloody things are called, Clive? How about some sprouts for good measure?' I launch sprouts like missiles at my unwanted visitor.

'Yoo-hoo! It's only me!'

Ah, it's my mother.

'Sammy, what on earth are you doing, dear?' She looks at me as if I'm completely bonkers, and given the sight she is looking at she has every right to assume that I have totally lost the plot.

Clive has disappeared and in his place a veritable feast of vegetables adorns my sofa and I am in mid throw, taking aim with a beetroot in my hand.

'Mum! Hi!' I say in a panic.

CHAPTER TWENTY-SEVEN

I managed to convince my mum that I am not going mad and that the reason my sofa was covered in an assortment of vegetables was a stress relief method that the Dalai Lama swears by. I know, but what else could I say and it was the first thing that came into my head.

After I had discussed the virtues of his Royal Highness Lama with my mother and thanked her for dropping off a bag of cat litter for my feline family, she left to allow me to finish my 'stress relieving programme' in peace. Little did she know I had been doing battle with her boyfriend's dead cousin.

I have worked out that Clive is still deeply fearful of vegetables and in particular the wonderful orange root vegetable, the humble carrot, and I decide it's time to take action and remove all the ornaments and vases from my window sills and replace them with bunches of carrots. That will sort the bugger out. I hang a bunch above the front door for good measure.

'What the f...?' Ange says.

'Ange! Where have you been?' I swivel round towards the sound of her voice and ... oh my God! There, standing in the middle of my living room, is Ange. And I mean really standing there in all her Essex glory.

'Ange?'

Ange does a twirl.

'What do you think? And why the hell are you hanging carrots above the door? Is it some kind of witchy ritual, because if it is I don't want to know,' Ange says, looking up at my choice of house decoration.

'Good Lord, look at you! You're real!' I squeak. I can't believe it. All this time I've been able to hear Ange, but I haven't been able actually to *see* her and she looks stunning. Her hair is golden blonde and curls all the way down to her bum and she's a real woman. By that I mean she is not a stick insect, but a normal size twelve to fourteen, with gorgeous womanly curves. She reminds me of a cross between Marylyn Monroe and Adele. Ange's fashion sense isn't quite what I would choose to dress myself in – short, stonewashed blue denim skirt, a pink lace vest top, with a purple leopard skin bra underneath it, the biggest pair of gold hoop earrings you could ever wish to own and a pair of fluorescent orange wedge sandals. She has an equally orange tan.

This reminds me a bit of that old eighties movie *Mannequin*, when the mannequin comes to life. I'm looking Ange up and down; Ange is looking herself up and down, both of us in awe of the sight before us.

'How did you do that?'

'*I have no idea!*' Ange says as she examines her shapely legs.

'But you look so … so real!' and she does; not like Clive or the other visiting spirits who all looked slightly washed out. I poke my finger at Ange and as you would suspect it goes right through her.

'Did you feel that?'

'*Nope. Do it again,*' Ange says excitedly, so I do and again and again. We're like two kids who have discovered something very interesting.

'*Look, I can do this too,*' Ange says as she closes her eyes tightly and concentrates. She actually looks as though she needs a poo.

'*Hang on, it's coming …*'

I stare at Ange as she concentrates hard on whatever she's trying to do and she suddenly disappears before my eyes.

'*I'm still here,*' I hear her say.

'Cool. Now come back, I want to see you in all your glory again.' I feel so happy for Ange right now because I know how much she has wanted to be able to show herself to me.

'*See! I'm here again,*' Ange says.

'Err, no you're not, Ange.' And she isn't.

'Oh shit, hang on a minute.' Ange makes a huge grunting sort of noise.

'Taadaa!'

There she is again. Amazing!

'Ange! This is brilliant! How did you do it?'

'I have no idea. Someone up there told me that we can show ourselves given the right frequencies, or something, so I thought I would give it a go. What do you think?' Ange spins around again, wobbling slightly on her six-inch wedge heels.

'I think you look bloody marvellous. Is this the sort of thing you used to wear, you know when you were ... you know?

'Alive? Yeah, why? Don't you like it?'

'I do...I just...' Oh crikey, how do you tell your spirit guide that less is often more without upsetting her? It's a bit like when your best friend bought that silver dress in the Next January sales and ended up looking like a turkey ready for the oven. Ange's large bosoms are almost hanging out of her lace top and the skirt could do with being a few inches longer. The diamante belt on her hips is a bit too glitzy for Bath, but other than that...

'You don't like the way I dress?' Ange snaps.

'No, no I do. You look very...'

'Classy?' Ange ventures.

'Um...very...fun loving,' I say, 'very Essex, like that girl off of TOWIE.'

'Oh good, because I love TOWIE – not as much as I love Mark Wright though, but he loved Lauren. Maybe if I paid him a visit he'd love me, wouldn't he?'

Eh?

'I don't think Mark Wright is looking for love at the moment, Ange. He's too busy presenting that new reality show, remember? And there's the little matter that he's alive and you're...well... you're not.'

'Well that's OK, because I have someone else in mind.' Ange smiles with sparkles in her eyes. *'Which is the reason I am here today,*

showing myself to you.'

'And this new guy, is he dead too?'

'He is!' Ange says with excitement.

'I didn't know you could date dead people when you were dead.' And I didn't. I mean, who'd have thought?

'I know! Me neither!'

'And this dead guy, where did you meet him?' I have visions of some speed dating club in the sky for dead peeps.

'Well, I was just wandering around up there, taking things in, when there was this great crashing sound. I thought it was thunder, as you do when you hear a great crashing sound in the sky. Anyway, next thing I know there's this guy on the floor in front of me dressed from head to toe in black leather with a crash helmet on his head,' Ange says as she settles herself down between the assortment of vegetables on the sofa.

' 'Ooo!' Ange shrieks as she produces a carrot from beneath her. *'That could have been unfortunate!'* She laughs her loud laugh.

'So? This dead guy?' God, this girl has the attention span of a goldfish sometimes.

'Oh yeah, well there he was, just lying there at my feet – probably looking up me skirt if I didn't know any better. Anyway I said, Who are you? And he groaned, opened his visor and said, "Who the fuck are you?"'

'A nice gentleman then?'

'Well I said, I'm Ange and who the fuck are you to ask who the fuck I am? I mean who the fuck does he think he is?'

'Quite.'

I am still in awe of the sight of my sassy little spirit guide, although I do wish she would pull her skirt down a few inches, you can almost see her knickers – that's if she's actually got any on. Ange was a great fan of going knickerless when she was alive, apparently.

'So, it turns out he's a guy called Danny, he's twenty-four, or should I say was twenty-four – he's dead see.'

'No kidding.'

'Yeah, he is. Anyway he died in a motorbike accident – hence why he was wearing the leathers, and he was in a right mood when we met.'

'Well, I expect he was, Ange,' I say. 'One minute he's out on his bike and the next he's flat on his back looking up at you. Oh God, you weren't wearing that skirt, were you?' I have visions of Danny waking up and getting an eyeful of Ange's privates.

'What's wrong with this skirt? It's my fave!' Ange looks shocked.

'Nothing. It's just a little - short.'

'That's what Danny said,' Ange says with a surprised tone to her voice. *'After he asked who the fuck I was! He's lush, mind, Sam, even if he is an arrogant git.'*

Oh no, where is this heading?

'So? Are you going to see him again?'

Ange's eyes light up.

'Well, that's where you come in.'

I thought as much. I sit on the sofa next to Ange.

'Go on, but it will have to be quick; I have a radio show to do today.' I say, looking at my watch. With Annette out of action it's all hands to the whatsit at the moment at Town FM, and with Jeff permanently wearing the carpet out with his walking up and down all the time, rather than reading the news, it's up to me and Liam to run the show. I have to say, though, it is good fun being a stand-in radio DJ and I keep name dropping Jack's band in the hope that it will encourage people to vote for Otherwise at the Vibe Awards – cheeky I know, but hey, you have to get the publicity where you can.

'Danny wants to hook up with me tonight, so I want you to take me shopping. I mean proper shopping. I want to look nice and sophisti-cated.'

'Okay, but surely you can't just roll up at Selfridges and try stuff on? I mean, when I poked you, my finger went right through you. How can you try on clothes?'

'Ah, well I can't, but if I concentrate hard enough on something I

can manifest it on me, but I need your advice on what looks sophisti-cated and what doesn't.'

'Right, well, OK.' I feel quite pleased that Ange values my opinion on fashion. No one has ever asked me for fashion advice before. I can't think why.

'Let me get the show out of the way and we will hit the shops.'

Ange beams a big smile, clicks her fingers dramatically and disappears, leaving me with a tonne of veg to put back in the kitchen.

CHAPTER TWENTY-EIGHT

'Good morning and welcome to Town FM. I'm Crystal Ball and I'm standing in for Annette today while she recovers in hospital. Thank you for all your good wishes, which we have passed on to her.'

'Get on with it. I want to talk to someone,' I hear a voice shout inside my head.

'Um...today we are going to have a much longer *Sixth Sense* show, so get your calls in now and I will do my best to answer as many as I can. First we are going over to the news desk with Jeff.' I hit the jingle button to activate the news jingle and mentally prepare myself for an hour and a half of chit-chat to the living and the not so.

'Are we on yet?' The same voice comes into my head.

'No, we're not and who are you?' I ask out loud.

'I need you to speak to my mum,' the young male voice says quite desperately.

'Who is your mum?'

'I need her to ring you,' the voice says.

'Does she listen to the show, do you know?'

'I don't know, but you must get her to ring in.'

The boy is almost hysterical and I don't know what to do.

'What's your mum's name?'

'Jan, and I'm Andy.'

'The thing is, Andy, if your mum doesn't phone in I can't pass on a message to her,' I say. I mean I'm good, but I'm not that good.

'You have to let her know I'm OK, before she does something stupid,' Andy says.

Oh blooming heck.

'OK, I'll see what I can do, but I will need your mother's full name.' I try to think of how I'm going to do this. The chance that his mother is listening to this radio station at precisely the same time as I am on is pretty slim, and as much as I'm in awe that real dead people can talk to me, they don't appear to be so clever that they can avert impending tragedies. Andy doesn't say any more, so I am left wondering how I am going to sort this out.

'…and that's the news and weather for the moment. Now get ready for the psychic to the stars, Crystal Ball,' Jeff says by way of introduction to my *Sixth Sense* show. Right,

focus Sam.

Poor Jeff, he looks so much older today, as if he's carrying the whole world on his shoulders. He's really worried about Annette. Despite the pair of them deciding that they are not going to be an 'item' as such, I have a funny feeling that they are.

As the mystical music fades out, Liam gives me the thumbs up that I'm on live. The lights on Annette's desk are lit up like a Christmas tree with callers all wanting to know where their loved ones are, when they will win the lottery and when they will find the man/woman of their dreams. Let's just hope that one of them is Andy's mum Jan, hey?

'Thank you, Jeff. Now it looks like we're in for a busy time, so I'm going to go straight to caller one. Hello, who am I speaking to?'

'Ha, you should know that, being psychic and all that,' the voice says.

'Oh another comedian,' I snap. 'What can I do for you, sir?'

Why is it always men who call with the wise cracks, I wonder? I shouldn't snap at them. It's just…oh I don't know, I miss Jack like mad and these comedians drive me mad when I feel like this.

'I want to know if Man U are going to win in the match on Saturday,' the man says. I sigh.

'Tony wants to know because he's going to put his life savings on it, the fool. The money he inherited from me,' Another much older man's voice says to me.

'Well, Tony…'

'Hey, how do you know my name? I didn't tell you my name. I didn't tell anyone my name. I didn't even tell the geezer who put me through,' the man protests.

'Well, I should know, me being a psychic and all that.'

'Just tell him to invest in premium bonds instead. He will win on those. Oh, and this is his uncle Charles, by the way.'

'Charles told me – your uncle.' I sigh again.

'My uncle? How do you know his name?'

'Oh, for goodness sake! Because I'm a psychic, that's why, Tony! Now your uncle has told me that you want to spend all your inheritance on a football match. He said he didn't give you that money to be foolish. Now, if you're wise you will listen to him and get some premium bonds instead,' I snap again.

'So how do I do that then?'

'What?'

'Get some premier whatsits?'

'Well, I don't know!'

'Well, you're the psychic, you should know,' Tony counterattacks.

'Precisely! I'm a psychic not a financial advisor.'

'Tell him to go online, type in premium bonds and Charlie's your uncle,' Tony's uncle advises.

How do you know? I ask in my head.

'Ha, I used to be an accountant,' Charles says.

'Your uncle says to go online and type in premium bonds,' I tell Tony.

'Oh right. OK then. Cheers.'

'You're very welcome. Now is there anything else?'

'Yeah, so what are Man U's chances on Saturday then?'

I hang up.

A familiar voice comes through again.

'Please get my mum to call in,' Andy's voice says.

'I can't make your mum call me, Andy. I'm sorry, but you will have to give me more information.' He's gone again.

The next few calls consist of a woman wanting to know where her mother put her will, two women wanting to know when their prince will come and a man wanting me to put him through to Jasper – his deceased ferret.

'And now I'm taking a break so that we can go over to Jeff on the news desk.' I click a series of lights off on the switchboard and slump back in my seat. It's quite exhausting all this psychic stuff, I don't mind telling you.

My mobile rings. It's Jack.

'Good timing! I just stopped for the news break. Are you OK?' It's so good to hear Jack's voice again and it only serves to remind me just how much I love him. We talk for a moment about when he's coming home and what's happening here and in London, and then I have to end the call because Jeff is finishing his news slot.

'...and now to the travel news. There are traffic delays on the Almondsbury interchange due to a broken down vehicle. And news just in, the B3129 is temporarily closed due to an incident on the Clifton Suspension Bridge and will remain closed for some time. That is all your Town FM news for now.'

'That's my mum! My mum's on the bridge! She's going to kill herself!' I hear Andy say in my head.

I hit the button that puts me directly through to Jeff and Liam.

'Jeff, that last bit about the Suspension Bridge?'

'Uh-huh?'

'Why is it shut?'

They never shut that bridge. It would cause all sorts of chaos to people trying to get to and from work.

'I dunno. Something about someone trying to jump off it again,' Jeff mutters back to me as he shuffles his news reports into some sort of order.

'Oh no! Jeff, I've got to go.' I grab my car keys and run out of the studio.

As I drive through the traffic heading towards Bristol I hear the news bulletin on the radio.

'...police liaison officers are at the scene now, trying to talk to the woman who is in her mid forties.'

I quickly dial Valerie on hands-free.

'Valerie, it's me. I don't suppose Donald's with you, is he?'

'Um - why?'

'Valerie, I don't have much time to explain, can you just get him for me?'

I know from talking to Donald many times while he checked my ID that he used to work for the Avon and Somerset Constabulary, up until a few years ago when he retired to become a security guard for the retirement homes where Valerie now lives.

'Oh, just a minute. Donald, it's Samantha for you.'

'Hello Samantha, how may I help you?'

'Donald, look, there's a woman attempting to jump from the Suspension Bridge and I think I know who she might be. I need to talk to her urgently.'

'You won't get past the police there, my dear,' Donald says.

'Donald, it's really important that I speak with her.'

Donald must hear the desperation in my voice.

'Leave it with me. I'll try and get you clearance,' he says in a very authoritative manner.

Thirty minutes later and I am at Bridge Road, which is cordoned off. There are several uniformed officers barricading the entrance to the Suspension Bridge and as I look past them I can see a tiny figure standing in the middle of the bridge that spans the Avon Gorge. It's a popular suicide spot and despite putting anti-climb rails up, people determined enough will still get over them. The drop is over two hundred feet down and I'm suddenly feeling terrified as I look at the woman. Another woman, who I assume to be a Police Liaison Officer, is several feet away, her arms stretching out as if to help the woman.

'I'm sorry, Mam, this road is closed.' An officer approaches my car.

I get out.

'I need to speak to that woman,' I say, not taking my eyes off her for a second.

'Do you know her?'

'No, yes, well, kind of.'

The policeman is having none of it.

'I'm sorry, Mam. You will have to turn round and go back and up to the junction and through the city centre.'

'No, you don't understand. I must speak to her. I think I know her dead son.'

'Yes, Mam, now if you could just do as you're told and...Oi!'

Too late, I've dodged under the yellow tape and am away. Damn these bloody shoes! I throw them behind me and run as fast as I possibly can towards the bridge. The policeman I was talking to is in hot pursuit and I look over my shoulder to see how quickly he's gaining on me. I do hope he doesn't have a Taser gun on him. As he runs he's shouting into his radio. Oh god, I am going to be in so much trouble!

Another officer runs towards me and I duck under his arms as he goes to grab me.

'Miss! Do not approach the bridge!' he shouts.

'Please get to her, Sam,' I hear Andy say. *'Please!'*

'I have to talk to that woman!' I shout back.

The commotion has made the liaison officer look round and she holds her hand up to me.

'Please! I have to speak to that woman. I have a message for her from her son,' I beg.

'My son? You cruel bastard! My son is dead!' the woman on the bridge shouts at me.

'I know he is, Jan. It is Jan, isn't it?' My god, that would be embarrassing wouldn't it, if I got the wrong woman!

'He's dead.' The woman slumps to her knees and sobs. You can hear an intake of breath from me and all the officers, all praying that she doesn't let go of the bridge.

'Please, let me get nearer to her. You can arrest me later, but I really have to speak to her,' I beg the female officer.

'You're what's her name, off the telly,' she says, keeping one eye on the woman on the bridge.

'Crystal Ball, yes, which is why I must speak with Jan. Please!'

'Jan? Jan? This is Crystal Ball, the psychic. She needs to talk to you. Can she come closer?' the woman officer asks kindly.

'She can't make anything better!' Jan shouts back. 'No one can!'

'I can't make him come back, Jan, but I can let you know what he's saying. He doesn't want you to do this. He's been begging me to get a message to you,' I shout as I move slowly forward.

'He's dead, you stupid woman! How can you possibly tell me anything?' Jan shouts back between sobs.

'Tell her I know about the pills she took this morning. I also know about the note she left. What's going to happen to Mollie if she's gone? Who's going to pick her up from school? Is she that selfish that she would let her come home to an empty house and a dead mum?'

I relay the message to Andy's mum who continues to cry very loudly.

'Who's Mollie, Jan?'

'She's my daughter,' Jan confirms through huge sobs.

'How old is she?'

'She's fourteen.'

'And how do you think she will feel about this, Jan? Andy is very concerned about her.'

Jan just cries again. I think of how Jan's daughter will feel if her mother decides to jump. The poor kid. Imagine coming home expecting your tea to be on the table and being greeted with grim-faced neighbours at the door waiting to tell you that your mother has taken her own life.

'Jan, don't you see, he's here with us, with you! Talk to him, Jan, through me. Tell him how you're feeling,' I urge. Bugger, my feet hurt.

'I...I miss him so, so much. It hurts, like a real physical pain. It's not fair; he tried so hard to keep positive and was so brave.'

'Maybe I just didn't try hard enough, Mum. You always said I was a lazy so and so.' Andy laughs. *'Tell her my body just couldn't keep going through the treatment. It's no big deal, I'm fine here. In fact it's pretty awesome!'*

Again I pass on the message to Jan. She smiles slightly.

'That was his favourite saying, it's no big deal.' She says, 'It didn't matter what obstacles he was up against, or how much he went through at the hospital, he would always say, it's no big deal, Mum.'

'Tell her she's got to stop this. It won't solve anything. I will always be around her, every day of her life. It's not the first time, you know, Sam. She's tried this three times now and I'm getting a bit sick and tired of it, if I'm honest.'

'Jan, this isn't fair on Andy or Mollie,' I say. 'Andy said this isn't the first time either, is it?'

I can see Andy, a good-looking young man, standing beside his mother. Tears roll down his cheeks.

'I'm sorry,' Jan sobs and looks down at the vast expanse of mud, two hundred feet below her. Oh no, please don't jump. Please don't jump.

'Please Jan. Don't do this to them. You can talk to me any time if you want to talk to Andy. He knew you were here. He was the one who contacted me and told me you were here, Jan. You know how it feels to lose someone so special to you. Think about how Mollie will feel if it happens to her again.'

Jan looks at me, her eyes red and swollen from crying. She looks desperate.

'Jan, please! I'm in enough trouble as it is for breaking through the police barrier, now will you get the fuck off this bridge before I get arrested!'

I know, but the gentle approach doesn't seem to be working

and I'm getting mightily pissed off now, and I think I've cut my foot running up to this stupid bridge!

Jan turns towards the liaison officer and reaches out for her hand. She looks as though she's aged twenty years in the time I've been speaking to her. The officer gently guides her back over the railings.

I rush towards Jan and hold her in my arms. I rock her and she cries and cries, until she can cry no more.

CHAPTER TWENTY-NINE

It's early afternoon and the shops in Bath are heaving. Having saved Jan from an untimely death I then rushed back to the studio to explain to my listeners why I had suddenly gone AWOL and was unable to take their calls leaving Jeff and Liam in charge of rest of the show.

So here I am in the changing room, in the shopping mall, standing in my undies and looking like I am talking to myself, when I'm actually on my shopping expedition with Ange. So that I don't look as though I'm a mad woman, talking to herself, in her undies, I have attached one of those Bluetooth gadgets to my ear, so that when I'm talking to her in my role as fashion stylist, it actually looks as though I'm having a conversation with the living, rather than a dead person.

We're in H&M now, trying on outfits – well, I say we, but actually all the sales girls have seen is me going into the changing rooms with armfuls of clothes that are a) too big for me and b) nothing that I would be seen dead in, but then I'm not the dead one, am I?

'What about this?' Ange says, as she twirls around the all too small communal changing room in a pair of black and pink polka-dot leggings, a turquoise vest top and an orange tutu.

'Lovely – if you're five years old.'

'I think I look gorgeous!' Ange admires herself in front of the mirror, which incidentally doesn't show her reflection to anyone else. I thought it was only vampires that happened to – you learn something new every day, don't you.

'Try this.' I hand Ange an outfit of a just above the knee skirt, a white t-shirt with gold buttons on the shoulders and a pair of blue and white polka-dot shoes. Ange holds the items up against her.

'I'll look like a friggin sailor! All I need is a bloody sailor's hat to

complete the look!'

'Well, it's a darn sight better than what you chose,' I retort, just as three teenage girls enter the changing room. I wish I'd put on better undies than the off-white bra and knickers I'm standing in.

I must look and sound like a right nut job, holding up garments for Ange to try on. She has a nifty little trick where I only have to show her the clothes I've chosen and she can transfer the images of them on to herself. How handy is that? Just imagine, you could just look at something and 'poof', you're all dressed, although we have discovered that I have to have the items next to her in order for her to duplicate them and they have to be in the same size as her body. We found this out when Ange tried to magic herself into a size eight, lemon crop top, which covered just one of her ample boobs.

'What about this one?' I ask as I hold up a black and red shift dress. 'You could wear this with those black killer heels you saw in Selfridges.'

I'm trying not to make it too obvious that I'm talking to a ghost, as the teenagers look at me and whisper to each other. They're probably saying, 'Have you seen the state of her underwear. What a skank.'

Ange looks at the dress, closes her eyes together and 'poof', the image of the dress is on her – and she looks fabulous.

'It suits her, doesn't it?'

I spin round to see a middle-aged woman, with short white hair and a kind smile, walk into the changing rooms with an armful of clothes to try on. I feel as though I'm about to have a panic attack, as my head swivels from Ange to the woman and back again.

I hold the dress up against me and look in the mirror. It's obvious it's miles too big for me.

The woman puts her hand on my shoulder.

'Don't worry; I can see her too, dear.' She smiles. 'And she does look lovely.'

'You can see her?' I whisper, for fear of the teenagers ridiculing me.

'Yes. I've been able to see spirits ever since I was a child,' the woman whispers back.

'Oh...I...Ange, this lady can see you too,' I say to my dead buddy.

'Cool. Now do you think I should wear tights or just bare legs with this? I mean tights are a bit tricky to get off once you're, you know, in the throes of passion.'

Oh my god, do they really do that sort of thing in heaven?

The lady by my side laughs and pulls a curtain around a small dressing room cubicle for the self-conscious or those that are without a dead person to dress.

We decide on a lovely pair of stockings for Ange; that way, if she and Danny do get to the you-know-what stage, then she won't have too many problems tackling the getting the tights off situation. I, on the other hand, am all in favour of tights and the woollier the better, especially as it's blooming freezing outside.

'Come on, let's go and see if Selfridges still have those shoes you liked,' I suggest to Ange, who is at this moment twirling round and round in her new dress. I am getting rather cold standing here in my underwear, and quickly change into my jeans and jumper.

'Right, we'll go to...what's that noise?' I say as we leave the H&M store and head right towards Miss Selfridge.

'Ha! I don't believe it!' Ange squeals.

I don't believe it either. There, standing on a bench, wearing a pair of dark shades and playing a guitar and singing 'I Will Always Love You', is Jack.

'Oh My God!' I shriek. 'Jack! What are you doing here?' I run over to him.

'I thought I might find you here,' Jack smirks, as he jumps down off the bench and hugs me. 'Well, that's a lie, actually. Your mother told me you'd gone shopping and seeing as you're a lousy cook, I guessed it wouldn't be groceries you'd gone shopping for.' Jack laughs as I punch him on the arm and then hug him to me. It is so good to see my lovely fiancé once again and I inhale the familiar smell of Lynx and old leather jacket. I can't believe it. This feels like a dream. Jack is back. My Jack is back.

'I'll go and get those shoes and see you two lovers later then,' Ange says.

'Yes, that would be good, Ange. Thanks,' I whisper as I kiss Jack passionately on the lips.

CHAPTER THIRTY

'Err, Sam?'

'Yeah?'

'Question: why do we keep vegetables on the window sills and not in a vegetable basket?' Jack asks, holding up a carrot and looking somewhat puzzled by it.

'Ahh! Quick, put it back!' I rush over, grab the carrot from his clutches and put it back on the window sill.

'Long story short: that Clive chap, you know, the lachanophobic who took a shine to me?'

Jack nods, still looking puzzled by the arrangement of vegetables not in their rightful place.

'He died.'

'Shame.'

'But he came back again - to haunt me.'

'Oh, right,' Jack says, 'and that explains the vegetable décor how?'

'Because he hates them, remember? He's a...he was a lachanophobic. The only way I can keep him out is to leave vegetables out. Well, at least I think it works. I haven't seen him since I put them out.'

'Oh right, but won't they start to smell a bit?' Jack sniffs a turnip and pulls a face.

'I'll renew them every couple of days,' I say matter-of-factly. 'Or I suppose I could get some plastic veg?'

'Right.' Jack shrugs.

After he surprised me with an impromptu visit to Bath, Jack and I rushed home to *our* home for the first time together and it was pure magic to see the look on his face when he saw the cottage.

'This is amazing, Sam!' he shouted as he ran around the house, taking in each room. I have to admit, I was a little nervous because, after all, I'm a girl and he's a boy and being a boy, Jack's idea of interior design is the biggest plasma TV in the world, an Xbox and a fridge.

'Whoa! A train set!' I hear Jack shout from upstairs. Personally I have my reservations about the train room, for obvious reasons, but Jack loves it.

'I was never allowed a proper train set up when I was a kid. I used to save up my pocket money and buy bits of track. Every time, some little bastard at the home would break it or nick it. It wasn't until I moved in with Dave and Maureen that I could buy some without fear of it being snapped in two, but there was never enough room in the flat to set up a track.' Jack stares in awe at the miniature village I've created for him.

It's funny to see Jack like this; one minute he's a rock and roll star with thousands of adoring fans and the next he's here, with me, getting all excited about his train set. Bless him.

'So where did you put my Rubik's Cube beanbag and the didgeridoo?' Jack asks, looking around the room.

'Ah...um...' Oh bugger, I thought he would have forgotten about those by now. The answer is they are currently residing in the Mind charity shop in town. 'Oh look! Come and see what I've done to the bedroom.' I grab his hand and pull him along the landing into our bedroom and we stay there for, oh, a very good two hours.

'Well, I'm very glad I came home for the weekend, instead of going to the VIP party with Dillon and the rest of them,' Jack smirks.

'And I'm very glad you did too,' I smirk back. God, you'd think we were two Cheshire cats, with all this smirking going on!

'I had no idea you were coming home.' And I didn't.

'You're not a very good psychic then, are you?' Jack laughs, for which he receives a punch on the arm.

'Well, I wish you'd given me some notice; I'd have got us

something nice to eat.'

'What, you don't eat when I'm away?'

'I try not to, if I can help it. I don't want to put any weight on. I keep having dreams that I won't fit into my wedding dress.'

Jack kisses my stomach.

'There's nothing to you. You are beautiful in every single way, words can't bring you down…'

'You're quoting the lyrics to that Christina Aguilera song, aren't you?'

'Yes. Ouch! What was that for?'

'For being lazy and plagiarising someone else's work instead of serenading me with your own words.'

Jack props his head up on his elbow, deep in thought.

'OK, how about this? You're the woman of my dreams, you're my wish upon a star, you're my rock, my soul mate rolled into one, from my thoughts you're never far…'

Jack spends the next few minutes singing to me one of the most beautiful songs I have ever heard and I have to close my eyes to stop tears from spilling out of the corners of them.

'I wrote it for you. It's going to be our next single,' Jack says shyly.

'I love it, Jack. Thank you. I have missed you so much, you wouldn't believe.'

And I have. It's hard being part of a couple and being on your own ninety per cent of the time.

'Hey, what's up?' Jack can sense something's wrong.

'I just…I just don't want today to end. I know it's your dream job being in a band and…I just miss you so much, Jack. When you're not here…'

'I'll give it up then,' Jack says as he sits upright.

'Oh god, no I didn't mean that!'

'No, seriously, Sam. If this is making you unhappy then I'd much rather be with you than anything else and if you're not happy, I'm not happy either.'

God, don't you just love this guy?

'No. I wouldn't dream of it and besides, we've only got another - one, two, three, four, five, six weeks until we get married...Oh shit!' I spring out of bed.

'What's the matter?' Jack jumps up too.

'Six weeks, Jack! We've only got six weeks left and I haven't even got my dress finished, let alone the flowers, or sorted out the reception! Holy crap, I haven't even given the printer the guest list!' I rush around the room (stark naked) like a wailing baboon.

Jack is nearly wetting himself with laughter at the sight of his bride to be. I, on the other hand, am still running around the bedroom (still stark naked), reeling off the list of things I still need to do before we get married, which is imprinted on my memory, while looking for my phone and knickers, in no particular order.

'Oh stop it, it hurts!' Jack can barely speak for laughing and is now doubled up in bed, laughing hysterically at me and I can see why. I've just caught a glimpse of myself in the full-length wardrobe mirror and yep, I look like a naked, mad woman. One half of my hair is stuck to the side of my face from where I was snuggled in to Jack and the other half is sticking out at all sorts of strange angles; my wobbly bits are wobbling all over the place and there is so much mascara down my cheeks that I look like a Gene Simmons tribute act. Yes, Jack has good reason to laugh.

I have found my knickers and phone and other items of clothing to make me presentable to the rest of the world – and more importantly, not in danger of getting arrested – and Jack has just about managed to hold himself together to get to the bathroom before he wets himself from laughing.

'Come on, Jack. While I've got you here I want to check that your suit still fits and organise when the band members can come over to have their suits fitted.' God, what do I sound like? One afternoon of sex and I've come over all bridezilla!

'What the f…? Sam!' Jack shouts from the bathroom.

'What's the matter? Oh my…'

As I turn the door knob on the bathroom door, I notice that the room is filled with a fog-like mist.

'Sam!' Jack shouts. 'What's going on? I only came in for a wee.'

'Oh no! Not again!'

'What do you mean, not again?' Jack shouts through the mist.

It's then that the writing appears on the mirror – again.

I'm so sorry, Jack. I love you.

'What's that supposed to mean?' Jack asks as the mist in the room clears.

'I…I…'

Oh dear, Jack looks cross now.

'Sam? How did that happen? Who's that message from? Is it from you?'

'No… no, it's not from me. It's…' I can't say it.

'It's what, Sam? What the hell is going on?'

Jack slumps down on the edge of the bath. He looks stunned.

'I don't… I don't understand.'

I don't understand either. I don't know how to tell Jack what is happening here, so I stall for time and grab hold of his hand, pulling him back out of the bathroom.

'Marianne, Jack doesn't know yet,' I whisper.

'Doesn't know what? What don't I know?' Jack asks, looking somewhat paler than he did five minutes ago.

'Come on, Jack. I think you need to sit down.' I guide him to our bedroom and sit him down on the edge of the bed. Poor Jack. It's bad enough having a girlfriend who can see dead people, let alone anything else.

'What don't I know, Sam?'

I sit on the floor, holding his hand.

'It's your mum, Jack…'

'What about her?'

'She's...she's dead, Jack.'

Jack looks at me as if he's seen a ghost, which is a bit ironic really given the situation.

'Jack?'

'Uh-huh.'

'Are you OK?' Stupid question, I know.

Jack looks up, his eyes sparkling with tears.

'How do you know? You know, that it's her?'

'I've seen her. I recognised her...' I'm about to say from the photo in Jack's special box, but then realise that he doesn't know that I know about the special box.

'...because she looks like you. You have her eyes and Ange confirmed that she's your mum.'

'Oh right.' Jack sniffs. 'So what happened to her?'

'I have no idea, Jack.'

We sit there for some time, with me holding Jack's hand and him staring off into space.

'Will you, you know, do whatever it is you do? You know, contact her? Jack suddenly asks, breaking my thoughts.

'I...um...I can try. If that's what you want?'

Jack nods.

I have to say, aside from doing the Halloween séance, I've never actually made the first move when it comes to contacting the dead. It's always been the other way round; they've always contacted me, whether I've liked it or not. And up until now I can honestly say I've had no intention to voluntarily make contact with the other side. I don't really know what the protocol is for contacting dead peeps, but it looks as though I'm going to find out, doesn't it?

'Are you OK?' I ask Jack.

'Yeah. I'm good. You go downstairs and put the kettle on. I'll be down in a minute. I just want to...you know... make the bed.'

As I walk down the stairs to give Jack a bit of time to himself, I hear him sobbing into the pillows.

CHAPTER THIRTY-ONE

My weekend with Jack has been all too brief, not to mention marred by the fact that Jack's mum decided to make an impromptu visit to our bathroom. Sunday was spent trying to make arrangements for our wedding, but in a half-hearted way, and we haven't really got any further than had we not bothered.

My heart aches for Jack now that he's gone back to London and I'm determined to help him find out what happened to his mum.

'Ange, please help?'

'There's nothing I can do if she won't talk to me. It's not like down there, you know! If they don't want to talk, they won't,' Ange says.

'But I need to find out for Jack.'

'I'll do my best, but like I say, if they don't want to talk, they won't. Anyway, let me tell you how I got on with Danny.'

Ange goes into great detail about her date with Dan the motorcycle man and I mean *great* detail, including how she was right about choosing not to wear tights. Way too much information if you ask me. I haven't heard her this happy in ages and he's asked her out again! Well, I say asked her out again: according to Ange he actually said, "I s'pose we'll have to do this again sometime; nowt else to do up ere, is there?' Romantic, eh? Still, she's happier than she's been in ages and the only reason she's been talking to me is because her new beau said he had to go to the Regent Theatre in Stoke because psychic Mystical Monica was going to be there with her show and his mother and sister were going to try and get her to get in touch with him.

'Sammy Puddleduck. It's Dad here.'

Oh! My dad was a man of few words when he was alive and even fewer now that he's on the other side, so I'm a bit taken aback when just as I'm tidying up the living room after Jack's brief visit – why are men so messy? – his voice suddenly comes into my head. Dad is another one who refuses to talk unless he wants to and from past experience the only time he contacts me is to warn me of something, so it's one of those uh-oh moments.

'Dad? Are you OK?' Sounds stupid, doesn't it? Are you OK? Hum, let me think, what do you think? I'm dead, of course I'm not *OK!*

'Sammy, it's about Amy, she's in trouble.'

'What? What do you mean, Amy's in trouble? What sort of trouble?'

'Sammy, Amy's in trouble.' Dad says again.

'Yes, Dad, you said. Think you can expand on that?' I say as I plump up the cushions on the sofa and rearrange the veg on the windowsills.

God, it's frustrating talking to the dead sometimes! And besides, why is my dad telling me about Amy after all this time?

My ex-best friend and I haven't spoken for over eighteen months now, since she went to the papers and sold a story about me, claiming that I was a fraud and that I made all this psychic stuff up. It resulted in me being hounded by the press, ridiculed and made to prove myself to the nation live on TV. My so-called best friend temporarily destroyed my career and my life and if it hadn't been for Jack, my brothers and my agent Larry, I wouldn't be where I am today. In some respects you could say it was a blessing in disguise and that she did me a favour, and a big fat one at that. If Amy hadn't caused so much trouble, Jack wouldn't have come to my rescue and I wouldn't have realised just how much I loved him. So maybe Amy did me a favour in the long run. But that doesn't make it right, does it?

The last I heard she had gone to live with her mum in Spain and was planning to find herself a rich footballer to date so that she could become an official WAG. Failing that she was going to follow in her mother's footsteps and find a rich plastic surgeon to marry. The relationship with "The Lovely Kenzie" – son of some lord or other and the photographer who contributed to my downfall by taking the picture that every national newspaper featured on their front page – didn't last long, so Amy was young, free and desperate once again and in search of someone new, and preferably rich.

'She's in trouble, Sammy. She needs your help,' my dad suddenly pipes up.

'Ah, has she chipped a nail or pulled a hair extension out?' I mutter as I plump the cushions again with frustration. 'I mean, why should I help her, Dad? She ruined my life!' I snap as I try to coax the kitten named Tin Man into the litter tray. A typical man; misses the target every time.

'And besides, I don't even know where she is,' I huff. 'Funnily enough she didn't leave a forwarding address after she'd ruined my career!'

And why should I help her? My best friend of more than twenty years deliberately stitched me up, tried to discredit me and never gave two thoughts to how I might feel.

'Huh?' I say to the ceiling in the hope that my dad is still listening to me and hasn't gone off to plant some hanging baskets outside the Pearly Gates or something.

'Dad?'

Nothing.

'Great, now what am I supposed to do?'

It's all very well giving me cryptic messages, but when you can't even work out a riddle that a five-year-old would find a piece of cake then it's all a bit pointless, isn't it? And talking of cake...no, Sam, control yourself. You will only live to regret it when Valerie has to take out your wedding dress again.

I drum my fingers on the kitchen worktop. Missy and Spencer curl round my legs in a synchronised fashion, waiting to be fed.

'So, what do you two think I should do?'

The pair of cats meow in unison, which I take to mean, give her a call, what's the worse than can happen? And stop holding a grudge, Miss Grudge-holder. They are probably saying is, for the love of God, will you shut up and just feed us?

I scroll through my contacts list until I come to L for Lorraine, Amy's mother. I no longer have Amy's number in my phone for obvious reasons. Chewing my lip I wonder what sort of trouble Amy could be in. My dad has only ever contacted me when there has been trouble with a capital T – the time when I had to prove live on TV that I wasn't a fraud and the time when Jack almost died in the sea come to mind.

Checking the time I press call and let it ring. If she doesn't pick up after four rings I'll...

'Hello?'

'Oh hello, is that Lorraine?'

'Yeah?'

'Um...hi Lorraine, it's Sam here...Samantha Ball...Amy's...' How do you explain that you're her daughter's ex-BFF? '...old school friend,' I add.

'Samantha! How are you? God, I haven't seen you since you were a little nipper,' Lorraine says in her half London, half Spanish accent.

'Um...yes, I'm good, thank you. How are you?' Yes, I'm stalling for time, but it's only polite to ask, isn't it? And the reason she hasn't seen me since I was a nipper was because she was never at home. I could never understand why Lorraine always palmed Amy off on other people when we were kids.

'Oh, you know, life's a bitch and then you die,' Lorraine cackles. 'No seriously, I'm great. Still living the high life 'ere in Spain. You should try it sometime, get some sun on those pale sticks you call legs.' Gee, thanks for that. I look down at my legs. They're not pale sticks, actually! Okay, so they could do with a bit of spray tan, but they're not *that* bad. I did say I never liked Lorraine, didn't I?

'Anyway, I just phoned to see if Amy was there? I'm getting married in a few weeks and...'

'Married? What *you*?' Lorraine laughs. Now I really don't like the woman.

'Yes, me and…'

'My gawd, who on earth to?'

Aghh, I just want to punch this woman!

'Um, Jack. You probably don't remember him,' I add.

'What, the kid you and Amy used to hang around with – spotty little thing? Looked like Harry Potter without the glasses?'

Now she's just being insulting.

'Well I never.' The witch cackles again.

'I was wondering if you knew where Amy was living now. We want to invite her to the wedding,' I lie. 'I know she came to stay with you a while back when…' I'm tempted to tell her the whole sorry story, but knowing Lorraine she would just laugh, '…when she, you know, lost her job over here.'

'Amy? Oh she stayed with me for a bit, then she got herself a new boyfriend: a Spanish football player, Demetrio Covas no less. Plays for some premiership club somewhere. A lovely fella…'

'*He isn't, Sammy.*' My dad's voice comes into my head.

'Doesn't speak much English, but you know our Amy, that's never stopped her!' Lorraine shrieks. Like mother, like daughter then. 'She moved in with him a few months back. Have you got her new mobile?'

'Um, no, she must have forgotten to give it to me.'

'Hang on…it's 07799 8899221. I bet she'll love to hear from you. Oh, and when you speak to her, tell her to give her old mum a ring sometime, will ya?'

'Yes, of course. Nice to speak to you, Lorraine.'

'You too, love. Cheers.'

The line goes dead and I tap the number Lorraine gave me into my phone and wait for it to ring.

'*Hola*?' a man's voice answers.

'Oh hello. Is Amy there, please?'

'No,' the voice snaps and the line goes dead.

'You have to help her, Sammy!' my dad urges.

Hello, dad, have you not been listening? Amy's mum doesn't know where she is. Just that she's living with some footballer called Demetrio.

'You have to go and find her, Sammy.'

Great! As if I haven't got enough to do as it is!

CHAPTER THIRTY-THREE

'So if you could keep an eye on the kittens and the possessed villagers for a few days...' As conversations go, this is one of those strange ones and anyone listening in on me and Gem would think we were a pair of psychiatric patients on a day out.

Not only is Gem with me in the café, but so too is Simon. He is around her all the time, and while she obviously misses him like crazy she's comforted by the fact that he's with her every moment of every day, and we often have a three-way conversation with her talking to him through me and vice versa . Their baby is due any day now and she really is blooming. It's going to be hard for her, being a single mum and still coming to terms with Si's death, but she's doing well and as she says, it's like Si hasn't left her; he's just in the next room.

'No problem, but how are you going to track this Amy down? You don't even know where she lives,' Gem says. I'm booked on the next flight to Malaga in a bid to find Amy, although I don't know why I should be concerned. Amy has always got herself in and out of trouble all her life, but my dad was so insistent that I feel I have to go.

'Ah, well, I did a bit of research on this guy she's living with and found out that he lives in an area called San Pedro de Alcantara, which is quite near to the airport, so hopefully, once I'm there, I can find out exactly where he lives, check that Amy's OK and be on the next flight back.'

'Well, you're a better woman than I am,' Gem says. 'I don't think I could forgive someone if they did to me what Amy did to you.'

'I know, but my dad was adamant I should go and find her. What else can I do? I've tried phoning her and the guy that answered just said she wasn't there.'

'But why would he have her phone?'

'Good question, which makes me think my dad might be right.'

'Well, don't worry about things here; if the village folk get too out of hand I'll push them all down the well in the middle of the village green.' Gem smiles.

I have to say, considering half the village are still possessed, they seem to be going about their lives pretty much as normal. Okay, so Mr Brent still has his moments with the tourists and my mother breaks out into song the moment she hears a drum beat, but aside from that, the spirits have kept their part of the deal and remained relatively quiet. I still haven't told Jack that we will be having more guests at our wedding than we intended, but then sometimes some things are best left unsaid, right?

And talking of Jack, I need to phone him and tell him that I am off to Spain for a few days.

'You're mad, you know that?' is Jack's response when I tell him what my plans are for this week.

'Gee, thanks.'

'Mad, but in a good way,' Jack adds. 'Don't you remember what that cow did to you?'

'I know, that's what Gem said, but I just have this feeling that Dad wouldn't have come through to me if it wasn't important. And besides, it's unhealthy to hold a grudge.'

'Well, don't get upset if she's mean to you again and don't go inviting her to our wedding just because you feel sorry for her,'

'*I'll second that!*' Ange butts in.

In another world Amy would have been my chief bridesmaid. We always said we would be there for each other's momentous moments.

'*Err, hello? New best friend here!*' I hear Ange say in my head.

'Oh, sorry, Ange.'

'Eh?' Jack says.

'Oh, sorry, Jack. Ange was just ticking me off for thinking

about Amy.'

'Right, well you go carefully and call me as soon as you're in Spain. And try not to look too much like a tourist; you know what you're like.'

'I do not look like a tourist!'

'Err, yes, you do, Sam. Be safe and I love you.'

'Loves me too!'

I hang up and huff. I do so not look like a tourist. OK, so I do carry a map around with me if I'm any more than five miles away from home, and I do have a habit of saying, 'Excuse me, speaky English?' even if I'm in London, but that doesn't make me a tourist, does it?

'Well, if you ask me, you're wasting your time,' a rather disgruntled Ange informs me as we land at Malaga airport. Considering it's mid November, it's still warm enough to wear just a cardigan. Maybe Jack and I should think about coming here for our honeymoon.

'You can't even speak Spanish!' Ange says.

'Look, Ange, I know you're not very happy with this, but there's no need to be bitchy, is there?'

Ange huffs loudly in my ear as we make our way through customs.

Right, now where do I go? I check my map and work out that I will probably be better off getting a taxi to San Pedro de Alcantara, so trying not to look like a tourist I jump into the nearest taxi – I do hope it is a taxi and not a pretend one with a Spanish axe-wielding murderer as a driver.

'*Hola!* Speaky English?' I ask as I jump in.

'*Si, Senora.* Where to?'

Phew, at least I don't have to get the phrase book out.

'Um…I'm not too sure. I'm looking for Demetrio Covas; you know, the football player? But I'm not sure quite where he lives. I'm…I'm here to do an interview with him for…News Times, it's a British newspaper. I seem to have left my diary on the plane,' I add for effect.

The taxi guy mutters something in Spanish, followed by the footballer's name – I'm not sure if he's a fan or not. As Ange kindly pointed out, I don't speaky Spanish.

'I take you,' the taxi driver says and speeds off.

Being typically British, I start gabbling away about the story I'm working on and why I need to interview Mr Covas. Being typically blokish, the taxi driver ignores me.

'Here,' the driver says as he screeches to a halt outside a huge white complex of luxury apartments that is dominated by gold security gates. They don't intimidate me. Having spent quite a lot of time in the company of Donald, I now know all the tricks in the book of how to get into a secure complex.

'Thanks.' I hand the driver a twenty euro note. 'Keep the change.'

'Not enough. Five more,' the driver says.

'Oh, sorry. Here.' I give him another ten euros.

'*See, you're hopeless!*' Ange laughs.

'Oh shut yer face, you.'

The driver looks at me.

'Oh, no, not you. Thank you. Bye!' I scurry quickly out of the taxi.

Right, now let's see. I scan the foreign names listed on the gold panel until I come to D. Covas. Good start. I press the discreet black button next to his name.

'*Hola.*'

'Oh, um…hello. Can I speak to Amy, please?'

'No. Not here!' the voice says.

'*She is there. She needs your help, Sammy.*' My dad's voice comes through to me.

'Are you sure? Could you please tell me where she is?'

'She no here! Now go!' the man snaps.

I press the button again, but this time it just buzzes.

'I would like to see Amy, please!' I say impatiently.

No reply.

Right, if he won't let me in then I will have to find another way in. Checking the number of the apartment on the intercom, I look up at the apartments. 5P. Now, how the hell am I going to get in there?

'Not the best of ideas you've had to date, Ange, I have to say,' I mutter as I hide behind what seems to be the only bush for a million miles. My bum aches from where I've been sitting for hours on my handbag as I wait on the off chance that the security gates will open. It's later than I first thought because I forgot to put my watch forward an hour, and the sun is starting to set.

'This is bloody ridiculous! I bet she isn't even...'

'Shhh! That's him!' Ange hisses.

I watch as a man in a dark suit blips his key ring at a silver Porsche that is parked alongside several other posh-looking cars. He looks around him for a moment and then gets into the car.

'How do you know?'

'I just do. Now shhh and get ready to run when he opens the security gates.'

I brace myself and sure enough the gold gates open. As he drives through them I crawl as fast as I can, sniper style, towards them, praying they stay open until I get to them. If they don't then I will have to resort to trying to climb over the top of them, and given my lack of fitness, it won't look pretty.

Just as the gates close, I squeeze myself through the gap.

The Porsche screeches to a halt.

Oh god, oh god, oh god! I do a quick tuck, duck and roll under a parked car and hold my breath.

'Hurry up, Sammy!' my dad shouts in my ear.

Jesus, Dad! I'm doing the best I can here, you know! And besides, why couldn't you have opened the bloody gates?

The Porsche pulls away from the complex again. Phew! I

exhale loudly. Right, now for the simple matter of getting inside the building.

'So? Any ideas, you two?' I whisper up to the sky. It's getting a bit cold now and I rub my arms to keep warm.

'The code is 88781,' my dad whispers back. I have no idea why he's whispering; it's only me that can hear him.

I tap the code into the security pad on the front door – and it opens. Nice one, Dad.

Posh is an understatement! The marble floor and chrome elevator only emphasise the richness of the complex. I decide to take the stairs up to the fifth floor. I don't want to have to explain who I am if someone else uses the elevator.

Taking two steps at a time – okay, one at a time – I eventually find floor five and push the internal door. It doesn't move.

'33978,' my dad whispers. Blimey, you'd think I was trying to get into Buck Palace!

I tap the code in and push the door.

It's all quiet on this floor and the aroma of vanilla fills the hallway. They must pump it through the radiators or something.

'Hurry up, Sammy!'

Okay, okay! I scan the corridor for apartment 5P. As I hurry, looking from side to side at the door numbers, I hear a groaning noise up ahead. Tiptoeing slowly I peer round the corner, but there isn't anyone there. I hear the noise again and notice the sound is coming from the next apartment - room 5P.

'Amy?' I run to the room and bang on the door, 'Amy, it's Sam. Are you in there?'

The noise stops for a moment.

'Amy?' I bang on the door again.

'Go… away,' a small voice from the other side of the door says. I'm positive it's Amy.

'Amy? Let me in! It's Samantha.'

'Please, just go away!' the voice says.

'If you don't let me in, then I'm going to call the police,' I snap.

'Please, Sam. Go!'

'No! I'll stay here all night if I have to! Something's wrong, let me in,' I hiss through the door.

The locks turn on the other side of the door.

'Oh my God! Amy!'

Amy looks nothing like the Amy I knew: her once beautiful long, blonde hair has been hacked short and the curvaceous Amy I knew has been replaced by an almost anorexic girl. What is most shocking are the bruises and black eyes on her once beautiful face.

Amy looks behind me nervously and opens the door slightly wider so that I can squeeze through the gap. She shuts it and quickly locks it again.

'Jesus, Amy! What the hell has happened to you?'

Amy, dressed in a dirty white tracksuit, limps towards the cream leather sofa, clutching her stomach.

'I... you can't be here, Sam,' she whispers, looking anxiously at the door again.

'What the hell has been going on?' I can't believe this is the same Amy that I knew and once loved.

Amy looks panic-stricken.

'You have to go; he'll be back...ouch...soon.' She clutches at her side. It's then that I notice that the dirty white tracksuit she's wearing has a red mark down the left hand side of it.

'Amy?' I lift her tracksuit top up and reveal a blood-soaked pad of tissue, secured with medical tape.

'*Uh-oh.*'

'You have to go...' Amy staggers to the door, then falls to the floor.

I'm sitting in the hospital, waiting for news about Amy's condition. It could be any hospital anywhere in the world – all hospitals are the same, aren't they? Stark, cold and busy places.

When Amy collapsed I kind of lost the plot a bit and couldn't for the life of me remember the number for Spanish emergency services, so I just opened the door to the apartment and screamed for help, until the cleaner, who thankfully spoke English, heard me.

My dad was right; Amy was in trouble. According to the neighbours in the complex, her relationship with Demetrio was a volatile one to say the least, and despite being showered in diamonds and beautiful clothes, according to one of the hospital porters, this isn't the first time that Amy's been a visitor to the hospital. By the sound of it, she's been a frequent guest of San Pedro de Alcantara Hospital with various bruises, breaks and black eyes.

It's horrible here; more so because all I can see between the hospital staff going about their business are the spirits of people who haven't had a happy ending. They wander the hospital corridors as if looking for something and the noise inside my head is unbearable. There's an elderly man, muttering something in Spanish. There's a middle-aged woman, limping and wearing a bewildered expression on her face.

'It's OK, Sam. They will find their way soon,' Ange whispers in my ear. 'I was the same – didn't have a bloody clue where I was. Bit of a shock I can tell you when you suddenly realise you're dead!'

I cover my ears with my hands and close my eyes tightly in the hope that they will go away and find the light, or whatever it is they are supposed to do next, but it's no good, I can still hear them inside my head.

'Dónde estoy? Dónde estoy?' the old man repeats over and over again.

'Estoy perdida,' the middle-aged woman shouts above the old man.

Aghh, just go away, please!

'Uh-oh.' Ange says. 'Sam?'

I open my eyes.

It's then that I see Amy, a few feet away, wandering the corridor and looking equally lost.

CHAPTER THIRTY-FOUR

'Amy? Oh my god, no!' I whisper.

I watch as Amy walks up the corridor, looking left and then right, as if she's looking for someone. She too is dressed in one of those shapeless hospital gowns and looks different, almost serene, as she glides up the corridor, which is ironic really because Amy has never glided in her life. She's not what you would call a glider. She's more of a 'Here I Am!' kind of a girl.

Tears sting my eyes. No, not Amy. It doesn't take a genius to work out that if I can see Amy, it means only one thing - she's dead.

It takes me back to when Jack drowned and I could hear his voice inside my head. He too had crossed over, albeit for only a few minutes, but it is the worst feeling I have ever experienced; to know that someone you love so much might not be in your life any more.

'*She isn't dead, Sam,*' Ange whispers in my ear.

'But she must be; I can see her. I wouldn't be able to see her if she...'

'*Disculpa, senora.* You come in with the girl with the stab wound, yes? Err, Miss Amy Evans, yes?' A nurse suddenly appears in front of me.

'Um...' I avert my gaze from Amy for a second, then look back again. She's gone.

'*Senora?*'

'Um, yes, sorry... I...Amy, she's...' I can't quite bring myself to say the word out loud. I can't believe this is happening. Why, oh why didn't my dad warn me earlier? Give me more notice? Maybe if I hadn't faffed about, waiting for that moron footballer to go out, or hadn't taken no for an answer in the first place, I would have got to her in time. I would have been able to get Amy to the hospital in time for them to do something and...

'Can I speak with you, yes?' the nurse interrupts my thoughts.

'What? Yes, of course, but...?'

The nurse leads me by the arm to a small room as I look behind us to see if I can see Amy. I can't.

The room is sparsely furnished with just a coffee table and three plastic chairs. I slump down in one of them.

'You're a relative, yes?' the nurse asks.

'No, I'm her...I was her best friend,' I whisper.

'She has family, yes?'

'Um...no, yes, but I'm not sure where her mum lives. Somewhere in Spain, but I'm not sure...oh my god, I'm going to have to tell Lorraine. How am I going to tell her that her daughter is dead?' The tears sting my eyes again.

'Your friend is not dead, *senora*. She is in a coma.' The nurse smiles kindly at me.

'A what? No, she can't be. I saw her, just out there. I saw her, in the corridor...'

The nurse looks puzzled and I realise just how mad this statement sounds. Even with the language barrier dividing us, it sounds mad.

The nurse sits in the chair opposite me and looks at me intently for a moment.

'Miss Evans is in a coma. At the moment her injuries are serious and we are doing everything we can to help her. Now we have to wait. She has severe brain trauma.'

'Wait? What for?'

'We wait to see if she comes out of the coma. I'm afraid it's not looking great. There's a one per cent chance that she will survive this,' the nurse explains. 'We have treated her injuries, and now we have to wait. You inform her mother, yes? And *la policía* will want to speak with you, yes?'

'Yes, of course, but I don't understand. I saw her; just out there.' I point to the corridor.

'Holy shit! Sam? Is that you? What the fuck is going on?'

'Oh my God. Amy?'

That was definitely Amy's voice I just heard. I swing my head round and the nurse jumps back a little.

'That was her! That was Amy. I heard her!'

'Would you like to see her? *Si*?' The nurse asks.

'Huh?'

I don't understand what's going on here. One minute I'm seeing Amy in the corridor and the next I'm hearing her voice inside my head and yet the nurse is insisting that she's in a coma.

'You like to see your friend? Sometimes it's good for them to hear a friendly voice.' The nurse encourages me.

'*Sam?*' It's Amy's voice again. '*Where the hell am I? And who the hell are you?*'

'*I'm Ange, Sam's best friend, actually!*' I hear Ange snap at Amy.

Oh God, what is going on here?

The nurse escorts me out of the room, down the corridor and into another small room where she squirts my hands with antibacterial gel and puts a gown and a mask on me. All the time I can hear Amy's and Ange's voices squabbling in my head.

'*What do you mean, you're her best friend?*'

'*I am. In fact, I'm more than that; I'm her spirit guide, her guardian angel.*'

'*Oh yeah, well I've known her for years, unlike some who have known her for, ooo, let me think, five minutes! And where the fuck am I?*'

The nurse escorts me to another room. It's full of machines bleeping and buzzing and it all looks very clinical, like something out of *Holby City*. And there is Amy, lying on a bed, eyes closed and very, very still. Despite the bruising and black eyes to her face, and the multitude of tubes attached to her, she looks just like she's asleep. Her stained tracksuit has been folded up neatly on a chair, along with her jewellery, including the silver bangle I bought her for her twenty-first birthday.

'Talk to her, *si*?' the nurse says quietly.

'Amy? It's Sam here,' I say self-consciously to her lifeless body.

'Sam. What is going on?' I hear Amy's voice in my head. She sounds very irritated.

'Durh! She really is a dumb blonde,' Ange mutters.

Amy's lips aren't moving. She's just lying there. I don't get it. If Amy isn't dead, how can I hear her? I make a living out of hearing *dead* people, but I'm being told that Amy isn't dead.

'God, did you learn nothing on that course you took recently?' Ange huffs.

'Ange, this isn't the time or the place, is it?' I whisper, as I push a stray piece of hair from Amy's face.

'Yer think? The reason you can hear her in your head is because she's on the other side, durh!' Ange says.

'But she can't be. The nurse said she's not dead.'

'Oh shit! I'm not bloody dead am I?' Amy suddenly says. *'Oh Jesus Christ, tell me I'm not dead!'*

'Jeez, will you stop screeching for one minute?' Ange replies.

'Ange? You want to explain?' I ask, looking down at Amy. She looks so peaceful and content and she's not cold, like I expected, despite only being covered in a white sheet. Ange sighs again.

'She's not dead. She's in a coma.'

'Who's she, the cat's mother?' Amy snaps.

'Well, if the cap fits and all that! Anyway, as I was saying before I was rudely interrupted, your so-called best friend is between worlds at the moment, Sam, which means she's not technically dead, but she's not technically alive either. She's kind of floating about up here.'

'I am not floating!'

'Yeah, whatever!'

'Oh God.' Tears form in my eyes again.

'See that machine there above her head? That's what's keeping her alive at the moment,' Ange whispers.

'What? So I'm not breathing on my own?' Amy wails.

'Not down there, luv, no.'

'But how do I get back down there?'

'How the hell should I know? Believe me, if I knew I'd help you go back down there in a shot. You're seriously getting on my nerves.'

'You are such a bitch! And OMG, look at the state of me!' Amy screeches again.

'Yeah, you do look a bit rough,' Ange agrees.

'Right, that's enough!' I can't believe I'm in a Spanish hospital, refereeing a slanging match between my spirit guide and my comatose ex-best friend, who isn't *technically* dead but isn't *technically* alive either.

'Oh Amy! What are we going to do with you?' I whisper, stroking her hair.

'Well, you could start by working out how I get back into my body!' Amy says. 'You're supposed to be the expert here.'

Aghh! This is so frustrating! I don't know whether I'm coming or going. One minute I'm talking to Amy's motionless body and the next I'm hearing her in my head. Or maybe I'm just imagining it and...

'You're not imagining it, Sammy.'

It's my dad's voice. And about bloody time!

'You did a good job getting to Amy in time, but as Andrea pointed out, her body isn't well enough right now for her to go back to it.'

'But...how long? She isn't going to...' I can't say the word.

Ange and Amy have both gone very quiet. It's as if we're all holding our breath.

'Who knows, Sammy? Who knows? Her injuries are bad, Sammy. When it's your time, it's your time, you know that.'

'Oh My God! No!' I hear Amy gasp.

I look down at Amy sleeping peacefully.

'I'm so sorry, Amy. We'll get you through this, sweetheart. Trust me, I'm a psychic.'

I kiss her on the forehead and then I cry – a lot.

CHAPTER THIRTY-FIVE

'So there's nothing more they can do at the moment,' I sniff into the phone to Jack at the other end, as soon as I get back to England. 'They said she will either come out of it or...or she won't, but in the meantime...' I swivel my head from side to side. 'Amy is...she's in my head, Jack,' I whisper, 'you know like when you drowned last year in Australia and you could speak to me?'

'You can whisper all you like, Samantha, I can still hear you!' Amy says.

Oh bugger!

'And apparently she can hear me if I whisper too!'

I can imagine Jack at the other end of the line, shaking his head.

'Yes, he is,' Ange says.

'Hey, he's my friend, not yours!' Amy says.

'Oh, yes, and we all know how you treat your friends, don't we?' Ange retorts. *'Anyway, haven't you got somewhere to be?'*

'No, actually, I haven't,' Amy snaps back. *'Unlike you, I'm not dead.'*

'Yet!' Ange says. *'And when you do die, you've got to go through a whole dead person process before you can communicate with the living.'*

'IF I die,' Amy snaps back at Ange.

'Oh, you are so naïve, aren't you? We're all gonna die someday, Amy.'

'Aghh! Will you two just shut up for one minute!' I snap.

'What?'

'Oh no, not you, Jack. These two – Ange and Amy. Since Amy went into a coma, she's kind of trapped in between worlds. She's kind of a...what would you call it? A part-time spirit? Until she comes out of the coma, *if* she comes out of the coma...' I try to explain, but the more I try, the madder it sounds. I bet Jack's thinking...oh my God, what must Jack be thinking? I bet he's having second thoughts. I mean, who in their right mind would want to marry someone who spends their whole time talking to dead people, huh? There's not going to be just the two of us in this marriage, there will be dozens, no hundreds, maybe thousands!

When I first met Jack, I worried about the usual kinds of things other young women worried about; you know, whether Maybelline was better than No7 or whether I could still get away with wearing a miniskirt, that sort of thing. Now I worry about dead people. I think about them from the moment I wake to the moment I go to sleep, particularly if they come through to me with a desperate problem. Bloody dead people!

'Sam?' Jack says quietly and seriously.

'Uh-oh,' Ange says.

'What do you mean, uh-oh?' Amy asks.

'I mean something's up. I can feel it in me waters,' Ange whispers back.

Oh no. He has had second thoughts. He's thinking I don't want a psychic for a wife. *I* don't even *want* to be a psychic wife. I only ever got into this to earn some money to pay my bloody rent and now look at me.

'Jack, you don't have to say anything. I know what you're going to say. It's all too much for you, this psychic malarkey…' My voice breaks with huge sobs.

'Sam?'

'Yes?' I snort.

'Ewww!' Amy and Ange chorus.

'Sam, I would love you even if you were Buffy the vampire slayer. Don't worry; you're doing a fantastic job. You have an amazing gift, whether you like it or not. Think I can't handle a few ghosts? Ha! I laugh in the face of them ghosts!' Jack does a theatrical laugh. 'What I was going to say was, don't forget that I'm…'

'But you must wonder what it would be like to have a normal

girlfriend. I mean this is hardly a conventional relationship, is it?' I babble on. 'What if I become possessed like my mother, or…or what if you decide you would much rather be with someone who is normal? Someone who doesn't talk to dead people?'

'Sam! Look, I love you, OK?' There's a lot of background noise and I can hardly hear him. 'Look, I have to go,' Jack says quickly.

'What? Where? What were you going to say?'

'It doesn't matter,' Jack says. I hear someone call out Jack's name, 'I have to go. I'll call you later. Loves ya.'

'*Ah, he is lovely, isn't he?*' Ange says.

'*Oi, he's spoken for! My best friend is about to marry him!*' Amy snaps back.

'*Your best friend? I think you'll find you lost that right when you did the dirty on Sam, didn't you?*' Ange has a point.

'*Well, we will soon find out who's her best friend when she chooses who is going to be her maid of honour, won't we? Besides, you might not be around when she gets married.*'

'*Listen, luv, whether I'm dead or alive, I'll be attending that wedding, so I should get your coat if I were you!*'

Oh great! I'm having a bit of an inferiority complex here about my boyfriend not loving me and these two are fighting like cat and dog, although I have to say, as weird as it sounds, it really is nice to hear Amy talk again, even if it is only in my head. As it stands, her body is still too weak to come out of the coma, but she's still the same sassy girl she always was and although what she did to me was beyond horrible, somehow that doesn't seem to matter any more. All that matters is that she gets better.

Her mother, Lorraine, has spent the past week hiring someone to sit next to Amy's bed. She couldn't do it herself, you understand: her time is much too precious to sit with her only daughter. No, instead she hired her maid to sit next to her bed, instructing her to call if there was any change.

The sleazeball of a boyfriend who hurt Amy was arrested by the police and is awaiting trial in some Spanish cell. I hope he rots in it. I also hope to God that Amy pulls through so that she can testify against him.

'I really loved him, Sam,' Amy whispers. 'I thought he was the one, you know. I thought he was like your Jack. I thought he was my Evermore.'

'You are frigging joking, aren't you?' Ange butts in. 'Have you actually seen what he's done to you? You look like shit. And I bet it's not for the first time, either. I tell you, if my Danny ever did anything like that to me, he'd be right out of the door!'

'Yeah, but he wasn't always like that.' Amy defends her dire choice in men. 'He was really nice to me – once.'

'Once a woman-beater, always a woman-beater,' Ange says sagely.

Err, girls, can you just bugger off a minute and take this elsewhere, please? I think.

'Oh, sorry, Sam. Yeah, we'll just …'

The voices stop. Thank God!

Once I've settled the kittens down, fed Missy and Spencer and had a nice relaxing hot bath, I flick the TV on and ring Miracle. I wonder who it was calling Jack away from the phone.

'You sound exhausted, Sam,' Miracle worries.

'I am.'

'You are going to have to shut the door on them sometimes, my love,' she advises.

'But, what if…'

'If Amy dies?'

'Yes. If I shut the door on them then I can't keep an eye on them all, can I?'

Miracle has warned me about this before; about mentally closing the door to the spirit world so that I can get a bit of peace and quiet and be normal again for five minutes, but I just can't do it. Even with Ange, I worry that something might happen to her if I'm not around, and what if my dad needs me urgently or someone else I know, you know, dies and I'm not there to talk to them and comfort them?

'If you don't, Sammy, then you will eventually exhaust yourself and you may lose your powers altogether. But more importantly, you may lose what you have here. You can't live to honour the dead, Sam. We're all entitled to a break, you know. You wouldn't be expected to work twenty-four hours a day, every day, in another job, would you – except perhaps in China.' Miracle laughs her throaty laugh.

'I suppose,' I shrug.

'So you promise me you will close the door on them when you get off the phone. Watch some TV, take the phone off the hook and just relax,' she advises.

'Yes boss. I'll call you tomorrow. And Miracle?'

'Yes, my love.'

'Thank you.'

'You're very welcome.'

I do as I'm told. Miracle's right. I can't keep worrying about people who are not in the real world. I apologise to Amy and Ange and explain that I have to close the door on the spirit world just for the night, but promise to be back in the morning. I put another selection of fresh vegetables on the windowsills, just in case Clive decides to pay another impromptu visit, and then I snuggle up on the sofa with all the kittens to watch the telly. As I flick through the channels something catches my eye. MTV are showing the Vibe Awards. The Vibe Awards? Wasn't Jack...oh my God, I completely forgot that tonight Jack is playing at the awards. That's what he must have been phoning about. Bloody hell! And there was I babbling on and on to him about my own worries. I completely forgot that tonight was his night. I turn the volume up.

After a few tracks from a band called Little Green Cells, the camera pans round to the crowd. There are numerous banners held up with different band names on them, several with

Otherwise written in huge letters, but the one that catches my eye is the one that shouts, 'I Love You, Jack!' and my heart does a flip. I should be the one in the crowd holding that sign. I shouldn't be here, worrying about people who are pulse-less and therefore technically not here. I should be with Jack, doing normal things like standing in a crowd full of adoring fans, screaming his name and feeling very smug that he's all mine.

'And now, let's welcome the new, up and coming band to the stage. It's Otherwise!' the presenter, clad from head to toe in black leathers, shouts out to the crowd. And the crowd goes wild, screaming and shouting.

And there his is. My man. Dressed in his favourite, 'If you were a shoe, what shoe would you be?' t-shirt and ripped jeans, guitar slung casually around his waist and embracing the atmosphere. He's loving it, and as he plays the first chord to the band's first hit he knows he has the audience eating out of his hand.

I was right. He doesn't need me. This is where he belongs: on stage with millions of adoring fans worshipping him. Not with a neurotic fiancée who spends her days talking to dead peeps.

Tears roll down my cheeks as his voice belts out track after track. The audience go wild for more and the band love it. Even Dillon, who, it has to be said, could turn milk sour just by looking at it is enjoying the adoration – between you and me, if he was a Spice Girl he'd be Moody Spice.

As they come to the end of the next track, Jack looks right into the camera, as if he's a pro.

'Thank you, you're too kind!' He winks his cheeky wink. 'Right, our last song tonight is for one very special lady out there. This lady has been the best thing that has ever happened to me and I'm sorry to say, girls, I don't care what our management company says, I'm getting married to her in a few weeks' time. This is our new single, 'Loves Me Too'. Sam, this is for you, kid.'

Jack strikes a long chord on his guitar, then he sings.

'You're the woman of my dreams, you're my wish upon a star,

you're my rock, my soul mate rolled into one, from my thoughts you're never far...'

I'm a mess. Snot is pouring from my nose in great long dribbles and I can barely focus on the screen due to the copious tears that have clouded my vision. I'm a blubbering wreck as I watch my fiancé not only dedicate his song to me, but sing it with so much passion *and* announce to the world that we are getting married. Am I one lucky girl, or what?

In the background I can hear Ange and Amy sobbing their socks off too.

CHAPTER THIRTY-SIX

'So, you're telling me that with your wedding just two weeks away, you're going on an all-night, celebrity ghost hunt?' Annette says between mouthfuls of Death by Chocolate cake. 'Are you mad?'

It's my turn to visit Annette who is bored out of her mind, on bed rest. She's been advised by the doctor not to go back to work until the baby is born, so is reliant on me to keep her up to date with all that is going on at Town FM. Between me, Jeff and Liam the *Sixth Sense* show has continued to be on air. And talking of Jeff: since Annette's scare, he has been the perfect father-to-be. He's insisting on doing everything for her and while this is very endearing (including the proposal of marriage), it's doing nothing but drive Annette round the bend. As Annette says, while it's all very romantic to be waited upon hand and foot, the chemistry just isn't there between them. It's a bit like pairing Mr Bean up with Lady Gaga, and I have a funny feeling that Jeff is going to be disappointed before long.

'Well, it's part of my contract with Living Today TV. I've already refused to do an investigation into a missing little girl because I didn't think I could cope with it, so I kind of felt obliged to do the celebrity ghost hunt thing this weekend, despite still having to chase up guests who haven't RSVP'd to their invites.' I huff. Once upon a time I was a reasonable woman. These days I'm turning into an obsessive bridezilla thanks to this wedding.

'Besides, it could be fun. I have a right mixed bunch. The line up's better than any celebrity Big Brother – I have a glamour model, a children's TV presenter from the eighties, a disgraced MP, and someone called Wilmore Pentlebrair, whoever he might be.'

'Oh, that's that TV chef who had an affair with that guy that played cricket for England, oh, what's his name? It'll come to me. I think this baby has already taken half of my brain cells.' Annette sighs. 'Anyway, let me know how you get on. How's your mother now?'

'As mad as ever, but we seem to have contained the Bob Marley impersonations. She's fine so long as we keep her away from a set of bongos. I'm just hoping that once the spirits have been to the wedding, they will quietly go home, like the rest of the guests, and let me get on with my life.'

'We are going to have so much fun tonight, Amy,' I hear Ange whisper as I get out of my car at the 'secret location', which is in fact an old mental hospital situated in the middle of nowhere. I didn't know this place even existed, but according to my research notes, it was a nineteenth century asylum where if you went in, you never came out again. Rumour has it that no one will buy it due to the paranormal activity going on in there, so it's an ideal location for a selection of wimpy celebs then. Having accepted that I can hear and see dead people and do so on a daily basis, the biggest thing that scares me these days is a spider in the bath. It's the living you have to worry about, not the dead.

'Now you two, I want you to behave yourselves, is that clear?' I whisper to Ange and Amy. I have to say, Amy is taking this coma business very well. After spending a day crying about how she looks back in the hospital – they had to take her false nails off along with all her make-up and hair extensions – and realising that there really is very little that she can do at the moment until her body repairs itself, she's adjusting remarkably well to being in what she calls 'no-woman's land', and despite their spats, Ange has kindly taken her under her wing and by all accounts is showing her the ropes of what it's like 'up there'. That's not to say that Amy doesn't freak out from time to time; I mean, wouldn't you, if you didn't know whether you were dead or alive?

'Don't know what you mean, do we, Amy?' Ange laughs.

Hum, I don't know what Ange has up her batwing sleeves, but whatever it is, it sounds mischievous.

'OK, hello and thank you for braving the elements tonight and welcome to Oaklands hospital,' I say to the freezing celebs, who are wrapped up against the bitter wind; well, aside from Suki, the glamour model, who I have to say has the most amazing breasts I have ever seen, which peep suggestively over the top of a tiny yellow crop top. Benny, the ex-children's TV presenter, already looks white and I have a feeling it's not because it's just three degrees out here. The disgraced MP, Kenneth Bowerman, is already so bored he's busy texting on his iPhone, and Wilmore Pentlebrair – do you think that's his real name? Nah, me neither – is checking his reflection in one of the many windows that grace Oaklands, brushing his bushy eyebrows down and checking for nose hair.

'Holy crap!' he suddenly shouts, 'did you see that?' The TV chef points to the window and takes a step back, bumping into Suki's breasts.

'Ow! Watch where yer going, will ya!' Suki shouts.

'Did you see that? Did you get that on camera?' Wilmore shouts at the crew, who already look fed up at the prospect of following four Z-list celebrities around all night with a camera and a cardioid microphone. The crew shake their heads in unison, as they adjust the settings on their equipment.

'Hee, hee!' I hear Ange giggle.

'I thought we were here to ghost hunt?' Wilmore-angry-chef rants. I think he believes he's Gordon Ramsey.

'Did you see something then, Wilma?' Suki laughs, her ample bosoms jiggling as she does so.

'I saw a horrible face in the window, staring back at me!'

'Sure it wasn't your reflection?' Kenneth laughs.

'No, it was not my reflection, you moron. I saw it with my own eyes and if this bloody crew got their act together…'

'Okay, right, let's stop the name calling and act like grown-ups, shall we?' I say, clapping my hands together like a primary school teacher trying to control a group of nine-year-olds.

'Right, as I was saying, we are here tonight at this wonderful building to see if there is any paranormal activity...'

'Err, hello? What does that count as then if it's not paranormal activity?' Angry chef rants again. This guy is really peeing me off now.

'Mr Pentlebrair, I'm sorry we missed your ghostly encounter, but I'm sure there will be many more to experience this evening. Now, if I may continue?'

The director goes for another take and I carry on with my introduction to the celebs, doing my best to create a suitably spooky atmosphere by emphasising the history of the building and the reported hauntings that have happened over the years. There's a lot of waiting around for it to get really dark and eventually we're allowed into the building, where they have set up infrared cameras all over the place. We make our way to a room on the first floor, which was originally the solitary room where disturbed patients were kept in isolation for days on end, with no food or water – it's no wonder they went mad. Tonight this room is to become our séance room and a round table with five chairs is the only furniture in the sparse room.

'This is so exciting!' Benny, the kids' TV presenter, whispers excitedly to Kenneth, who just sighs as though wishing he was back at his desk fiddling his expenses, rather than standing in a freezing mental hospital, waiting for ghosts to show. But hey, beggars can't be choosers, can they? If you're going to screw the public out of their money and get caught, you have to accept that your future source of income is going to consist of appearing on reality shows like this. I bet you anything his agent is in talks with the producers of *I'm a Celebrity, Get Me Out of Here* as we speak.

I eventually get the participants to sit down in a circle and hold hands.

'Ow! Your bloody nails are digging into me!' Angry chef complains about Suki's long talons.

'Oh, sorry, love,' Suki says with a gleaming white smile, and jiggles her breasts by way of an apology. You're wasting your time doing that, love, I think.

'I love the colour of her nails, don't you, Amy? Sam? Ask her what colour that is,' I hear Ange say. Not right now, Ange. I need to get on with the séance, I say in my head.

'Right, if you can all keep the link and close your eyes,' I say, as I close my own eyes. I'm praying this doesn't go like the WI séance and I end up with a whole bunch of mental spirits roaming around the earth plane.

'Then perhaps it would be a good idea to close the circle properly this time, eh?' Ange says. *'You'll never guess what she did, or to put it correctly, didn't do, the last time she held a séance, Amy...'*

Yeah, OK, thanks for your support, Ange! I ask any spirits to come forward and we wait.

CHAPTER THIRTY-SEVEN

I can hear Suki and Benny giggling and I open one eye and stare at them both with it.

'*Watch this,*' Ange suddenly says.

'Waaa! What was that?' Wilmore Pentlebrair shouts, looking around him, his moustache twitching as if it has a life of its own.

'Someone blew in my ear! Was that you?' he asks Kenneth, who is seated next to him.

I stifle a laugh, knowing full well just who is responsible for blowing in the chef's ear.

Ange, stop that, I think.

'*What?*' Ange replies, innocently.

I tut to myself. Right, let's get on with the show then. In my limited experience of working on TV, I don't think viewers are going to be enthralled with blowing in someone's ear, do you? They want to see these celebs jump out of their skins at the very least.

I have to admit that I'm a little petrified as to just who might come through, seeing as we're in a disused mental asylum. Mind you, I am a trained psychologist, which is always a bonus, I guess.

'Is there anyone there?' I say as spookily as I can.

The temperature in the room drops suddenly and the table starts to shake slightly – and no one human is moving it.

'*Uh-oh!*' Ange and Amy say in unison.

Uh-oh indeed. I open my eyes to see the room full of ghostly figures – and mental ones at that. I know this from the insane grins they are displaying to me. Talk about the lunatics taking over the asylum! Within seconds they've gone again. Disappeared into thin air.

'*Uh-oh!*' Ange says.

It's like that film, *Casper the Friendly Ghost*. The hospital patient spirits have all whizzed off in different directions. Oh heck, I hope this isn't going to turn into a mammoth ghost chase. When I first came to look around the old hospital, I asked the spirits if it was OK to visit. I mean, how would you like it if your home was suddenly taken over by a film crew? I think they were all cool about it, but we will see. You never can tell. What I do know is that more often than not, spirits are more than happy to have a bit of company and provide a bit of light-hearted entertainment for us mere earth mortals, but as with any good party, there's always one that takes things a bit too far at times, which is why I'm feeling a wee bit nervous.

'Right, ladies and gentlemen, I think we have some paranormal activity here at Oaklands, so we are going to divide up into pairs.'

'Ooo missus!' Benny says. 'Suki, you've already got a lovely pair, haven't you!' he titters. You've got to love him, haven't you? He's like a ten-year-old boy trapped in the body of a forty-five-year-old.

'Come on, Benny, I'll keep you warm; we'll pair up together.' Suki giggles, linking arms with Benny.

'Huh, I supposed that means I'm with him then, does it?' Wilmore huffs.

'What do you mean by that?' MP Kenneth snaps in a rather, bitchy kind of way.

'Nothing. I didn't mean anything by it.'

'So why did you say it then?'

'OK, can we just move out of this room?' I shout above the argument. I feel sick and tired and wish they would just shut up. 'Suki, if you and Benny can follow Scot our camera tech, he will get you rigged up with some infrared equipment and you two will be going into the surgery room. Kenneth and Wilmore, you two will be sent to the chambers downstairs. You will all have cameras and microphones attached to you, so if you do experience anything, it will get picked up.' I smile, wondering what the spirits have up their sleeves tonight.

I do my best impression of Yvette Fielding to the camera and explain the history of Oaklands and the reasons why the old asylum has never been sold.

'Um, hello? Excuse me? Can we start now?' A voice comes into my head.

'Who are you?' I ask quietly.

'Oh, sorry, dear, I'm Elsie. Elsie Colleridge. I'm a ghost, dear,' the well-spoken woman says. *'I don't like to ask, it's just that the rest of them are getting a bit restless over here and we wondered when you would like us to start...you know, the hauntings?'*

'Oh, err, yes, carry on, but can I just make one thing clear?'

'Yes, dear?'

'No one is to get hurt or scared to death, and once we finish filming, you all go back into the realm,' I insist.

'Of course, dear' Elsie replies. *'I was like you once, you know,'* she muses. *'I was a medium. I told them I could hear voices, I knew things they didn't. They didn't believe me, of course. They locked me up in here because they thought I was mad. I never got released.'*

'Aww!' I hear Ange and Amy chorus,

'That's awful,' I whisper, just in case the crew wonder who I'm having a little chat with.

'Ah, but I had the last laugh, didn't I?' Elsie says. *'I was right. They couldn't beat it out of me. I was right,'* she says defiantly. *'Right, let's get this party started!'*

'Oohh, this is going to be good,' I hear Ange say.

'This is bloody weird,' Amy replies. Ain't that the truth?

I follow the camera crew outside to the portable studio and look at the monitors that have been set up, covering every angle of the surgery room where Benny and Suki sit huddled together in the dark on a metal bench. They look like two little demon gargoyles sitting there, due to the infrared lighting.

'So, I was thinking of going one size bigger, what do you

think?' Suki asks Benny, pushing her bosoms up for him to see in the dark. There's already so much silicon in them, I'm surprised they're not luminous.

'I don't think you should. Have you not heard about implants exploding? Ahh! What was that?' Benny shouts as he jumps up from the bench and spins round, looking from side to side.

'What? Aghh! Was that you, Benny? Cos if it was, that's not at all funny!' Suki screams.

What my lovely page three model and children's entertainer can't see and I can are two spirits: a large man dressed in a hospital gown and a small woman, aged about forty, in a long dress. The two of them are poking Benny and Suki in turns and tapping them on the head, while howling with laughter. All of a sudden, the large man pushes a chair across the room, and as if on cue Benny and Suki scream and Benny tries to jump into Suki's arms. Next, the woman runs her finger along the many surgical instruments that are lined up along one wall, making them clang against each other, like an industrial wind chime.

'Holy crap! What was that?' Benny says – I bet he's never said that on TV before.

'Aghh!' Suki screams, as a pair of surgical scissors fly across the room and hit the opposite wall. These were thrown by the portly man, who is now roaring with laughter.

It's very funny when you have the ability to see spirits that other people can't. The crew are amazed at the live feed that is coming through. I can hear Ange and Amy in hysterics with laughter.

Benny demands to be let out and the crew switch the camera view to the chambers where Kenneth and Wilmore are staked out.

'What was that?' Wilmore predictably shouts, as we view the pair of them in the chambers. The chamber area is where the most dangerous patients were kept and it's appropriately spooky with lots of archways and dark corners. Kenneth and Wilmore are tiptoeing around the hallways as if they are cast members of a Scooby-Doo cartoon. I have to put my hand over my mouth to stop myself from laughing because behind them I can see three ghostly figures tiptoeing after them. The one at the front, a young man in his twenties, keeps flicking Wilmore's ear.

'I don't like it in here,' Kenneth says. 'It's too…aghh! What was that?' he spins round and collides with Wilmore.

'You blithering idiot,' Wilmore rants, 'will you get a grip?'

'But it's…oh shit!' Kenneth wails as a spooky figure breathes on his face. It's a young woman, about twenty, and her face is inches away from Kenneth's. She laughs and twirls around.

'I don't like this,' Kenneth says. 'Hold my hand, Wilmore.'

'Oh for goodness sake!' Wilmore huffs, but obliges. Hum, you think this could be the start of a beautiful relationship?

The men continue to tiptoe through the arches, hand in hand, as the three spirits continue to follow them.

'Don't forget to close the circle before you go,' Ange reminds me.

Good point. I make a mental note to send the spirits back when we finish and continue to watch the celebrities being appropriately spooked.

CHAPTER THIRTY-EIGHT

'Uh-oh!' Ange and Amy say in unison.

What the…?

By the time I get home it's one o'clock in the morning and as I pull up outside my cottage I stare at it in astonishment. There, painted in huge red letters, starting from my front window and extending across the front door to the second window, is the word BITCH! My front windows have been completely painted over in red gloss paint and the path that leads to the house has been daubed in more red paint.

Gem, who is on her hands and knees with a bucket of soapy water and a sponge, is desperately trying to scrub the writing off. My mum, Colin, Mr Brent, Mrs Jackson and Mrs Samuels – the one with one leg shorter than the other, although you would never tell – are there too, sponges in hand. My mum is barking orders to everyone.

'What's happened?' I gasp as get out of the car and look at my once lovely cottage.

'Sam!' Gem gasps. 'We didn't think you were coming back tonight,' she says with panic in her voice.

My initial shock turns to rage.

'Who did this?'

My mum rushes over to me.

'We don't know, sweetheart. Gem fed the kittens and locked up at about nine and Mr Brent said he went out around ten to pull his drawbridge up and it was then that he noticed the paint on your house.'

'But who would do such a thing?' I stutter, taking in the full glory of the graffiti. I feel a wave of nausea.

My mum squeezes my arm as the tears start to flow.

'I know who it was,' Amy whispers. *'It was that girl, Beth. The one on Facebook.'*

'*How do you know that?*' Ange says, impressed by Amy's deduction skills.

'*I have no idea,*' Amy says, sounding as surprised as Ange. '*I just thought about it and that girl's name came into my head.*'

I'm speechless. Why would she do something like that?

'*Because Jack announced your engagement on live TV maybe?*' Ange says. '*Don't worry, Sam. Leave it to us. We'll sort her out.*'

Gem waddles over to me and holds out her arms.

'Oh, Sam, I am so sorry. I only just locked up a few hours ago. I didn't see anyone out here and I checked the house before I left,' Gem is distraught. I just keep looking at the paint – jeez, she's even painted my bloody bay bush by the front door!

'Gem, it's OK. I know who did it. It's not your fau…Gem?'

Gem suddenly goes very pale. There's a great big whooshing sound and we both look down at the red path, which is now covered in a pool of water.

'Oh no! I think my waters have broken!' Gem stutters.

Oh heck!

'Mum!' I shout as I hold Gem around the waist.

My mum rushes over and seems to automatically know what has happened.

'Colin! Call an ambulance, quick! Mr Brent, stop that and run up to the airing cupboard and get some towels, quick as you can, my love. Mrs Samuels, look in my handbag, there's an SOS flashlight in there. Stand in the middle of the road and flash it with the SOS signal. You remember, dot, dot, dot, dash, dash, dash, dot, dot, dot. We did it at the WI meeting last year with that lovely man, Brian, from the Red Cross, do you remember? Keep going until the ambulance arrives. Colin, you have phoned for the ambulance, haven't you?' she barks.

'Why do you have an SOS flashlight in your bag, Mum? We're not on a snow-topped mountain, you know,' I ask as we slowly escort Gem back into the house.

'You never know when you might need one, girls. Always

keep a flashlight, a paperclip and a tampon in your handbag, ' my mother advises, as she bends her knees, grunts and takes all Gem's weight on her shoulder and carries her to the sofa.

'Now come on, this baby isn't going to wait all day. Have you been practising your breathing, dear?' she asks Gem as she throws all my scatter cushions to the floor and prepares my living room for a labour ward.

Gem nods and winces with pain – if this is what childbirth is like, you can forget any idea of becoming a grandmother any time soon, Mum.

'Mr Brent, we'll need more towels than that, dear,' my mum tuts. 'If this is anything like when I had you, Sammy, it'll be a blood bath in here any time soon.'

Gem looks terrified. Way to go, Mum.

'Right, let's have a little looksy, shall we?' My mum puts her reading glasses on and dives beneath Gem's long maternity skirt.

'Ah ha, uh-huh,' my mum mutters to herself.

'What is she doing down there?' I whisper to Mrs Jackson, who looks as though she's going to faint. Oh, spoke too soon, there she goes.

'Oh, for goodness sake!' my mother mutters. 'Mr Brent, come and move Mrs Jackson out of the way, will you? She's had one of her funny turns again. She can't stay down there. She'll be right in the way of the paramedics. That's it, levitate her legs – at least someone here remembers what Brian the Red Cross man told us,' Mum whispers under her breath. 'That's it; drag her by the legs out into the kitchen, Mr Brent. Oops, watch her head now. That's it; lie her on the floor with her legs in the air. Sammy, see if you can get her legs to reach the kitchen counter. She might be a bit short, but do your best; it will get the blood flowing to her brain again. Oh, and grab me a new packet of those Marigolds I bought you, love; they're under the sink.'

A rush of nausea comes over me.

'Aghhh!'

'It's OK, Gemma, I'm coming, dear. It's going to hurt a lot more than that before it's over, dear.' My mum sings as she happily snaps a pair of Marigolds onto her hands.

'Right, let's have another look.'

My mother dives under Gem's skirt again and I look around the lounge to see if I can find something to protect Gem's modesty. I'm sure she doesn't want all the neighbours seeing her lady parts this evening.

'Colin, can you get me the sheet that's in the tumble dryer,' I shout, 'and check on Mrs Jackson while you're there.'

Colin hurries in with the sheet and reports that Mrs Jackson has come round and is currently having a cup of sweet tea on the kitchen floor. I peg the sheet to the standard lamp and the doorframe on the opposite side of the room. It's then that I see Simon standing beside Gem. His image is almost like a real human and his face looks anxious. I smile at him.

'Aghh!' Gem screams.

I feel for him. He desperately wants to hold her hand and tell her it's going to be OK, but he can't.

'OK, my love, I don't think this little one is going to wait for the ambulance, so when the next contraction comes I want you to push as hard as you can. Can you do that for me, sweetheart?' my mum says softly but firmly to Gem. Gem looks terrified at the prospect but nods.

'She'll be OK, Simon,' I whisper, but I can't look. The thought of something so large coming out of something so small makes me feel quite queasy. I look the other way, mumbling really stupid things such as, 'You're doing great, Gem,' and 'That's it, breathe, good girl!'

'Here we go,' I hear my mum say with excitement in her voice.

'Aghh!' Gem cries again.

'Come on now, I can see the head, just a bit more, Gemma.'

Oh God, I think I might be dragged out by my legs myself in a minute.

'It hurts too much. Aghhh!'

'Of course it does, dear. You're trying to get a melon through a polo hole,' my mum trills. 'Now one more big p...'

'Aghh! Fucking hell!' Gem shouts.

'That's it dear, have a good old swear. Here we go. One more...'

'Wahhhhh!' a tiny voice interrupts my mum.

'Here we are! A little boy! Gemma, you have a beautiful little boy, dear!'

The last thing I see before I fall to the floor is Simon, with tears rolling down his face, smiling.

CHAPTER THIRTY-NINE

Today is a day where I can just chill out and catch up on my list of jobs-that-must-be-done-before-I-get-married. I recovered from my bump on the head, courtesy of the coffee table meeting my head when I fainted, when the paramedics arrived to tend to Gemma, her new baby, me and Mrs Jackson. Anyone looking out of their window would think we were all heading off to a party, given the number of people being pushed into the ambulance.

Gemma's little boy is absolutely gorgeous. She's decided to name him James Simon Green. She and Simon had already decided that if it was a boy he was going to be called James, but Gem wanted to hold on to Simon's name, so little James will always remember his hero father, Simon. And I know that Si is as pleased as punch about his little boy – as I passed the maternity ward, I saw Si stood by Gem's bed, watching her and baby James sleeping.

So, armed with my list of things to do, I start phoning around everyone checking that Valerie has finished making my dress, Jack's suit is ready to pick up, the flowers have been ordered and that all the guests are coming, including my brother Paul, who has still not booked his flight from Australia.

Missy and Spencer have abandoned their offspring in favour of hunting for mice, so I am now responsible for finding homes for the litter of kittens. I really want to keep them all, Dorothy in particular, but I know I can't, so next on the list is to advertise them on Facebook and see if anyone will give them a good home.

As I log in, I notice that on Jack's fan page, Busty Beth has had a change of heart. Her 'I LV Jack' comments have turned to hatred comments, which have in turn been rewarded with a ban from the social networking site. Ha! That will teach her and thankfully my lovely team of neighbourhood watchers managed to get most of the paint off, before Gem went into labour and before too much damage was done.

To my surprise the majority of fans on Jack's website are made up that he is getting married and many have sent their congratulations or said how lucky I am to be marrying *the* Jack Lewis, from Otherwise. And I am lucky, I know I am. I just wish I had more time to arrange our wedding. I'm sure I've forgotten something.

Just as I'm about to check my list for the umpteenth time, I see Ange standing in front of me.

'Hey Ange, you OK?' I ask absentmindedly, adding up the number of tables we will need at the wedding reception, which is kindly being provided by our old local, The Pig and Whistle, in Bristol. This was Jack and my favourite haunt when I went to college there, and when Steve and Bev, the landlord and his wife, found out we were getting married, they insisted holding the reception at their pub, all paid for by them. I just hope the venue is going to be big enough. We could have held the reception at the Abbey, but we both decided the atmosphere was a bit serious for us; great for taking our vows, but not really the sort of place where you want all your mates doing a drunken conga and besides, The Pig and Whistle has fond memories for us both. It was where Jack got his first paying gig and where I would sit with a pint waiting for him for when he finished.

'*Sam?*' Ange says quietly. She looks unusually sombre and serious, which is not like Ange at all.

I take my reading glasses off and look at her.

'You OK, Ange?'

'*Um, Amy needs to talk to you,*' she says. She looks uncomfortable and starts fidgeting.

'Where is she?'

'*She doesn't want you to be mad at her, so she's sent me in first, you know, to gauge your mood, so to speak,*' Ange says.

'What do you mean, gauge my mood? I'm not moody!'

'*Err, yes, you can be.*'

'Hang on, what do you mean she doesn't want me to be mad at her? What's she done now?' I sigh.

'She's... she's decided to stay here...in...well, what you lot would call heaven,' Ange stutters.

'You what? What do you mean, stay here in heaven?' I look at Ange who looks petrified.

'She...'

Suddenly Amy is standing next to Ange.

'I'm not going back, Sam,' Amy says.

I can't quite believe what I'm seeing. It's Amy, as real as she ever was. She's dressed in the latest designer gear: white, wide leg Chanel trousers, a bottle-green Christian Dior top, and the most amazing pair of Louboutin shoes you have ever seen. I know this not because I'm a fashionista who knows her Prada from her Primark, but because the trousers have the double C symbol on the gold belt, her shirt has a silver metal Dior tag attached to it and her shoes have the signature Louboutin red soles – see, I do take notice of what's going on in *Heat* magazine. In short, Amy looks amazing. Her long blonde hair flows down her back in glorious cascades, like she's just stepped out of a L'Oreal advert.

'Amy? Oh my God, Amy!'

Amy smiles at me and puts her hands on her hips.

'Looking good, huh?' she does a little twirl on her four-inch heels. She makes me and Ange look like the ugly sisters.

'But...I don't understand,' I stutter. I can't get my head around this. It's Amy standing in front of me and she looks just as I remember her, only thinner. I go to put my arms around her but it just feels like thin air. It's like a mirage; I can see her, but she isn't really there. Not physically, anyway.

Amy looks serious for a moment.

'I had to make a choice, Sam. I was told I could either stay on earth or stay here.'

'But...'

'If I stayed on earth, they told me that even if I came out of the coma, I would be in a vegetative state. I've suffered too much brain damage. I would have no…what did they call it, Ange?'

'Cognitive functions,' Ange says.

'I'd have no cog - thingies. Whatever they're called. Anyway, I wouldn't be able to do anything. I wouldn't be able to walk or talk. At best I would be able to blink. That's it. I'd be in a wheelchair for the rest of my life. I wouldn't even be able to pee on my own; I'd have to wear incontinence pads, you know…pee and poo myself all day long,' Amy whispers, just in case anyone else can hear her. *'I can't live a life like that, Sam.'*

'Hang on,' I interrupt, 'who are they? Exactly who has been telling you this, Amy?' This can't be right, surely. I mean, who knows what is going to happen to anyone? Who knows, with medical technology improving by the minute, what miracles might happen?

Amy and Ange look at each other with a knowing look in their eyes.

'The people up here, Sam. Our time on earth is decided long before we live our life. It's no accident when we die, you know. For some of us, like Ange, it's just our time.' Amy and Ange sit down next to me, one on either side. *'For others like me we get given a choice – go back to earth or stay here. When they showed me what my life would be like if I went back to earth I…well I can't do it, Sam. I can't live like that.'*

I have to say Amy is being remarkably calm about all this. I on the other hand am not.

'You don't know that, Amy!' I snap. 'You don't know for sure that the doctors won't make you better. We can bring you back home. Jack and I will look after you. We'll get you the best medical care money can buy and we will get you better again.' I know I sound desperate. Amy just smiles at me.

'It wouldn't make any difference, Sam. No amount of money will make me better again. You think I wouldn't jump at the chance to come back here, all mended and back to my normal self? It won't happen,

hun. It just won't happen. If I decide to go back, I face a life of never being able to talk to anyone. Never ever having my independence again. Never...'

'No! I will not allow this to happen!' I shout. 'Amy, please think about this. We can get you better, I know we can. I have plenty of money. We'll get the best doctors in the world to make you better.' I sob, 'You can't just decide you don't want to live any more. It's not fair on other people.' I want to add, you selfish cow, but I don't.

'And it's fair for me to be a vegetable forever more, is it? Is that fair on me and other people, Sammy? Is it fair for someone to have to care for me twenty-four hours a day? Is it fair on me never to be able to speak to anyone again? Never to be able to communicate, have another boyfriend, tell someone I love them? Is it, Sam? Is that fair?'

'But...' I can see Amy is getting impatient with me now.

'But nothing, Sam. It's my life we're talking about here. At least here I can be me. I can go on dates, I can look beautiful again. I can talk to people. I can always be with my best friend and I can help other people. Think of it as karma, Sam. I wasn't the nicest of people when I was on earth, was I?'

'That's not the point! Amy, you're not thinking this through.' If Amy wasn't a mirage I'd punch her in the arm right now.

'It is the point, Sam. That's exactly what it is. I am not prepared to spend a life locked in a vegetative state until the day everything just stops working. What's the point in that?'

'But...'

'Look, Sam, I've made the decision and that's final,' Amy says defiantly.

My phone rings and I give Amy and Ange a warning look to say don't you two go anywhere, this is not over yet.

'Hello?'

'Samantha? It's Lorraine, Amy's mum.'

No, no, no, no! I close my eyes.

'She's gone, love. My baby's gone.'

CHAPTER FORTY

It's been a little over a week since Amy 'died' and I'm still trying to get my head round all of this. How can anyone just choose to die? But then, if, as Amy says, your only other option is a life in a wheelchair, being fed and kept alive by tubes, would you want a life like that? I don't think I would. But it's very difficult to think that, in the real world, Amy has died, when she is constantly still with me. And constantly with me, she is – she doesn't shut up. I'd forgotten just how talkative and bossy she is – was – is!

'And I don't want any of those horrible yellow flowers...oh, what are they called? You know, the ones they always put in wreaths? Bloody horrible things.'

'Daffodils?' Ange guesses.

'No, not daffodils, oh you know...' Amy replies.

'Well, daffodils are yellow.' Ange states the bloody obvious.

'Durh, I know that, but it's not daffodils. Oh bollocks, what are they called?'

'Primroses,' Ange guesses again.

'No, not primroses. Sam, what are those yellow flowers that they use in wreaths? You know, the ones I don't like?'

'Dandelions,' Ange guesses.

'It's chrysanthemums you don't like, Amy,' I say, before Ange recites the name of every bloody flower in the flower dictionary.

'That's the ones!' Amy squeals, happy that we have finally worked out which flowers she doesn't like.

'And I don't like those purple ones, either. What are they called?'

Oh, for goodness sake!

'Tell you what, how about we decide on the flowers you do like?' I suggest as I finalise the list of Amy's funeral requests. Her funeral is due to take place in Spain next week, two days before my wedding to Jack, and I'm not altogether sure how Lorraine, her mother, is going to take the news that her daughter wants a Westlife tribute act to send her on her way, or that she also wants twelve pink turtle doves released. Mind you, according to my research, there are no turtle doves in Spain because they've all buggered off to Africa for the winter, so she might have to settle for twelve pigeons instead. We could always spray them pink, I guess, and no one would be any the wiser.

'*I would know!*' Amy says in my ear.

'Well, I can't find a bloody turtle dove, Amy, let alone twelve, and I do have a wedding to finish organising, if that's alright with you.'

'*Well excuse me for dying at such an inconvenient time!*'

Normally Spanish funerals have to be performed within seventy-two hours of the person dying, but because Amy is British, Lorraine managed to extend the time so that we could send her daughter off in the style she wanted. It's a good job she got an extension; Amy's funeral would give a Big Fat Gypsy Wedding a run for its money! So far her list consists of a pink, fur-lined coffin, the Westlife tribute act I already mentioned, and a full male choir, dressed in pink smocks, singing Katy Perry's 'Hot N Cold' while the pink pigeons, sorry doves, flutter around the church. We've now established that she wants a mixture of white orchids and orange tiger lilies for her flowers.

'So, is that all?' I ask Amy, as I read through the list.

'*I think so. Oh, I don't want my nosey neighbour, Chelsea, coming to my funeral either. She'll only be coming for the food, the fat pig!*'

'Right, no Chelsea,' I mutter as I write it on the list.

Now for the difficult bit – phoning Amy's mum and telling her what Amy wants. While she knows what my job is, she's still not convinced that it's been Amy's decision to leave the earth plane and remain in heaven or that Amy talks to me every day.

'*Just tell her I know all about Doctor Agapeto. Another surgeon she met when she came to the hospital to turn off my machine. She's dating him now, but she thinks no one else knows about it.*'

I laugh, wondering if this new information will finally convince Lorraine that I really can talk to her daughter.

'So, have you decided if you're coming? To your own funeral, I mean?' I ask.

'*We're going to watch from the side lines,*' Amy says. '*Ange is coming with me, then after that we're going shopping for bridesmaids' dresses.*'

I keep forgetting my wedding is next week. The shops are so chock-a-block with Christmas stuff that the last thing on people's minds is sourcing a hundred and twenty eight silver boxes, to put Shamballa crystal watches in, for me, which is the last thing on my to-do list. Thankfully, Vicky, a very kind regular on my website forum, has offered to make them for me. In the meantime I have my hen night planned for tonight, so as soon as I've called Lorraine and given her Amy's instructions, I am heading off for a hot bath in preparation for my night on the tiles. I just hope it doesn't end like Ange's last night out did!

CHAPTER FORTY-ONE

Well, what else would you expect with twenty-three women (and that doesn't include the non-living ones) out on a hen night and on a boat? Not the best of combinations, is it? But Miracle, who was in charge of organising my hen night, thought a party boat cruise would be a top idea. I, on the other hand, have had my reservations confirmed – yes, it has turned into a very wet nightmare!

It all started well: Mum, Miracle, Valerie and Marjorie and her WI buddies came aboard The Shakespeare, a barge type boat, complete with its own very well stocked bar, music and dance floor. Even new mum Gem managed to get time off from feeding baby Si, as he is now known, and turned up in the most stunning, full-length red dress. Within days she's got her tiny figure back – lucky bugger – and was looking forward to a night out, where she could just let her hair down and forget all that's happened this year.

After hours of changing into different outfits, I decided on a long black, sequinned dress, which I have to say made me not only look taller than I really am, but the fitted corset also made me look much slimmer than I really am. I wonder if I could get away with wearing it as my wedding dress.

Having boarded the boat in the Bristol harbour, The Shakespeare slowly chugged its way up the Floating Harbour, while we danced to the likes of Jessie Jay and Rihanna. Mrs Horsham – the one who tried to kill her sleepwalking husband and then turned into a serial speed dater – was the first one on the dance floor, quickly followed by Mrs Horsham – the one with one leg shorter than the other, although you couldn't tell – who was bobbing up and down like a good un to 'Price Tag' by Jessie Jay. My own mother thought it would be a great idea to take over the bar and create our own cocktails, which resulted in the most lethal drinks known to woman.

'Marjorie, dear! Try this one!' my mum yelled, passing to a now very pissed Marjorie her fifteenth cocktail of the evening, consisting of vodka, rum, gin, Martini and a splash of lime, that my mum named a Volcanic Tropicana and which almost blew Marjorie's head off.

'I think I've drunk a bit much, Sammy,' Miracle slurred, at the same time slipping on the slice of lime that Marjorie had thrown out of her drink, resulting in Miracle having hysterics and being unable to get back on her feet. One bottle of VK blue and I already felt sick, bobbing about on the boat.

'Oh for goodness sake! Look at the state of them!' I heard Amy say to Ange. Mind you, they did look a bit of a state. Miracle decided to remain sitting on the floor, while my mum, Marjorie and Mrs Jackson danced around her, like she was a human handbag.

Annette, still on bed rest, couldn't make it, so she decided to send a stripper in her place.

This was all well and good, until the WI members spotted him.

'Ooo look, Cathy!' Mrs Samuels screamed, as she tried to jump on the poor fella as he writhed around on the small stage in his silky, black boxer shorts. Have you ever witnessed seven women of a certain age with a twenty-something hot-looking man? It's not a pretty sight. The poor guy looked terrified and despite trying to maintain an air of dignity – if that's at all possible when writhing around in your underpants – he was outnumbered and on the floor before you could say, 'Hey big spender!'

Not only did the poor chap suffer being smothered by Mrs Horsham, who it has to be said is not the lightest of women, but he also managed to lose his pants in the process and ended up jumping off the boat, with six middle-aged women in hot pursuit.

I, on the other hand, behaved impeccably and spent much of

the evening holding Miracle up, controlling my uncontrollable mother and her friends, and reuniting the stripper with his undies.

Once the tears and puking arrived – and that was just my mother – we decided to call it a night.

'Just think, Sam, in a week's time you and Jack will be married,' Amy whispers in my ear. *'And I will officially be dead,'* she adds as I tidy up the bar and pick up slices of lime from the dance floor.

I don't want to think about it. In just one week I will be Mrs Jack Lewis. That's scary in itself. I will officially be a grown-up and expected to do grown-up things, like get a pension, life insurance and write a will. Not that I don't want to marry Jack; of course I do. It's just a new milestone in my life and one that Amy won't be sharing with me.

'Of course I will!' she says, reading my mind. *'I'd be no good to you as I was there on earth, would I?'*

'But you won't really be there, Amy.' I busy myself tidying away cocktail mats, because if I don't do something then I will cry.

'You still don't seem to get it, Sam,' Amy says, slightly frustrated. *'I will always be around you. Just like Ange is always with you, and your dad. Just because we're not physically there, it doesn't mean we've gone anywhere. You forget; the bodies we have are just a shell for our souls to live in for a certain amount of time that we're on earth. Think of the body as a kind of vehicle. Would you really prefer to see me in a wheelchair, unable to speak or communicate with you? That's why I made the choice to stay here. I can do more good here than I could ever do down there.'*

I stop shuffling cocktail mats and look up to see Amy with her arms out in front of me. I then cry a lot. Which I seem to be doing a great deal of at the moment.

Why can't I just be a normal woman, living a normal life, doing a normal job in insurance or something, instead of dealing with all this dead stuff? It's mentally and physically exhausting. I seem to be in tears practically every day over something or the other and I don't know if I can do this any more.

'*Lady?*' a little voice comes into my head. Then I see a small figure in front of me, just in front of the bar. It's Tom, the little boy from the WI séance. He looks sad.

'Hello again, Tom.' I smile and look at him. He looks so much more real today.

'*You can't not do this any more, Lady,*' Tom says. '*We need people like you. Imagine being dead and not being able to talk to the people you love ever again.*' He says wisely, '*Dead people like me need you.*'

'*Me too,*' Mrs Jackson's daughter Alice appears.

'*And me,*' Andy says. '*What do you think would have happened to my mum if you hadn't got to her at the bridge in time?*'

'*And we need you more than ever, Sam.*' Amy and Ange appear.

Strange: I'm on an empty boat and yet I feel all-consumed by the most amazing love from these people.

'*Yeah, so snap out of it and stop feeling so bloody sorry for yourself, girl!*' the Viking booms in my ear.

Well, that told me, didn't it?

CHAPTER FORTY-TWO

Despite it being the middle of winter, the sun is shining in Marbella where Amy's funeral is to take place. Jack, Mum, Colin and I flew out yesterday and stayed in a hotel near to the San Pedro Alcantara cemetery where Amy is to be cremated. I shudder at the thought of it, but she insisted she didn't want to be buried. Well, what she actually said was, *'What and have all those worms crawling all over me, eating me up? Fuck that! Nah, pop me in the oven!'*

My stomach turns over. Cheers for that thought, Amy.

While this is the norm in the UK, cremation is not widely practised in Spain, so we've had a bit of a problem getting the authorities to allow us not only to cremate Amy but also to give us enough time to arrange everything. Usually the Spanish like to have their deceased buried as soon after death as possible, but because Lorraine wanted to keep Amy in Spain with her, it took a while to inform everyone in the UK – although it has to be said, she didn't have much of a fan club here after she left for Spain, having tried to publicly destroy my career.

So here we are, standing outside the crematorium waiting for Amy to be officially cremated – no one is allowed in the actual crematorium – and the pastor will then perform a service for Amy. Her coffin was to her specifications – bright pink, with the words 'Amy' and 'Reem' written in diamante crystals on both sides - and despite seeing her just feet away from me, I shed a few tears as I see my friend's coffin go past me. Jack hugs me to him.

'You OK?' he asks.

I nod, sniff and wipe my nose on his lapel. He doesn't mind – that's love for you, isn't it?

'Ooo, I do like the way they've done your flowers on the top of your coffin,' Ange, who is also standing on the sidelines, says. *'Did you tell Sam you wanted the ivy to run all the way down?'*

'No, the florist just thought it would look nice if it was. Can you see she's sprinkled silver glitter on the orchids?' Amy adds.

'Yeah, nice touch,' Ange muses, as the very pink coffin goes into the crematorium and the Westlife tribute act breaks into 'Flying Without Wings' – actually they're pretty good as tribute acts go, although the one who's supposed to resemble Shane Filan looks more like Louis Walsh's younger brother, and they still have the Brian look-a-like, who really does look like Brian McFadden, and he left the band years ago. Or maybe he actually left Westlife and joined the tribute band?

I've only ever been to one funeral in my life and that was my dad's, which was obviously a sombre occasion, but had I known then what I know now, I wouldn't have spent weeks crying my eyes out. Instead I would have known he hadn't really gone anywhere and he would always be in my life, even though I can't see him. In fact, in some ways, I feel quite honoured that I have this 'gift' and wish everyone had it. Don't get me wrong, of course I would prefer that everyone could live forever, but they can't – can you imagine the problems with getting a parking space in Sainsbury's for starters?

'Sorry, sorry!' a woman's voice interrupts my thoughts. It's Lorraine, Amy's mum, and she's late.

She totters on the highest of heels, flanked by three men in their fifties. I'm not sure which one is her latest beau, but they all fawn over her as if she's a precious diamond.

'Typical!' I hear Amy say. 'She can't even be on time for her own daughter's funeral!'

You would think Lorraine had come to an eighties disco the way she's dressed: she's wearing a Barbie pink skirt with a red vest top – even I know that red and pink don't go – a white jacket, with the biggest shoulder pads ever to have graced a catwalk, and a multicoloured fascinator which looks as if she has a parrot on her head. Her eyes are covered by a huge pair of sunglasses and the minute she sees me and Jack she slumps as if she's going to faint. Her boyfriends hold her up and offer her a tissue.

'Oh Sammy,' she sobs as she reaches me, 'thank you all for coming. Amy would have been so pleased.' She sobs again. 'Have I missed much? You don't know what it's like, having to bury your only daughter. I nearly didn't make it, did I, Roger?' she says to one of the men beside her. He solemnly shakes his head and pats her hand.

'The reason she's late was because she was screwing the guy at the back!' Amy snaps. *'Come on Ange, let's have some fun. This is just too depressing for words!'*

'Sammy! Look!' Lorraine suddenly gasps as she spots a tortoiseshell butterfly fluttering around our heads. 'It's a sign! It's our Amy!' she sobs, lifting her sunglasses, revealing a new set of black eyes: the after effects of her latest nip and tuck.

What she doesn't see, but I do, is that Amy and Ange are having a great game of chasing after the butterfly. Oh very mature. How old are you two? I think to myself.

'Well, it's better than listening to that silly cow whine on about how she misses me, blah, blah, blah!' Amy says. *'Right, Ange, you go that way and I'll go to the right. We'll get the little bugger this time!'* she squeals.

This is all very odd and it feels as though I'm in two worlds: on the one hand, I'm like everyone else attending a funeral, sad that my friend is no longer with us, but on the other hand, I can see her prancing around in front of me in a turquoise-blue tracksuit with the words *'Well Jel'* emblazoned across her bum in silver writing. Why can't other people see what I can see? It would be so much nicer for everyone if they could see that their loved ones were well and healthy and chasing butterflies, instead of having to remember the way they looked the last time they saw them on earth. I daren't say I can see her. Can you imagine it: me pointing and shouting, 'There she is!' Instead I keep quiet and try not to laugh when Ange and Amy collide and fall to the ground during their bid to catch the dastardly butterfly.

'*Senorita*. The cremation is complete. If you will all come this way, we will begin the service,' the Spanish priest says and directs us to a building where Amy's service will be performed.

The building is not too dissimilar to a church: it has several pews in lines and a huge cross at the altar, with the Virgin Mary kneeling and praying by the cross. The room echoes to the clip-clop noise from Lorraine's heels and as we all take a seat, the band follows us in, singing 'You Raise Me Up'. Jack and look at each other and try not to laugh.

'Dearly beloved, we are here today to celebrate the life of Amy. A vibrant young woman who was taken from us all too soon...' the priest begins. He's reading from a script, which annoys the hell out of me. He didn't know Amy. He had no idea whether she was a vibrant young woman or whether she preferred to slob out in her pyjamas until noon. He doesn't know that she can (could) bend her thumb right back to her wrist.

'*I can, you know, look.*' Amy demonstrates her party trick to Ange.

He doesn't know that her tongue is so long, she can touch her chin with it.

'*Look!*' Amy shows Ange her other party trick.

And he doesn't know that Amy once stole a pair of knickers from Lipsy because she wanted to be arrested by the sexy security guard, or that she knows all the words to every one of Westlife's hits. He doesn't know the real Amy at all.

He goes on to say what a trooper she was and how the hospital did everything they could to save her, and I want to say, No, you are so wrong, but I don't. I look around the room and just see a sea of sad faces. It's only then that I notice Amy's ex standing, handcuffed to two police guards, at the back of the room.

'What the hell is he doing here?' I stand up and shout out. Everyone turns to see who is at the back of the room.

'Why, the little bastard. Get him out of here, Sam!' Amy shouts.

'Get him out of here!' I snap, marching up to the footballer.

'I do nothing wrong. I am innocent. I just want pay respects to Amy,' Demetrio Covas says. He's dressed in a smart Armani style suit and looks well groomed – police cells in Spain must be more accommodating than those in England then.

'Yeah? Well, this is from Amy, you slimeball!'

Thwack!

'You go girl!' Lorraine shouts.

'Oh my!' my mother says.

'Oh crap!' Jack says.

Ouch! I didn't think a Spaniard's face would be quite so bony, I think as I shake my painful hand.

'Arrest this mad woman!' Demetrio demands of the guards. 'She assaults me!'

'And you'd know all about assaulting people, wouldn't you? This is the man who killed Amy, and if they don't find him guilty of that and throw away the key, then perhaps you should look into his drug dealing affairs. He's got a garage full of drugs on the Solara Avenue. Apartment 28.' I repeat what Amy told me a few weeks ago, when reminiscing about her ex-boyfriend.

One of the guards talks into his radio and they pull Demetrio out of the room and haul him into the back of a police van.

'Sorry about that, people,' I say as I sit back down and regain my composure.

'Nice right hook, kid,' Jack whispers, 'I didn't know you had it in you.'

'Me neither,' I whisper back, 'but I think we'll need to pay a visit to the hospital when we finish here – I think I've broken my hand.'

CHAPTER FORTY-THREE

Finally the day has arrived – Jack and my wedding day. I would love to say everything is going swimmingly, but it's not. Far from it, in fact.

Having packed Jack off to his uncle Dave's last night, I came back to the cottage to find Clive sitting on my sofa, waiting for me. Damn it! With Amy's funeral I'd forgotten to tell Gem about putting the vegetables on the window sill. Mind you, it's not the normal thing you say to your house-sitter, is it? 'If you can feed the cats for me, collect any post up, oh, and pop a few carrots on the window sills that would be great, thanks!'

'*Hello Samantha.*' Clive grins.

'What do you want, Clive?'

I will not be intimidated by this man, ghost, whatever.

'*I told you, we have unfinished business,*' Clive says.

'And I told you…'

'*To sod off, you moron! Now if I have to tell you again…*' Ange suddenly appears.

'*You'll what? Get your scary new friend to say boo?*' Clive laughs. He really is an irritating man.

'*No, I'll get my new boyfriend to sort you out. Danny!*' Ange whistles. The noise of a motorbike roars into my living room. There in his full leathers is Ange's boyfriend, Danny. Clive looks as though he's just wet himself as Danny climbs off his bike and slowly takes off his helmet. I have to say, as ghosts go, this is one cute one!

'*So you're still annoying my girlfriend's friend then, are you?*' Danny bends down and looks Clive in the face. Clive goes white – well, whiter than he normally is, considering he's also a ghost.

'*No…I…I just…*'

'*You just what?*' Danny says, still glaring at Clive.

'*Nothing,*' Clive says, dropping his head.

'I thought as much. Now don't let me see you bothering Sam again. Is that clear?'

'Yes, sir,' Clive mutters and disappears.

'There, job done. If he bothers you again, just whistle.' Danny winks at me, climbs back on his bike and zooms off through my patio doors.

'My hero!' Ange swoons. 'Now come on lady, we have a big day tomorrow, so off to bed with you and get some much needed beauty sleep,' Ange instructs me. I'm not sure whether that's a compliment or not, but I did as I was told and the morning has arrived and I'm all of a dither! I've been sick twice this morning with nerves and the house is chock-full with people, both dead and alive, swarming around me with hair curlers, straighteners and make-up.

'Now, did you decide whether you want your hair up or down, Sammy?' my mum enquires, pulling my locks this way and that.

'Ouch, Mum! Will you stop pulling my hair!'

'You haven't got much time, dear, so chop, chop, or you're going to have to wear a hat!'

The doorbell rings.

'Oh, that will be your brothers!' my mum says, discarding my hair to answer the door.

'Hey sis!' Paul and Matt say in unison.

'You're not going like that, are you?' Paul asks, looking me up and down.

'Yes, Paul, I'm going to my wedding in my dressing gown with a red wine stain down it, and my Minnie Mouse slippers.'

'Really?' he pulls a face.

'No, stupid. Anyway, you can talk. What happened to the suit I ordered for you?'

Paul is wearing a pair of surf shorts and a Hawaiian shirt.

'What this? I'll have you know this is my best outfit!' Paul mocks outrage.

'Don't worry, Sam. I have his suit safe in the back of the car,' Matt assures me.

I swore I wasn't going to turn into one of those hysterical brides, but I'm now hyperventilating at the thought of my wedding all going wrong at the last minute.

'I think I'm going to be sick again,' I say as I rush past the throng of people in my living room and into the bathroom.

As I'm bent over the loo, I feel someone smooth the back of my head.

'You'll be just fine, Sammy Puddleduck. Jack's a very lucky boy.'

It's my dad, smoothing my hair as he always used to do when I was poorly.

I take a deep breath, stand up and compose myself. Right, let's get this wedding started.

I'm being pushed and pulled in several directions as Valerie ties me into my dress and Mum dresses my hair with tiny red roses.

'You don't think I look ridiculous?' I worry.

'Sam, you look beautiful, darling. Now will you please stand still while Valerie does the last hook on your corset?'

'I'm sure it wasn't as tight as this two weeks ago when I had a fitting. I've put on weight, haven't I?'

'No, dear. It's probably because you didn't have the slip on when you last tried it on. Don't worry, we'll make it fit,' Valerie says, through a mouthful of silver pins. 'There we go. Turn round.'

I do as I'm told and everyone gasps.

'Oh Samantha, you look beautiful!' My mum starts to cry. 'I wish your dad was here to see you.'

'Oh, I'll be there, Sammy Puddleduck. I wouldn't miss it for all the tea in China,' I hear my dad say and I smile, blinking away a tear before it threatens to roll down my cheek, spoiling my make-up.

'The cars are here!' I hear one of my brother's shout.

Oh heck. This is really happening, isn't it?

Oh crap; I think I'm going to be sick again.

CHAPTER FORTY-FOUR

To the outside world it looks as though I only have two brides-maids – Gem and Annette, who waddles rather than walks behind me. I have in fact got fifteen bridesmaids and two maids of honour, all dressed in long white Grecian dresses and they all look beautiful. Mrs Jackson's daughter, Alice, looks adorable and is so pleased to be one of my bridesmaids. I just wish Mrs Jackson could see her as I do. Ange and Amy look absolutely stunning and take their maid of honour duties very seriously, ensuring that all the dearly departed are seated in the correct pews in the Abbey.

'You look beautiful, Sammy,' my mum says. 'Now you're quite sure about this? There's still time to change your mind if you want, you know.'

'I've never been more sure of anything in my life, Mum,' I say as we walk up the steps towards the Abbey where Matt and Paul are waiting for me, to walk me down the aisle. They both look so smart and thankfully Paul isn't wearing his surf wear, but a smart morning suit, with a white silk handkerchief folded into a small triangle poking out of his pocket.

My mum lets go of my hand so that my brothers can stand either side of me. I look behind me and there he is – my dad – in the flesh – well, kind of. He's here. He promised he would be and here he is, dressed in the same suit as my brothers. He winks and smiles. He looks better than I have ever seen him before and seems to radiate a warm glow.

'Matt, Paul,' I whisper, 'Dad's here. Do you mind if he walks me down the aisle?'

My brothers look at each other for a moment and then smile and step aside and stand next to my mum.

My dad looks down at me.

'Look at my beautiful little girl. I told you I wouldn't miss this for the world.'

I want to cry. I want everyone to see that my whole family are here, standing with me, sending me off into married life.

'Now come on, let's get you married.' My dad smiles and hugs me and it feels like a real hug. I must look rather strange though because not only does it look as though I'm walking down the aisle on my own, with my mum and brothers behind me, but I'm also aware that I'm leaning at a slight angle as I walk up the long aisle.

'Sammy, straighten up!' Paul whispers from behind me. 'You look like you've had a stroke.'

I push back my shoulders and stand up straight. My dad laughs and looks over his shoulder at his sons and his wife. He looks so proud right now.

As I approach the altar it's then that I see Jack, standing with his uncle Dave and best friend and best man, Dillon. Jack looks gorgeous. I haven't seen him in his morning suit and he looks as though he's just stepped out of the pages of *GQ* magazine.

'*Wow! He's scrubbed up well!*' Ange says. And he has, he looks so handsome – oh God, I'm going to cry. Don't cry, Sam, don't cry, I tell myself as I approach him.

'You look absolutely gorgeous,' Jack whispers, as I stand next to him.

'You don't look too bad yourself,' I whisper back.

'We are here today to witness the marriage between Samantha Louise Katherine Ball and Jack Peter Lewis...' the vicar begins.

I can't believe we have finally made it. I feel giddy with excitement at the prospect of spending the rest of my life with Jack. I look around the Abbey and see a sea of friends and family, both dead and alive. There are all the spirits I accidentally let into our world, all dressed from different eras: little Tom the urchin, the Rastafarian, Simon, Gem's husband, Pearl, Petra's mum and the Viking, who I'm sure has a tear in his eye. They're all here, along with many spirits that I have come into contact with on the radio station or in TV work. The pews are packed with my living and dead friends and I feel truly blessed.

When I look back at Jack, I see standing behind him is his mum, Marianne. She looks beautifully serene and so proud of her son. Despite trying to contact her, I haven't been able to, and I have never found out exactly what happened to her, but it doesn't seem to matter now.

'Look after my boy for me, Samantha,' she whispers.

I will, I think, and she smiles, wiping away a tear.

'...If anyone here knows of any reason why these two people should not get married, speak now or forever hold your peace.'

'Aghh!' a voice shouts from behind us and both Jack and I spin round. It's Annette.

'So sorry! Don't mind me. I think the baby's coming! Carry on...I'll just...aghhh!'

Smashing.

CHAPTER FORTY-FIVE

All heads turn back to the vicar.

'Carry on, she'll be fine, she's done this before,' I say, as I see my mum, Miracle and Florence Nightingale rushing Annette out of the Abbey doors, while my mum is calling for an ambulance on her mobile. My dad looks as proud as punch at his wife taking charge of the situation. I have a feeling Mum could be heading for a career change as a midwife before long.

'Shall we continue?' the vicar asks.

'Yes, yes, come on, or we'll be here all day,' I say. Jack looks at me and laughs.

'What? We've been waiting for this day for ages.'

'So, if anyone here knows of any reason why these two people should not get married, speak now or forever hold your peace.'

We all hold our breath, waiting for someone to shout out something again.

'Great, now that's out of the way, I proclaim you man and wife. You may kiss the bride.' The vicar looks as relieved as I feel.

Jack cups my face in his hands.

'I love you so much, Mrs Lewis,' he says, before kissing me passionately on the mouth. 'I love me too, Mr Lewis!'

You know people say they go weak at the knees? Well, I think I will soon need a new pair of kneecaps. I close my eyes and fall into Jack's arms. The stress of the past year melts away and I wish I could just stay here, in his arms, forever.

'Uh-hum,' the vicar coughs.

'Oh, sorry.' I come up for air and smile at Jack.

Our guests cheer and clap as we turn to them and proceed to walk back down the aisle. I look over my shoulder at my dad, who waves at me, blows me a kiss and then disappears. My non-living guests cheer as we pass them and one by one they disappear too, leaving just my friends and family who have a pulse clapping and sending their good wishes and I feel like I'm floating down the aisle as I hold Jack's hand.

And yes, I'm the happiest and luckiest girl in the world!

EPILOGUE

Larry, my agent, managed to set up a diversion so that the press thought we were getting married in London. By the time they realised just where we were getting wed, we were long gone.

Steve and Bev at the Pig and Whistle did us proud: when we arrived at the pub on Jack's motorbike, the reception guests were all standing in the pub garden with confetti and streamers to greet us. But first we made a diversion to the hospital to make sure that Annette was OK. Thankfully she was, and thanks to my mum's quick reactions, they made it to the hospital just in time for Annette to give birth to the most beautiful baby girl, who she has named Angel. When we arrived, Jeff was by her side, cradling his newborn daughter in his arms and holding Annette's hand. Call me psychic, but I have a feeling that despite Annette's protests, this relationship could blossom very soon.

My deceased guests stuck to their word and went back to their own world as soon as we had taken our wedding vows, apart from Amy and Ange, of course. They spent the evening dancing on the tables in the pub and flirting outrageously with the male guests. Thankfully Dillon couldn't see Amy exposing her breasts, or Ange bumping and grinding to Madonna's 'Vogue' in a suggestive manner. If he had, I think he would have had a heart attack.

My mum's wedding present to us was to send us off to Molokai in Hawaii for a fortnight and we had the best time ever. Just being able to wake up together and do nothing but lie on the beach all day was simply magical.

And the weight gain and sickness? Yes, you've guessed it, Jack and I are expecting our own pitter-patter of tiny feet in seven months' time! How I will cope with childbirth is a different matter – I just hope my mum's qualified as a midwife by then!

Soul Rocks is a fresh list that takes the search for soul and spirit mainstream. Chick-lit, young adult, cult, fashionable fiction & non-fiction with a fierce twist